... ...heat quickened. The courte... ... ...ct variance with the b... ... his manner and his prese... ...e of undress.

Darting a swift look around her, she became more acutely aware of her present isolation and the remoteness of the stream. If she screamed no one would hear. Besides, it was a mistake to show fear.

Ban saw the dainty chin tilt. Far from being embarrassed or afraid, the look in her eyes was bold—challenging, even. It satisfied him. His gaze travelled downwards, mentally removing the cloth again. When she saw this, the colour rose in her face.

'How long have you been watching me?'

'Long enough.'

The blush deepened and the hazel eyes sparkled with anger. 'How dare you spy on me?'

'Unforgivable, I know,' he admitted, 'but impossible to look away.'

HIS LADY OF CASTLEMORA

Joanna Fulford

MILLS & BOON

First published in Great Britain 2013
by Mills & Boon, an imprint of Harlequin (UK) Limited.
Harlequin (UK) Limited, Eton House, 18-24 Paradise Road,
Richmond, Surrey TW9 1SR

© Joanna Fulford 2013

ISBN: 978 0 263 89833 0

Harlequin (UK) policy is to use papers that are natural, renewable and recyclable products and made from wood grown in sustainable forests. The logging and manufacturing process conform to the legal environmental regulations of the country of origin.

Printed and bound in Spain
by Blackprint CPI, Barcelona

Joanna Fulford is a compulsive scribbler with a passion for literature and history, both of which she has studied to postgraduate level. Other countries and cultures have always exerted a fascination, and she has travelled widely, living and working abroad for many years. However, her roots are in England, and are now firmly established in the Peak District, where she lives with her husband, Brian. When not pressing a hot keyboard she likes to be out on the hills, either walking or on horseback. However, these days equestrian activity is confined to sedate hacking rather than riding at high speed towards solid obstacles. Visit Joanna's website at www.joannafulford.co.uk

Recent titles by the same author:

Prologue

Isabelle threaded her way among the trees and came at length to the wall at the far end of the orchard. It afforded a fair view of the wood and the hills above Castlemora, though in truth it was not these she saw. All she could think about was the last interview with her mother-in-law…

'Had you fulfilled your wifely duty and produced an heir, you would have retained your place among us. As it is, my son's death removes any requirement for you to remain.'

Isabelle stared at her in stunned disbelief. Alistair Neil's demise in a hunting accident had been shock enough, but this was beyond everything. 'But this is my home.'

If she hoped to appeal to Lady Gruoch's compassion the notion was wide of the mark. The

*blue eyes regarding her now were cold, the stern
face pitiless.*

*'Not any longer. A barren wife has only one
future open to her: to take the veil and disappear
from the world of men.'*

*Isabelle's stomach knotted. 'It is not my fault
that I am childless. My late husband must share
the responsibility for that.'*

*The furrows in Gruoch's brow deepened.
'How dare you attempt to cover your own fail-
ings by besmirching the name of the dead? My
son was eager for an heir. I have good reason
to know that he never neglected his duty to you.'*

*Isabelle's hands clenched at her sides. So they
had discussed this behind her back. She could
well imagine what spiteful and lying tales her
late husband had told to cover his own inepti-
tude. Mortification vied with anger.*

*'Since he was assiduous in undertaking his
part,' Gruoch continued, 'it is only reasonable
to expect that you should have done yours.'*

*Isabelle bit back the heated reply that leapt
to her tongue. Alistair was dead; what use to re-
count the embarrassed fumbling that had blighted
the marriage bed in the early part of their relationship; fumbling that became frustration and,
eventually, violence when he took out his failure
on her?*

Seeing her hesitation Gruoch nodded. 'I

note that you do not deny it. The shame is doubly yours. You were married a year. Any self-respecting wife would have a babe in arms and another in her belly by now.'

'I wanted that as much as my husband did. How can you doubt it?'

'It may be so. However, that does not alter the fact of your failure as a woman and as a wife. You will go back to your father and he may dispose of you as he sees fit. If he has any sense he will place you in a convent as soon as possible.'

Isabelle didn't care to think about her father's response to this development. Quite apart from the insult, her return would be a burden that he would scarcely welcome. Nevertheless, it would have to be faced. Knowing that further argument was useless, she lifted her chin. 'In that case I demand that my dowry be returned to me.'

'You are in no position to make demands. It is our family that has been wronged. We made a bargain in good faith and we were cheated.'

'This isn't just.'

'Do not speak to me of justice.'

The words created the first fluttering of panic. 'Keep part if you will, but return the rest.'

'We will keep what is ours.'

Isabelle swallowed hard. With no dowry, and a reputation as a barren woman, she would have no chance of remarriage. Sick with repressed

shame and fury she made a last desperate at-
tempt.

'It is not yours to keep. The Neils have wealth
enough; they have no need of more.'

'Do not presume to tell the Neils what they
need.' Gruoch's voice grew quieter. 'You may
count yourself fortunate to leave here at all, my
girl. There are those at Dunkeld who favoured
a quicker and neater end to the embarrassment
you represent.'

Isabelle experienced a sudden inner chill.
When first she came to her husband's home she
was accorded courtesy, albeit not warmth. Her
new kin were not given to displays of affection.
However, as time went on and she failed to con-
ceive a child, their attitude changed until their
scorn was scarcely veiled. The thought that they
might do her physical hurt had not occurred,
until now.

'Would the Neils risk incurring the wrath of
Castlemora?' she demanded. 'My father would
not let such a deed go un-avenged.'

Gruoch's lips tightened to a thin line. 'We have
no fear of Castlemora.'

'You would be wiser if you had.'

For all that the words were defiant Isabelle
knew they were futile. In this argument all the
weight was on the other side of the balance.

Gruoch's lip curled. 'We are content to put it to the test. You leave first thing in the morning.'

And so she had, under the disdainful gaze of her erstwhile kin. The recollection was bitter. All the high hopes she'd set out with at the start of her marriage were ashes, and her pride lay among them. At the same time it was hard to regret leaving a place where she was so little valued or wanted. The trouble was that she couldn't imagine how the situation was going to change in the foreseeable future. Unwilling to let the Neils see any tears she contrived to put a brave face on it.

She'd worn a brave face when eventually she had to confront her father. Archibald Graham was fifty years old. Formerly a strong and active man his health had failed in his later years until even small exertions tired him and any significant effort brought on the pains in his chest. However, his grey eyes were bright and shrewd, his mind as sharp as it had ever been. He made no attempt to hide his anger and disappointment. When he learned that they had refused to return her dowry his wrath increased tenfold.

'Those scurvy, double-dealing Neils are no better than thieves.'

Her brother growled agreement. At sixteen Hugh was grown to manhood and, as the only surviving son, was now the heir. He also possessed a keen sense of what was due to kin.

'This is an insult to our entire family. It should be avenged. Let me take a force to Dunkeld and burn out that nest of rats.'

'The rats are numerous and strong, boy. We'll bide our time.'

'You mean we're to swallow this outrage?'

'This outrage will not be swallowed or forgotten, I promise you.' Graham paused. 'However, revenge is a dish best tasted cold. If you're to be laird one day you need to remember that.'

Hugh nodded slowly. 'I'll remember.' He turned to Isabelle. 'You're well rid of the scum, Belle.'

That much was true, but it didn't change the fact that she was now a dowerless widow. It hung there, unsaid, like the subject of her alleged barrenness. Her brother was fond of her and would never throw such an accusation in her face, but it wasn't going to go away...

Being thus lost in gloomy reflection, she was unaware of the approaching figure until she heard him speak.

'Well met, Lady Isabelle.'

Recognising the voice she turned quickly. 'Murdo.'

The master-at-arms was standing just feet away. She eyed him uneasily, repressing a shiver.

The black-clad figure was entirely shaven-headed. A scar seamed the left side of his face from cheek bone to chin, though it was partially hidden by a beard close-trimmed and dark as night, as dark as the predatory gaze watching her now. He reminded her of nothing so much as a hunting wolf, lean, powerful and dangerous. A strong odour of stale sweat enhanced the impression of lupine rankness.

He bared his teeth in a smile. 'I thought I might find you here.'

Suddenly she was aware that the orchard was some way from the house and that it was entirely private. Apprehension prickled. Unwilling to let him see it she remained quite still and forced herself to meet his gaze.

'What do you want?'

'To speak with you, my lady.'

'Very well, what is it you wish to speak about?'

'The future.'

The knot of apprehension tightened a degree. 'What of it?'

'Your honoured father is a sick man. He cannot live long. That must weigh upon your mind.'

'It does,' she replied, 'but you did not come here to tell me that.'

'When he dies you will need a strong protector, Isabelle.'

She knew what was coming now and sought

desperately for the means to evade it. 'My brother will protect me.'

'A new husband would perform the role better.' His expression became intent. 'I would be that man.'

Isabelle's stomach wallowed but she knew better than to anger him deliberately. 'What you are asking is not possible, Murdo.'

'Why not?' He held her gaze. 'Who better than me? I may be a younger son but I come of good family. I have risen to my present rank on merit and served your father well. Thanks to my efforts Castlemora is strong and feared.' He paused. 'And you cannot be entirely unaware of my feelings for you.'

'I regret that I cannot return them.'

'Not yet, but you might come to return them, in time.'

She shook her head. 'I will never feel about you that way.'

'You say so now but I know how to be patient.'

'Time will not change this. Do not hold out hopes of me.'

'If not me, who else, Isabelle? You are no longer the prize you once were, only a widow returned in disgrace to her father.'

Her chin lifted at once. 'I wonder then that you should wish to make her yours.'

'I have long wished it. The present circumstances change nothing, except to work in my favour since there will be no more suitors coming calling now.'

'Never tell me you speak out of pity, Murdo.'

'Far from it.' He smiled. 'I know the truth, you see.'

She stared at him. 'What do you mean?'

'That Alistair Neil was no man at all.'

'You have no right to say such things.'

'You don't have to pretend to me, Isabelle. 'Tis common knowledge among the local whores: your late husband was but meagrely endowed, and that he couldn't get a cock stand either. If you have no children the fault is not yours.'

Had it been anyone else this vindication would have been balm to her spirit. As it was, her cheeks burned.

Murdo drew closer. 'I can give you children.'

She stiffened. The thought of intimacy with him was utterly repellent. 'It's impossible.'

'Come now, would you not prefer to be ridden by a real man for a change?' Seeing her outraged expression he laughed softly. 'One night in my bed and you'll forget Alistair Neil ever existed.'

'I'll never share your bed.'

If her reply had dismayed him it was not apparent for his expression did not change save that his gaze became more intense. 'When I set myself a goal I always achieve it.'

Despite the warmth of the late afternoon sunshine goose bumps started along her arms, and she wanted nothing so much as to be free of his presence.

'I regret that you will be disappointed this time.'

'You're wrong, Isabelle. This time you will be my wife.'

'That I never shall.' With that she turned to leave, but a strong hand on her arm prevented it.

'I never take no for an answer,' he replied. 'You should know that well enough by now.'

She tested the hold but it didn't alter. 'Let go of me, Murdo.'

'You escaped me once before but I'll not let it happen again.'

The tone was casual but its implications were not. Her heart thumped unpleasantly hard but she forced herself to meet his gaze. 'You forget yourself. You may have a trusted position in this household, but it does not give you the right thus to presume.'

'Not yet perhaps,' he replied, 'but know this: I intend to have a husband's rights over you soon enough.'

That quiet assertion snapped the last fragile strand of her self-control. 'Never!'

Tearing herself free of his hold she turned on

her heel and ran off through the trees. He watched but made no attempt to stop her.

'Aye, run from me, Isabelle,' he murmured. 'You won't escape.'

Chapter One

Three months later

Isabelle urged the horse to a canter, wanting only to put space between herself and Castlemora for a while. In theory she ought not to ride out alone but Murdo and her brother had gone out hunting earlier so there was no one to prevent her. All the same, freedom was going to be short-lived. Her father might have decided to bide his time over the Neils, but he had not been tardy in seeking another husband for her…

'Glengarron is an old ally. Marriage will serve to strengthen the tie.'

Her stomach turned over. Somehow she managed to control her voice. 'Forgive me, but I thought the Laird of Glengarron was already married.'

'So he is. I was speaking of his brother-in-
law, Lord Ban.'

'I see.'

'He's a Sassenach but that canna be helped.'

'A Sassenach?'

'It's not ideal, I admit. On the plus side he's
a respected warrior with strong family connec-
tions, but, having no land, he canna be so particular in his choice of a bride.'

Her jaw tightened. 'Nor I so particular in my
choice of a husband?'

'You canna afford to be choosy now.'

'Perhaps it is the Sassenach thane who will
be choosy.'

'Why should he be?' He eyed her appraisingly.
'You've looks enough and the Graham blood to
boot. No doubt some small financial inducement
could be found as well. It should be enough.'

With an effort she held fury in check. 'And if
it isn't?'

'There's always a convent.'

'I have no vocation for the religious life.'

He regarded her steadily. 'Murdo looks at you
a good deal. You could do worse.'

'I hardly think so.'

'In that case I advise you to put on your finest
gown and make yourself agreeable when Lord
Ban arrives.'

Her mouth dried. 'When is he expected?'

'Very soon now. See to it that all necessary preparations are made to welcome him.'

The recollection of that conversation filled Isabelle with roiling anger. Nevertheless, she didn't dare to disobey. Castlemora was ready to receive the guest. Meanwhile, she needed time alone to gather her composure and ready herself to face what was coming. For that she required some peace and quiet.

Holding her mount to a steady pace she followed the burn until it widened out into a pool beneath a stand of trees. Although it was just within the bounds of Castlemora land it was a secluded place and, ordinarily, she would not have come here alone. If Murdo ever found out, the fat would be in the fire. Over the years the master-at-arms had evolved a highly efficient system of intelligence. Almost nothing happened at Castlemora without him knowing. The hunt was a fortunate distraction.

Isabelle dismounted and tethered her horse. The sun was high now and the day hot. Her clothing was sticking to her back and the water looked inviting. She glanced around but the land was still; there was no sign of human presence as far as the eye could see. The temptation grew stronger. It ought to be safe enough for a while at least.

Ban smiled and leaned back against the tree, glad to be out of the saddle for a while. He and his companions had been riding since early morning, albeit at an easy pace to spare the horses. Their mounts were dozing in the shade while the men, having partaken of bread and cheese and slabs of dried meat, stretched out awhile at their ease. A little way off among the trees Davy stood watch. For all that the country seemed peaceful it never paid to be complacent. Ban had learned that through long experience. For five years he had ridden with Black Iain of Glengarron, watching, learning, training, his body growing hard and lean and strong, his mind sharp and focused. The stripling youth who had been saved after the destruction of Heslingfield was long gone and in his place the man, now a respected warrior in his own right. Being Iain's brother-in-law had won him no favours. Ban was expected to prove himself like all the rest. He applied himself wholeheartedly, for by concentrating on the new life he could forget the old. Here the past mattered not. He was judged by what he did now. Though he was treated with civility enough by his companions he knew they watched him, judged him. It had been a matter of pride to be found worthy, to win their trust and acceptance.

He glanced across at his companions: Ewan, Jock and Davy, good men all, men he trusted at his back in a fight. They would stand by him as he would by them. They had been through

enough adventures together to know it. Not that
he expected to do any fighting in the near future. Delivering some horses to an old friend was
hardly likely to be fraught with peril. He did it as
a favour to Iain. Of the other, more personal, matter he had said nothing to his men. After all, he
had not positively decided yet; could not decide
until he knew more. A few days at Castlemora
would doubtless clarify matters.

Unbidden his mind returned to the conversation a week earlier. *He was playing in the courtyard with his young nephews when Iain appeared
on the scene. For a while Iain watched the bois-
terous game, an indulgent smile hovering on his
lips. When eventually they stopped for breath he
dismissed the two children with the intelligence
that he wanted private speech with their uncle.*

*'Is anything wrong?' asked Ban when the
youngsters had gone.*

'No, 'twas merely that I would ask a favour.'

'What kind of favour?'

*'I need someone to deliver some horses to Cas-
tlemora. Archibald Graham asked me for some
good breeding stock a while ago. I told him I'd
look out for some likely animals.'*

*'The brood mares from Jarrow by any
chance?'*

'The same.'

Ban nodded. They were fine animals. How-

*ever, it wasn't a challenging undertaking and any
of Iain's men could have delivered them, so why
was he being singled out for the task? As so often
he sensed there was more here than appeared
on the surface.*

*'Would you mind?' Iain's tone was casual.
That more than anything else set off alarms in
Ban's brain and he couldn't help but smile.*

*'Of course not.' The assertion was sincere.
Castlemora was no more than two days' ride and
the weather fine. Besides, he owed his brother-
in-law a great deal and was glad to return a favour when he could.*

'Good.'

*Ban waited certain now that there must be
more to come. He was right, though he could
never have guessed its import.*

*'The journey may be made to serve two ends,'
Iain continued. 'Archibald Graham is an old
friend and ally but, sadly, his health is failing.'*

'I am sorry to hear it.'

*'He has a daughter. The last time I saw her she
was a child, but she must be eighteen or there-
abouts by now. She was widowed a while back
and he seeks a new husband for her.'*

*Ban's expression grew more guarded. When
he'd guessed at some ulterior motive he could
never have suspected anything like this. Yet it
was typical of Iain that he should, with such un-*

*ruffled ease, let drop some small but incendiary
piece of information.*

'By that you mean me?'

'Not at all,' was the imperturbable reply. 'I
merely suggest you should go and take a look.'

'She's a widow so there will be children as
well, Iain.'

'Apparently not.'

Ban raised an eyebrow. 'Not?'

'She was married but a year, and the mortal-
ity rate among infants is high.'

'As you say.' Although he didn't pursue it, the
matter still left a question in Ban's mind.

'The woman is reputed fair and, being Graham's daughter, will have a handsome dowry to
boot.'

'Better and better. And of course I am five and
twenty and single yet.' Ban paused. 'Did my sister put you up to this?'

'No, though I know she would like to see you
settled.'

'She told you that?'

'She may have mentioned it once or twice.'

'An understatement if ever I heard one. She
has been matchmaking these last five years.'

'Aye, well, what do you expect? You're her only
brother.'

'And being the last surviving male of the family I must get an heir.'

'Have you any objections to marriage?'

Ban shook his head. *'None—in principle.'*

It was true as far as it went. The idea of marriage did not displease him. It was a necessary
step in a man's life, a responsibility that must
be undertaken to ensure that his name and his
line continued. The woman should be compliant
and, ideally, pleasing to look upon although, as
he knew to his cost, beauty was no guarantee of
a warm and generous heart.

His brother-in-law nodded. *'Well then.'*

Considered dispassionately, Ban knew the
scheme made sense. All the same he couldn't
quite repress a twinge of envy when he compared
it with what Iain and Ashlynn had found in marriage. He saw the love and the passion in their
relationship, heard the shared laughter and the
witty banter. Iain was a devoted husband and a
good father. Recalling how he had once doubted
the man, Ban was ashamed. Ashlynn could not
have found a better. Among married couples they
seemed to be the exception that proved the rule.
To his knowledge Iain had never strayed from
his wife's bed. He had eyes for no one else and
that was as it should be. A vow once made should
be kept.

'Of course this commits you to nothing,' Iain
went on. *'The woman may not be to your liking.'*

Ban schooled his expression to neutrality. It

was far more likely that a landless thane would not be to her liking. 'As you say.'

'If so, you were merely delivering horses. On the other hand...'

'I might fall in love?'

'Stranger things have happened.'

Ban grimaced. In his experience love was a chimera, the stuff of boyish dreams. It also made a man dangerously vulnerable. If he married it would be a business arrangement, essentially. If affection followed later well and good. It was as much as one could hope for. *'Indeed.'*

Again the lazy smile appeared. *'As I said, she is reputed fair.'*

'Damn you, Iain.' The words were uttered without rancour.

'Then you'll go?'

'Aye, confound it. I'll go and look over the goods but I warn you now, I'm hard to please.'

'So was I.'

A gentle nudge brought Ban back to the present with a start and he realised Jock was passing him the water bottle. He took it with murmured thanks, realising guiltily that he hadn't been taking in any of the conversation thus far.

'We should be assured of a warm welcome anyway,' said Ewan. 'Archibald Graham has a reputation for hospitality.'

Ban and Jock exchanged glances and grinned.

One of Ewan's prime concerns was his stomach.
Yet no matter how much he ate it made not the
slightest difference to a frame that was small and
wiry. There wasn't an ounce of fat on him, but
he was surprisingly strong. At eighteen he had
ridden with Ban for three years now, at his side
in whatever adventure came their way.

'Good. A well-cooked meal and a comfortable
bed will suit me fine,' replied his leader.

'The old man was ailing last I heard,' said
Jock.

'I heard that too.' Ewan took a swig from the
leather costrel in his turn. 'Fortunate then his son
is of an age to manage things after him. He has
a widowed daughter too, accounted fair forbye.'

'She'll no lack for suitors then. Graham is rich
enough.'

'She's marriageable all right.'

'Do ye think she'd look my way?' Jock's craggy
face split in a grin revealing a missing front tooth.

'No,' replied Ewan. 'She could have her pick
of men. Why would she bother with an ugly brute
like you?'

'You can talk. If ugliness were a crime, lad-
die, ye'd no be in prison; ye'd be ten feet under it.'

Unperturbed, Ewan grinned. 'I'm thinking
she'll no marry either one of us, but what about
Davy? He's handsome enough.'

'Aye, he is, but he and Lachlan's daughter have

reached an understanding. Besides, Davy's a commoner too.'

'Then what about you, my lord?' said Ewan.

Ban was almost taken by surprise for it came so near his private concerns, but he managed to return the smile.

'I have nothing against marriage, though heiresses are almost invariably ugly.'

'I've never met any so I'll have tae take your word for that,' replied Jock.

Ban plucked idly at a strand of grass, thinking that, ugly or not, no heiress was likely to consider a dispossessed English thane to be a good catch. His fortunes had mended considerably in the last six years and he had gold enough but his lands were lost, perhaps in the hands of some Norman lord now. It was beyond mending, like a father and brother slain along with his brother's wife and their infant son. King William's men had laid waste to a huge swathe of the north of England, leaving a charred desert where nothing lived, and the bones of the dead lay bleaching amid the ruins of their villages for there were too few left alive to bury the number of the slain. All for the death of one man, and that man a fool. Robert De Comyn's brutality had led to the uprising in which he was killed. However, he was one of William's most favoured earls, and the king had taken a terrible revenge. Ban wondered whether the land and the people could ever recover from it.

'Perhaps Graham will have her matched with a Norman lord,' said Ewan.

Once again Ban was jolted out of his reverie. 'A Norman?'

'The Treaty of Abernethy has effectively made Malcolm a vassal of King William.' Jock spat into the dirt. 'What better way to create strong political alliances than to wed Scot to Norman?'

They digested this in silence, recognising the unwelcome truth of it. King Malcolm's raids into northern England in 1070 had been all too successful and called forth an uncompromising response from William, who raised an army and marched north to confront the Scots. Though brave and eager their army was routed by the Norman host. As a result Malcolm was forced to pay homage to William and sign the treaty at Abernethy two years later.

Ewan was scandalised. 'The lassie deserves better than that surely?'

'That she does, lad. Under all their pomp and titles the Normans are just treacherous bastards.'

'Aye, and led by a bigger bastard.'

It drew a laugh for King William's lowly birth was well known. It was also known to be a sore point with him.

'Dinna let him hear ye say that. He'd cut out your tongue.'

'He isna here though, is he?' Ewan reasoned.

'No, but he's left his mark has he not?'

'Aye, he has. Northumbria's naught but a wasteland.'

Silence followed this for they knew something of their lord's past and none cared to dredge up a subject they knew to be painful. Aware of their discomfiture, Ban adopted a lighter tone.

'So tell me, Ewan, is there no lass you've set your heart on?'

'Not yet.'

'There's no lassie in her right mind would have ye,' said Jock.

'Why not? You managed.'

'Aye, for my sins.'

Ban and Ewan grinned. Jock's wife, Maggie, was known for her acid tongue. She and Jock argued often and loud, but none doubted for a minute that they were devoted. They'd had a brood of eight children, of whom five survived infancy. Three were fine strong boys already showing the promise of their sire in their skill with weapons. Jock was rightly proud of them.

However, the subject of marriage came too near the knuckle and presently Ban excused himself on the pretext of wanting to stretch his legs, wandering away from his companions to follow the burn. He found the tenor of the conversation strangely unsettling and he wanted some time alone with his thoughts.

For the first couple of years after his arrival at Glengarron all he owned were the clothes on his back and his sword. He had been in no case to support a wife. Gradually he'd carved out a reputation and amassed wealth by the strength of his arm and the use of his wits. However, a name, even backed by gold, wasn't enough. Land was what mattered. Land was what gave a man position and power. Without it he was effectively little more than a hired blade. Women of noble blood might indulge him with a brief dalliance, but it was beneath them to marry such a man. It was a lesson he'd learned the hard way.

There had been female companions, of course, in the past six years, women of a certain class who filled a need. They were transient and soon forgotten, unlike Beatrice. Her image was still vivid, although he'd long since understood what she was.

Deep in thought Ban had been wandering along the edge of the burn, winding among the trees, paying little heed to his surroundings. He had left his men some way behind, being happy enough with his own company. Now he paused in the dappled shade beneath a mountain ash and looked about him. It was a pleasant scene with hills and trees and burn. The summer had been unusually warm and dry and the flow was slightly less now, but still the stream sparkled and leapt over the stones in its bed, the water a clear peaty brown. Presently, it fell over a rocky shelf and tumbled into a wide pool below. It looked cool and inviting and a swim would be most welcome. Ban sat down and pulled off his boots. As he did so a movement caught his eye and he saw that he was not the first to think of the idea. Someone was swimming on the far side.

Instinctively he ducked behind a boulder, watching. He could see a horse tethered to a bush and a pile of clothing at the water's edge. Then his eyes widened and a smile dawned. The figure in the water was unmistakably female. He had an impression of a slender waist and long shapely legs. Long brown hair trailed after her like some exotic weed. Who was she? Where had she come from? There were no dwellings near. She was no commoner; one look at her mount established that. She was clearly no blushing maiden either. Such girls were carefully chaperoned and certainly not permitted to ride out alone, or to swim naked in lonely woodland pools. Only one kind of woman would display her charms in such a way. Ban grinned. Doubtless she had not expected to find a client in so remote a spot, but this was a ready-made opportunity and no red-blooded man would pass it up. If she was amenable they could spend an enjoyable half-hour together on the river bank, time for which she would be amply recompensed afterwards.

Stripping to his breeches Ban waded into the pool. The water was cold enough to make him gasp but he plunged in, all sound concealed by the fall above. Then, duck diving, he swam under water towards the far side of the pool. By the time he surfaced near the other bank the girl was out and drying herself with a linen cloth. She was younger than he'd first thought, eighteen perhaps or a little more, but her body revealed the rounded curves of early womanhood. Having removed much of the water she wrapped the cloth around her and sat down on a rock to let the sun do the rest. Its heat was already drying her hair and he saw now that he had been mistaken: it was not dark brown but deepest auburn and it framed a lovely face. Ban's smile widened. This really was too good to miss.

Chapter Two

It was the horse that alerted Isabelle to his presence for the animal threw up its head and whinnied as it scented him. She looked round following the direction of the horse's gaze, and then drew in a sharp breath. Hazel eyes widened as they registered the figure moving towards her and she jumped up and backed a pace, ready to flee. Though the stranger was apparently unarmed he was fully six feet tall and possessed of the broad shoulders and hard-muscled arms that bespoke the fighting man. His waist had not a hint of fat about it, nor the long powerful legs currently accentuated by the clinging breeks. He stopped a few feet away. She had an impression of tawny hair and blue eyes and a clean-shaven face with strong lines and a square jaw. Then he smiled, revealing even white teeth.

'Good afternoon.'

Her heartbeat quickened. The courteous greeting was at distinct variance with the boldness of his manner and his present state of undress. Darting a swift look around her, she became more acutely aware of her present isolation and the remoteness of the place. If she screamed no one would hear. Besides, it was a mistake to show fear. He had clearly formed the wrong impression about her, but if she kept calm she might be able to talk her way out of this.

Ban saw the dainty chin tilt. Far from appearing embarrassed or afraid the look in her eyes was bold, challenging even. It satisfied him. He hadn't been mistaken. Unusually though, she lacked the hardness he associated with harlots. Perhaps that came with time. As yet she was unmarked by her experiences and, at closer quarters, even more desirable. The strength of his reaction surprised him. His gaze travelled downwards, mentally removing the cloth again. Seeing this, the colour rose in her face.

'How long have you been watching me?'

'Long enough.'

The blush deepened and the hazel eyes sparkled with anger. 'How dare you spy on me?'

'Unforgivable I know,' he admitted, 'but impossible to look away. Figures like yours are all too rare.'

She drew in a sharp breath at the sheer effrontery of it. Undismayed he waited, surveying her with keen enjoyment.

'You spy on me and then you insult me,' she said.

'No insult, lady, I swear. Consider it rather in the nature of homage to your beauty.'

'Such homage I can do without.'

'But it must be paid anyway.'

She shrugged. 'A cat may look at a king.'

'Or a queen,' he replied.

'I do not aspire so high.'

'Why, no, for if you were a queen you would not be alone in such a place as this; nor would you swim naked in the burn.'

Isabelle's heart sank and she backed another pace. The stranger came on, moving with apparent nonchalance.

'You need have no fear of me, lady. I won't hurt you.'

'What do you want?'

'Half an hour of your time, for which I will pay in gold.'

Her cheeks so pink before turned pale. He couldn't be serious. Another look at his expression disabused her of the idea. His intentions were unmistakable. Talking her way out of trouble was no longer an option. There was only one possibility now: to run for it.

He caught her in three strides, swinging her up into his arms. Isabelle shrieked. There followed a few seconds of furious struggle but his hold didn't alter. If anything he seemed amused. For one brief instant he looked into her face, then bent his head and brought his lips down on hers.

Her stifled cry of protest was ignored, and the kiss became more insistent, his mouth seeking her response in a more intimate embrace. Being crushed against him it was harder to breathe. Naked warmth pressed close. He drew back a little and again the blue eyes burned into hers, their expression unmistakable. Her heart lurched painfully.

'Please, I beg you…'

The construction he put on the words was quite other than she had intended. 'Have no fear, my sweet, you'll get what you want I promise you.'

Panic-stricken now, she redoubled her efforts. 'Let go of me! Put me down!'

He retained his hold with difficulty. 'What the devil…?'

'I said let me go!'

In another woman he'd have suspected playful protest and half-hearted struggle to increase his ardour, but there was nothing coy about her tone or expression and nothing half-hearted about her struggles. He frowned.

'Hold still, you little hellion. I'm not going to hurt you.'

'Then put me down.'

Hearing the note of fear beneath her command he hesitated. 'What is it? What's wrong?'

'How can you ask me that, you clod?'

'Clod is it? Perhaps I should show you otherwise.'

She almost lunged out of his arms. 'You'll have to kill me first.'

'I have no intention of killing you, you little fool, only of pleasuring you.'

'Never!'

The challenge was there and the temptation. He gritted his teeth, only too aware of the hot ache in his loins, of understanding that he wanted her more than any woman he could remember, and knowing how easy it would be to see his will met. Then he looked into her face. It reaffirmed the fear and reluctance he had seen before. Passion began to ebb. He'd seen enough of violence and violation to last him a lifetime. He wouldn't inflict that on any woman, least of all this one.

'For one who desires to escape a man's attentions you are very scantily clad.'

She made no reply to this but the look in her eyes was eloquent enough. His frown deepened.

'Have no fear. I'll not take a woman against her will.'

To her unspeakable relief he slackened his hold and set her on her feet. Grabbing the linen sheet she drew it higher, clutching it close. Her face was very pale, her heart thundering against her ribs.

He glared at her. 'I think you'd better explain.'

'I… It's not what you think. In truth it is not. I thought only to bathe.'

'A foolish thought,' he replied. 'Does your husband know you ride out alone?'

'I am not married.' That much was true at any rate and she had no intention of enlightening him about the rest.

The news surprised him. She was of more than marriageable age and fair besides. 'Your father then?'

She shook her head. 'He does not know.'

'He should keep a closer watch on you. It's madness for a woman to ride this country alone. Anything might have happened; rape is the least of it. You could as easily get your throat cut.'

Her cheeks burned, as much for the knowledge of her own folly as for the justice of the rebuke. The stranger's expression was thunderous, his strength frightening. When she thought of what he could have done, what he might still do, her stomach wallowed. She just had to pray he'd meant it when he said he'd never forced a woman.

Though she could not know it, much of his anger was directed at himself, realising what he had so nearly done, what he would still like to do. Imagination sent another surge of heat to his groin. With an effort he controlled it. Then he bent and retrieved her clothes, tossing them to her.

'Get dressed.'

She caught the garments awkwardly. He made no move to turn away. Annoyance mingled with fear.

'Are you going to watch?'

'It's a little late for modesty now, sweetheart.'

Biting back the hot reply that sprang to her lips, she hurriedly slipped on the kirtle and let the linen towel fall before donning her gown. The stranger's gaze never wavered. He handed her the woven girdle and watched her fasten it. She turned away from him to put on her stockings, tying her garters with shaking hands. Then she slid her feet into her shoes. He surveyed her critically.

'A little dishevelled but decent at least,' he observed.

Isabelle glared at him. Ban smiled faintly, acknowledging her courage, but his blue eyes held a dangerous glint. 'You are haughty for one who reveals her charms so freely.'

Anger began to replace anxiety. 'I did not deliberately reveal myself to you.'

'The outcome might well have been the same.

Fortunately for you, I have no taste for raping virgins.'

Virginity was a state long lost though she had no intention of sharing the irony. If he thought her experienced he might well change his mind and finish what he'd begun.

'No,' she retorted, 'only for gloating.'

He stared at her, incredulous. 'You ungrateful little vixen! I ought to warm your backside for that.'

'You wouldn't d—' Seeing his expression alter she bit the words off abruptly, recognising thin ice.

'Wouldn't dare? Try me, and you won't sit down for a week.'

Isabelle didn't care to put the matter to the test. She'd suffered quite enough humiliation at his hands.

'I'm minded to take you home myself and tell your father to thrash you,' he went on. 'It would teach you better sense.'

She paled a little, in fury now as much as fear. She'd experienced quite enough thrashings at the hands of men who thought it their God-given right to mete out punishment to the weaker sex. Resentment welled but she repressed it. Caution was needed here. If her father found out so would Murdo. The consequences didn't bear thinking about. No matter how much it went against the grain it would be better to play the part of the contrite, young virgin.

She lowered her eyes. 'Please, don't. I won't do it again, I swear it.'

Ban had no trouble believing that. She'd had a fright but the lesson had been well learned. Now she seemed only young and vulnerable.

'I suggest you go home and stay there,' he said.

Taking her arm in a firm clasp he led her to the waiting palfrey. The hold didn't hurt but it would not be resisted either. She could feel its heat through the stuff of her gown. They reached the horse but he didn't wait for her to mount. Lifting her with the same insulting ease as before, he tossed her up into the saddle instead. Then he handed her the reins.

'I doubt if we shall meet again, so I'll bid you Godspeed.'

She threw him an eloquent look and turned the horse's head. 'We shall not meet again. At least, not if I see you first.'

With that she touched the horse with her heels and it leapt forwards from a standing start to a canter. Quite unexpectedly, Ban found himself grinning. With grudging admiration he acknowledged her spirit, his gaze following her progress until she was lost to view.

Isabelle urged the horse to a swifter pace and only when she had put considerable distance be-

tween her and the stranger did she slow the animal to a walk. Even though the initial shock
had worn off she was still trembling. When she
thought of what might have happened she shuddered. He had been so strong, could so easily
have forced her. What had stopped him? From
his treatment of her it was clear he had taken her
for a slut. It didn't help to know she was responsible for that misunderstanding.

Her cheeks flooded with hot colour when she
thought of that passionate embrace. His kisses
burned: she could still feel the pressure of his
mouth on hers; her nakedness against his; strong
warm hands on her skin. He'd frightened her but
the memory of that intimacy was not entirely
repellent even though it should have been. She
quashed the realisation, quietly appalled. There
could be no place for such thoughts. They made
her feel like the slut he'd taken her to be. She'd
had a lucky escape and couldn't afford to be complacent about it. Neither her father nor her brother
must ever get wind of this. Above all, Murdo
must never find out.

Isabelle reached Castlemora without further
incident and, thanking the fates that the men were
elsewhere that afternoon, threw her horse's reins
to a groom and hastened to the women's bower
by the back route. In her present state she dared

not risk being seen. As she'd hoped the room was empty at this hour and having reached its safety she swiftly divested herself of the green gown, exchanging it for blue. Then she began to comb her hair into order. It was quite dry now and the auburn strands leapt beneath her fingers, fiery in the afternoon light. As she was engaged in this process Nell bustled in.

'There you are, my lady. Wherever have you been?'

'I went out riding.'

'Alone again I'll warrant.'

Nell gathered up the discarded gown. Plump and grey-haired, she was in her early fifties. Having known Isabelle since she was a baby, the older woman claimed the privileges of a trusted retainer. One of these was considerable freedom of speech. Nevertheless, she had a kindly nature and, despite an occasionally critical tongue, was also genuinely concerned. Seeing the younger woman's guilty look now she shook her head.

'You shouldn't do it, my lady. In these lawless times it's not safe. All manner of desperate rogues ride the border country and a woman alone would be easy prey.'

Recalling the events of the afternoon Isabelle shuddered inwardly. More than ever she was resolved not to ride out so far again. Only a fool would risk that twice. The desire for solitude must be balanced against the need for much greater caution.

'I'm sorry, Nell. I promise to be more careful in future.'

The tone was genuinely contrite. Surprised that she did not even try to argue the point, Nell regarded her keenly for a moment. However, Isabelle was apparently absorbed in removing a tangle from her hair and thus avoided the knowing eye.

'It were as well you did,' the nurse went on. 'Who knows what you might suffer at the hands of outlaws or marauders?'

Isabelle's colour became a shade more pronounced and she concentrated harder on her task. Nell crossed the room towards her.

'Here, best let me do it.'

She surrendered the comb and sat still while Nell took over, braiding the wilful mass into a thick plait and interweaving a ribbon to match the gown.

'If Murdo finds out he'll compel you to take an escort next time,' Nell went on, 'and you know fine well who it'll be.'

'I will not let him force his company on me in that way.'

'Do you really think you'd be able to avoid it?' The nurse paused. 'His power is second only to your father's now. No one dares to challenge his orders or his actions for fear of retribution. His thugs swagger about as though they own the place.'

'I know, but things will change when Hugh is Laird of Castlemora.'

'Your brother is full young. It remains to be seen whether he can be his own man. In the meantime it's Murdo who will control Castlemora, make no mistake about that. His ambitions don't stop there either.' Nell paused. 'His interest in you has not abated.'

'I have none in him. He knows that.'

'He has spoken on the matter?'

'He has.'

Nell pursed her lips. 'The brute grows bolder.'

'I told him plainly that he could have no hope of me.'

'He's not a man who takes no for an answer.'

The words were an uncanny echo of a former conversation, and Isabelle inwardly acknowledged their truth.

'You must marry again and soon,' Nell continued.

'By that you mean Lord Ban.'

'Who else?'

For a moment Isabelle saw the face of a stranger with tawny hair and blue eyes. Resolutely she tried to banish it, but it was not so easy when the memory of his kiss lingered on her lips.

He had held her in his arms. He had seen her naked. Again she grew hot with shame. It was a mercy she would never see him again.

'If you do not,' Nell went on, 'you may be compelled to wed Murdo later.'

It was the plain truth and Isabelle inwardly acknowledged it. The thought filled her with dread. 'I'd rather take holy orders.'

'That's the other choice.'

'I might as well be a bale of goods for all my opinion matters.'

'A woman's opinion never matters when it comes to marriage. You know that perfectly well.'

'At one time my father would never have countenanced such a husband for me, even to please Glengarron.'

Her father received several offers for her hand before settling on Alistair Neil. Nor had she been averse to such a glittering match. Her bridegroom appeared to be all that a maiden could desire: handsome, brave, rich, courtly. Being young and naïve it never occurred to her to look deeper, until it was too late.

'That was then,' replied Nell. 'Things are different now.'

'If the Neils had returned my dowry this wouldn't have happened.'

'It was wrong of them to act so.'

'Hugh wanted to go and get it back. I almost wish he had.'

'It would have meant bloodshed and death. Is that what you really want?'

Isabelle sighed and shook her head. 'I loathe the Neils for a pack of cold-hearted, rapacious thieves, but Castlemora doesn't need a blood feud. Nor would I have my dowry returned with blood on it.'

'Neither should you. No good could come of it.' Nell tied off the heavy braid. 'And if you're wise you'll not reject Lord Ban out of hand. He's all that stands between you and Murdo.'

Isabelle repressed a shudder, yet the unspoken fear persisted that she might be jumping from the cooking pot into the fire. Would history repeat itself and Glengarron prove to be the mirror of Dunkeld; her prospective husband a brute like Alistair Neil? Even if he was not, there was still the matter of producing heirs. What if the fault had not been wholly with her late husband? What if she really was barren? A man could put his wife aside for such a reason. Perhaps the cloister might be her lot after all.

These gloomy thoughts were interrupted by a knock at the chamber door. Then a servant entered.

'My lady, your father bade me tell you that the

riders from Glengarron have arrived, and that your presence is required below.'

She took a deep breath and composed herself. 'I will come directly.'

The servant bowed and withdrew. Isabelle rose from her seat, wondering if Lord Iain would be among the visitors. It had been many years since she had set eyes on him, not since she was a little girl, but she remembered the powerful charismatic figure very well. Now *there* was a man. Would Lord Ban be such another? Would he find her attractive? What if he did not? She had been so preoccupied with her own misgivings that she hadn't given any thought to possible doubts on the part of her intended groom. What if he rejected the match? Murdo's image returned with force. Her stomach knotted.

'Do I look all right?'

Nell smiled. 'You look beautiful.'

Isabelle smoothed the front of her gown and then quit the chamber, heading for the hall where her father would be entertaining their visitors. Already she could hear the sound of men's voices. No doubt they would be refreshing themselves with a mug of ale and delivering messages from their lord. On reaching the doorway she paused a moment to take in the scene. With her father was Hugh and beside him another man, several inches taller than both, who had his back to her.

Isabelle took a deep breath and then, summoning her courage, moved towards them. Her father saw her approach and, after a swift appraising look, he nodded.

'Ah, there you are, lass. Come and greet our guest.'

As he spoke the stranger turned and Isabelle's heart lurched. In a flash all the adventure of the afternoon returned with awful clarity as she found herself staring into a pair of very blue eyes—eyes that conveyed both recognition and amused surprise. And then her father was introducing them.

'Lord Ban, may I present my daughter, Isabelle?'

Chapter Three

For a moment she could neither move nor speak and her heart thumped so hard it seemed they must all hear it. Worse, she could feel a crimson tide rising from her neck to her cheeks as the blue gaze swept over her. Then she saw him smile, a mischievous smile that lit his face and spoke more clearly than words of huge enjoyment. For a moment she wished the ground would open up and swallow her; then indignation came to her rescue. Gathering her wits she dropped a proper curtsy and gave him her hand which he took with every sign of pleasure. He brushed it with his lips. The touch seemed to scorch her flesh.

'Lady Isabelle.'

The tone was courteous but she could not miss the amusement beneath. Isabelle felt perspiration start on her forehead. Would her father notice aught amiss? Would her brother? Thank heaven Murdo wasn't present for very little escaped him. Striving for self-control she summoned a smile.

'Welcome to Castlemora, my lord.'

'I thank you.'

'Your men too are most welcome.' Isabelle looked towards the door where stood a small group of retainers who immediately made their duty to her. Nothing in their expressions revealed that they knew anything about the incident at the pool. Why should they? Even if he had told them they could not know her identity.

If her father noticed aught amiss it was not apparent. 'Lord Ban has brought some fine horses, Isabelle.'

'I look forward to seeing them, Father.'

'Presently.' He turned back to their guest. 'My daughter is a keen rider. She has a way with horses.'

Ban smiled. 'I hope the animals will meet with the lady's approval.'

'I'm sure they will,' she replied. 'My father has often said that the Laird of Glengarron has a good eye for a mount.'

'Quite right. Not just for a mount either; breeding stock too.'

Isabelle's stomach churned. The subject was uncomfortably close to home and she hastened to redirect it. 'His reputation goes before him.'

'So it does, my lady.' Ban hadn't missed that fleeting expression of unease and was surprised. Experience suggested that she was no prude.

Her father nodded. 'He has made Glengarron strong.'

'As Castlemora is strong,' replied Ban.

'There's even greater strength in unity, eh?'

The allusion was impossible to miss and Isabelle's discomfort increased. Lord Ban didn't bat an eyelid.

'As you say, my lord.'

'We'll speak further on that in due course.' Her father beamed. 'In the meantime I'd like to see the new horses. Would not you, Isabelle?'

'Yes, very much.'

He held out his arm for her and she took it gratefully, allowing him to lead her outdoors. Lord Ban stood aside to let them pass and as they did so she saw the mischievous smile on his lips once more, could feel his gaze burning into her back as he fell into step with Hugh and followed them out. The knave was enjoying himself. Isabelle's chin tilted in militant fashion. The past could not be undone, but if he thought to discompose her again he was very much mistaken.

As they reached the courtyard they could see the horses standing by the trough; three lovely mares, strong and clean of limb. Hugh surveyed them approvingly.

'You have brought fine horses, my lord,' he observed.

Ban inclined his head. 'My brother's choices in this case.'

'Fine choices they are too.' Archibald Graham had paused some feet away, surveying them through narrowed eyes that missed nothing. 'What say you, Isabelle?'

'They're beautiful,' she replied and, relinquishing her father's arm, moved forwards to the nearest, a glossy bay mare with a white star on her forehead. The horse turned towards her, testing her scent through flared nostrils. Detecting no threat she relaxed again and lowered a velvety muzzle into Isabelle's hands.

'Your father spoke true. You have a way with horses, my lady,' said Ban, who had come to stand beside her. All too keenly aware of him she kept her attention focused on the mare.

'My daughter could ride almost as soon as she could walk,' said Graham, glancing her way. 'There are few to rival her in the chase.'

'I am sure the lady is unrivalled in many ways,' replied Ban. The tone was decidedly ambiguous though as far as she could tell only the two of them knew it. She threw him a swift and reproachful glance which apparently left him quite undismayed.

Graham ran a practised hand over the mare's

shoulder, back and flank, letting his gaze move down the legs to the hocks.

'Clean limbs. Plenty of bone,' he observed.

Isabelle dutifully followed his gaze. 'And stamina too, I'd say.'

'Aye, likely.' He turned to Ban. 'They are all broken?'

'All, my lord.'

Isabelle looked at her father. 'May I try her tomorrow?'

'Why not? Try them all.'

For the first time her spirits lifted a little. It would be fun. Indeed, if her assessment was correct, she was in for a treat.

Graham turned to his guest. 'You'll stay a while, my lord, and see the beasts settled in. Besides, I am sure Isabelle would be pleased if you would consent to ride out with her. I'm afraid my own health rarely permits it these days.'

Ban caught the expression in the girl's hazel eyes before they were swiftly veiled, and knew that pleasure was not what he had seen registered there. With a nonchalant smile he turned to his host.

'Delighted, my lord.'

Isabelle bit her lip. The knave was clearly amusing himself at her expense. She could guess what he thought of her. Was he already envisaging another tryst in some remote spot? The thought turned her hot all over but he should not have the satisfaction of seeing her discomfiture.

'I should be glad to accompany you both,' put in Hugh. 'If you have no objections.'

With a feeling akin to gratitude Isabelle threw him a warm smile. 'None at all. Come by all means.'

'I shall, with pleasure.'

'In the meantime I look forward to hearing news of my friends at Glengarron,' said Graham. 'You shall tell me as we dine, my lord.'

Ban bowed in acquiescence.

'Excellent.' Graham paused to look at his daughter. 'It will be good to have company. We tend to live a quiet life here and with little excitement, eh, Isabelle?'

'I have no complaint to make, my lord.' The tone was even enough though a tinge of warm colour appeared in her face.

'Excitement can be a double-edged sword, can it not?' said Ban. 'Fun, but dangerous at times.'

Her colour deepened but she turned and met his eye, now gleaming with sardonic humour. 'It may be as you say, my lord. I have always found it to be transient and thus quite easily forgotten.'

A widening grin acknowledged the hit. 'Now I have always been of the opposite opinion, my lady. Some forms of excitement leave an indelible impression on the mind.'

The hazel eyes widened in feigned surprise but he did not miss the flash of anger there. 'With such an appetite for excitement you must have had many such experiences.'

Ban fought the temptation to laugh. If they'd been alone, he'd have taught her the folly of impertinence. For a moment or two he indulged that pleasurable notion. Unfortunately, they weren't alone—yet.

'They add a certain spice to life,' he replied, 'and thus my appetite remains undiminished.'

'I can well believe it, my lord.'

His eyes gleamed. He had thought he'd known what to expect from his visit to Castlemora, but he'd been wrong on every count. It was far from being predictable or dull. Instead he found himself intrigued. Feistiness in a woman did not displease him: after all, his sister possessed the quality in abundance. It didn't displease Iain either apparently. Furthermore, his brother-in-law handled it supremely well: while he had never attempted to break her spirit he knew exactly how to bend Ashlynn to his will and have her enjoy the mastery too. Knowing his sister's fiery temper Ban could only marvel at how that had been achieved. His gaze rested speculatively on Isabelle. Could he bend her thus to his will? The thought was unexpectedly titillating.

* * *

The meal that evening provided Isabelle with new insights where their guest was concerned. Much to her relief he made no further reference to what had passed between them earlier and, because of her father's desire for news, the conversation was mostly about Glengarron. Required to say little she listened with close attention. Like everyone else at Castlemora she had long known of Lord Iain's marriage to the Lady Ashlynn, but the circumstances were intriguing. Rumour had it that he'd carried her off and married her by force which, knowing the man's reputation, was not at all beyond the bounds of possibility. However, that didn't tally with the stories of a mutually happy union. Moreover, Ban would surely not be on such friendly terms with a man who mistreated a beloved sister. Hearing him speak of his two young nephews she could detect real pride and affection in his expression. It was a side to him that she would not have suspected. Her curiosity increased.

'Have you no family besides your sister, my lord?' she asked.

There followed a fractional hesitation and his face was shadowed as though by some unwelcome memory, but when he spoke his tone was courteous. 'No, my lady. She and I are the last surviving members. The rest were slain by King William's mercenaries.'

'I am truly sorry to hear it.' The hazel eyes met and held his steady gaze. 'And your home?'

'Burned, my lady.'

'A bad business,' said Graham, shaking his head. 'I think King William has much to answer for.'

'But who will make him answer it?' asked Isabelle. 'Surely his grip on England is too strong to be challenged.'

'You are in the right of it, my lady,' replied Ban. 'And Northumbria has paid for its defiance.'

For a moment there was silence and then the conversation turned to other topics, but Isabelle pondered what she had learned. Their guest had not gone into details but her imagination was good and she had heard many tales about the brutality of the king's soldiers in Northumbria. They had cut a sixty-mile swathe through the land and reduced a once-great kingdom to ashes. No mercy had been shown to the population: men, women and children alike slaughtered in the wake of William's wrath. It had been some years ago, when she was little more than a child, but hearing it mentioned now brought back the shadow of that fear. Those who could flee did, heading for the border, seeking safety with kin if they had any or selling themselves into slavery if they did not. Even that was preferable to facing William's anger. How had Ban and his sister escaped? Had they been pursued or had they been lucky? How had they met Lord Iain? Suddenly she wanted to know. However, from his obvious reticence she guessed the subject was a painful one, and in any case it would have been discourteous to probe.

Now that he was engaged once more in conversation with her father she had leisure to observe. Even reclined at his ease there was something almost feline about the lithe power of the man. She knew his strength all too well. The recollection of that humiliating scene was sharp. She had been completely at his mercy and yet he had not taken advantage of it, or not as much as he might have anyway. It was plain though that he had believed her to be a whore, or as good as. His whole behaviour pronounced it. For that she was to blame and the knowledge aroused a feeling much akin to regret. That in turn led to other, more troubling thoughts: after what had passed between them he might not wish to offer for her hand. No man wanted a wife of suspect virtue. Double standards operated with regard to what constituted acceptable behaviour for men and women, and she was not naïve enough to think herself exempt. If only she had not been so reckless.

She darted a swift look at their guest. What

must he now be thinking? The very fact that he had come here at all suggested a willingness to marry if what he found pleased him. Isabelle felt suddenly sick realising then that, had things been different, she would not have looked with aversion on Lord Ban. As it was she had likely destroyed her chances this day with one ill-judged act. She had been so intent on outwitting Murdo that she had effectively played straight into his hands.

Having been so intent on their guest she had temporarily forgotten about the master-at-arms. He had taken no part in the conversation this evening, apparently content just to listen. She glanced across the table. For a moment Murdo's gaze met hers but his expression was unreadable. All the same it made her uneasy and she looked away again. If nothing else, this projected alliance with Glengarron would have removed her from his sphere. Her folly today was like to cost her dear.

After a decent interval she rose from the table and excused herself from the company, bidding them a courteous goodnight. Ban, who had risen with her, replied in kind. Then he smiled.

'I hope our arrangement to ride tomorrow still stands, my lady.'

His gaze met and held hers. In it she read both

speculation and challenge. He was playing with her. Isabelle bit back the refusal that sprang so readily to her lips. It would be impossible to get out of this without causing her father's displeasure, for he would take it much amiss that she snubbed one who was both guest and prospective suitor.

'Of course,' she replied.

'Then I suggest we leave early before the day grows hot,' said Hugh.

Ban smiled. 'A good suggestion.'

He bowed over her hand, brushing it with his lips, holding it for just a moment longer than was necessary. The warmth of his touch sent a tingle along her skin. Feigning calm she turned away and then took her leave of them all.

On returning to the bower Isabelle found herself in no mood for sleep and, dismissing Nell, went to the window. The evening was still and scented with warm earth and cut grass. Some light yet lingered in the western sky, the horizon soft with lemon haze beneath the deepening blue where the first stars shone clear. Bats flitted among the orchard trees and somewhere a dog barked. Then the silence dropped again. The sweet air that was usually so soothing now only added to her feeling of desolation.

She could well visualise the scene in the hall.

On the surface all would be smiles and good-will. Lord Ban would not offend her father intentionally; the friendship existing between Castlemora and Glengarron was too valuable to risk. He would handle the matter more tactfully: the horses would provide the means for all to save face. He had come to deliver them and, having fulfilled the obligation, he would depart without ever making an offer for her hand. Tears pricked her eyelids and for perhaps the tenth time that evening she silently cursed her own stupidity.

Chapter Four

If she had entertained any hopes that his lordship might oversleep next morning, Isabelle was disappointed for when she neared the stables he was already there, the horses saddled and ready. Hugh was with him and, she noted with disfavour, so was Murdo. Seeing her approach they turned towards her, causing Ban to look round. He greeted her with a smile. Somehow she managed to reply with the usual courtesies. Then her gaze went to the horses.

'You are before me, my lord. I hope I have not kept you waiting.'

'Not at all. You are prompt.'

To avoid the searching gaze she moved towards the bay mare, stroking the velvety muzzle and running a practised eye over bridle and saddle, satisfying herself that it was in good order.

'Allow me.'

Lord Ban came to the mare's near side and held the bridle while she mounted. Once she was safely ensconced a strong hand slid her foot into the stirrup, lingering briefly on her ankle. Only too conscious of his touch, she avoided his eye and occupied herself with the arrangement of her skirt.

He left her then and went to mount his own horse, a powerful and mettlesome chestnut which he reined in alongside her a few moments later. Murdo and Hugh fell in behind leaving Lord Ban's men to follow at a respectful distance.

'Quite an escort,' she remarked. 'Are you expecting trouble, my lord?'

'A precaution only. It is unwise to ride alone in these troubled times.'

Isabelle reddened and threw him a sideways glance but his face gave nothing away. Even so the rebuke had been plain. He wasn't going to let her forget about what had happened. The knowledge that she deserved it didn't help. However, she would not rise to the bait and touching the horse with her heels cantered on ahead.

The mare had a smooth even gait and a soft mouth that responded to the lightest touch of the rein. A long open stretch of turf beckoned and she gave her mount its head. Immediately the spirited creature leapt forwards, flying hooves skimming the ground, mane and tail streaming. Revelling in the speed neither horse nor rider paid heed to the thudding hoofbeats behind. The chestnut drew level and catching a glimpse of its rider's anxious expression, Isabelle raised an eyebrow. So he thought she was out of control, did he? His lordship made a good many assumptions about her. It was time to dent his self-assurance a little. Leaning forwards she urged the mare on.

Ban realised then that his earlier alarm had been unfounded. Isabelle hadn't lost control at all. Furthermore he realised he was being tested. The long greensward led into a copse and the narrow track meant he had to rein back, following in the mare's wake. Ducking low branches and jinking round bends in the path, they sped on. The mare took a fallen log in her stride and fifty yards later leapt a dry streambed. The chestnut followed suit, never altering its stride. Then, as they neared the edge of the copse Ban saw it, a great tree uprooted by an ancient storm, the centre section of its trunk lying across the path. It was high and solid. Isabelle didn't hesitate. Heart in mouth, he watched the mare gather herself and leap, soaring over the obstacle into the open land beyond.

Setting his jaw, Ban collected the chestnut a little. The big horse stood back and took off, clearing the jump with ease and landing safe beyond it. Then for the first time Ban let the animal have its head. The chestnut responded, lengthening its stride. Almost two hands bigger than the mare and far more powerful, it steadily narrowed the gap until eventually they drew level again.

Isabelle looked round, her face registering surprise for a moment. Then it was gone. She pulled up a little further on, he following suit. The blowing horses snorted, their great muscles trembling with effort and excitement. Ban, catching his own breath, was torn between reluctant amusement and annoyance for the anxiety she had caused him. That innocent expression didn't deceive him for a moment. The vixen was thoroughly enjoying herself. Moreover, the pace had heightened the bloom on her cheeks and brought a lovely sparkle to the hazel eyes. Strands of hair, loosened from the sober braid, played around her face in an artless halo that enhanced the suggestion of innocence. It was also unwittingly alluring and conjured more erotic thoughts. Ever since the episode at the burn they'd continued to tease his imagination. With an effort he suppressed them and nodded towards the mare.

'How do you like her?'

'Very much.' Isabelle patted the glossy neck. 'It's like riding the wind.'

'In truth I thought you were. Do you always set such a pace?'

Her face registered apparent concern. 'Was it too much for you, my lord?'

For a second or two he was speechless with incredulity. Then he fought a desire to laugh. If they'd been alone, he'd have exacted a penalty for barefaced cheek. It was a pleasing notion, but unfortunately they weren't alone. Instead he asked, 'Where did you learn to ride like that?'

'From my father, and a groom called Hamish.'

'They taught you well.'

'So I think.' She turned her attention to the chestnut. 'That is a fine animal. What is he called?'

'Firecrest.'

'It suits him. Did you break him?'

'I did, but he was a rare handful.'

'I can believe it.'

Before he could make any other observations their companions hove into sight, reining in nearby.

'How do you like the mare, Sister?'

'I like her well,' replied Isabelle, 'as I was just telling Lord Ban.'

'She can certainly move, eh, Murdo?' said Hugh.

'Indeed she can,' replied the other. 'All the same, you took a dangerous risk, my lady.'

His tone was perfectly level but she heard his unspoken disapproval. It irked her. He had no right to criticise; he had no rights over her at all, nor ever would have.

'I did not ask you to follow, Murdo. You were always free to go around the obstacle if you felt it too dangerous a challenge.'

Her brother drew in an audible breath and chuckled appreciatively. 'Oho! A hit! Most definitely a hit.'

The master-at-arms inclined his head. 'My lady's wit is sharp.'

For a moment the dark gaze glinted as it met hers, his expression quite unmistakable. Isabelle lifted her chin in silent defiance even though, inwardly, she regretted letting her temper get the better of her. She knew she had annoyed him and that it behoved her to be more careful; Murdo was not possessed of a forgiving nature and it didn't pay to cross him.

Ban had observed that brief exchange and felt his curiosity stir. The tension between the two was evident. He wondered what lay behind it. Apart from a brief introduction he'd had little to do with the man thus far, but Ban was fully aware of his presence none the less. From the seating arrangements at the table the previous evening it was apparent that Murdo enjoyed a privileged position in the household, as though he were a member of the family rather than a servant. However, such things were not uncommon. A rich house-

hold might well take in poorer relations and find
a place for them. In this instance an influential
place, he thought, but then a capable man who
worked hard might do much to better himself.

He had no doubt whatever that the master-at-
arms was capable; he'd met too many fighting
men not to recognise the trait. In combat Murdo
would be ruthless and deadly. He was also a natural leader. To judge from the way his men acted
around him he evidently commanded their respect, no mean feat when the men themselves
were hardened mercenaries. Castlemora's reputation had been well earned. Perhaps too Murdo
saw it as part of his role to be protective of Lady
Isabelle even if she did resent it as interference.
That would explain much. The more Ban thought
about it, the likelier it seemed.

Before he could dwell further on the matter the
party set off again, albeit at a more sober pace,
and the conversation turned to other things. Isabelle didn't speak to the master-at-arms again or
even look in his direction, and the remainder of
the ride passed without incident.

When, about an hour later, they returned to
Castlemora, Archibald Graham came out to meet
them. Then he looked quizzically at Isabelle.

'Well, how did the mare go?'

'Very well, Father. She has speed and stamina as we thought.'

'Good. Perhaps you will find the time to ride the others.'

She returned a non-committal smile and dismounted. Lord Ban followed suit and came to join them. Standing so close to him now she was forcefully reminded just how much taller he was and how strong. Thence it was but a short step to recalling their first meeting. The memory burned. Glancing up she saw him smile as though he somehow divined her thought. Of course, that was impossible. Even so, her face, pink before from the fresh air, became a much deeper shade.

Apparently unaware of her discomfiture her father turned to Ban. 'I trust you enjoyed your ride, my lord.'

'Very much, sir.' He looked at Isabelle. 'Who would not in such company?'

Her father beamed. Isabelle thought he'd look a lot less gratified if he knew the truth. They made their way indoors for the sun was hot and the cooler air of the hall was a welcome contrast. Graham bade the servants fetch refreshment and then poured the ale with his own hands before offering his guest a cup.

'It is most pleasant to have company again.'

'You are kind,' said Ban. 'In truth Castlemora is a most delightful spot.'

'Thank you.' Graham clapped him on the shoulder. 'I am glad you think so. I trust you will not find our hospitality lacking.'

'I am sure I shall not. One day I hope to have the honour of returning it.'

'If my health were better I'd like nothing more.' Graham threw him a wry smile. 'However, this hot weather is most tiring I find. It only seems to aggravate my condition.'

'I am sorry to hear it.'

'Never mind, I have strength enough to show you round Castlemora, if you would like it.'

Ban regarded him in concern. 'I beg you will not over-exert yourself, my lord.'

'No such thing,' replied the other. 'I'd be delighted.'

'Then I thank you.'

Isabelle's heart sank as she watched them head for the door, feeling certain this wasn't just about showing their guest around. Her father almost certainly intended to talk business and it had nothing to do with horses.

Strolling to the end of the orchard the two men stopped to survey the view beyond.

'A fine prospect,' observed Ban. 'Truly Castlemora is most happily situated.'

'Aye, it is.' Graham smiled. 'And I'll leave it to my son stronger and richer than ever it was when

I became laird.' He paused. 'But it is not of my son I would speak, as I think you know.'

Ban remained silent, waiting. Now they would come to it. He was quite ready, knowing what needed to be said. It wouldn't be an easy conversation but it must be unambiguous. There could be no room for misunderstanding.

'As I told you,' Graham continued, 'my health is not of the best. It is my ardent wish to see my daughter married again before I die.'

'A laudable aim, though I hope your lordship will live many years yet.'

'That is not likely I fear. The pains in my chest come more often now. It is a penalty of age.' He paused. 'As I intimated, your coming here is not just about bloodstock, though indeed the horses are very fine.'

'It is of Lady Isabelle you wish to speak.'

'My daughter's first marriage was ended untimely, a circumstance none could have foreseen.'

'A hunting accident, wasn't it?'

'Aye. A stray arrow from the thicket.' Graham shook his head. 'The culprit was never found. Most likely it was a poacher who fired without looking carefully enough, and then panicked and fled when he realised what he had done.'

'That is quite possible. The fellow must have known he'd hang otherwise.'

'At any rate it was a bad business and it has left Isabelle vulnerable.'

'Did she not wish to remain among her husband's kin?'

'To be honest, there was little love lost between Isabelle and her late husband's mother.'

'I see.'

'When the match was arranged it seemed good but subsequently...' Graham paused, eyeing his companion warily, as though deciding how far to commit himself. Then he took a deep breath. 'Subsequently I have had cause to repent the alliance. The Neils refused to return the balance of my daughter's dowry.'

Ban stared at him. 'Refused?'

'Aye, God rot them.'

The news gave Ban pause, though not for the reasons his companion might have thought. He didn't care about the gold. The point was that if Isabelle had only a small dowry it greatly reduced her chances of making an illustrious second match. At the same time her father wanted her off his hands. The strengthened tie with Glengarron began to look like a convenient pretext; the real reason was more concerned with the bridegroom's own lack of expectations. Such a man could not look too high for a wife. The more he thought about it the more certain Ban became. The realisation brought with it a raft of mixed emotions. It was a bitter reminder of what had been lost, but, at the same time, this match offered a glimmer of hope—for his house at least.

'She will still have a dowry of course, though it will not be as great as I'd have liked,' Graham went on. 'In spite of my representations the Neils have refused to return any part of the original portion. Until they can be persuaded otherwise that is how the matter stands.'

'On what grounds did they refuse?'

'On the grounds that there was no issue from the marriage.'

The question Ban had carried in the back of his mind now loomed large. However, it was a sensitive matter and he chose his words carefully. 'No issue because the child died, perhaps?'

'There was no child. My son-in-law was often from home in the king's service. No doubt he thought he had time aplenty to sire heirs.'

That threw up more queries in his companion's mind. Why would a newly married man leave his bride's bed, particularly when the bride looked like Isabelle? Even the king would not demand such a sacrifice, unless for dire political emergency. As far as Ban was aware there hadn't been any of those in last year or so. There was more to this matter for certain. While he didn't think that Graham was trying to mislead him—the man had been frank thus far—he knew they hadn't got to the truth yet either. Perhaps that resided with Isabelle herself.

'It surprises me that Neil should have shirked so serious a responsibility,' he said.

'He was a fool.' Graham hesitated. 'Isabelle will breed, my lord.'

'Will she?' Ban didn't want to antagonise his host but at the same time he had to make his own position clear. 'You know my family history so I need not repeat it now,' he continued. 'The essential point is this: as the last surviving male member of my line it is imperative that I get heirs to continue it.'

'Of course it is. I understand that.'

'Then you will also understand that I need to be sure.'

Graham frowned. 'What exactly are you suggesting?'

'A secret betrothal. Later, if matters turn out as planned, the arrangement would be formalised publicly.'

'It is not without precedent but it would not be easy to keep the matter quiet.'

'You may rely on my discretion.' Ban paused. 'It's a risk.'

'A calculated one, since you have already said you are certain of a favourable outcome.'

'If I agree to this I expect the matter to be expedited with all possible speed.'

'As soon as you like.'

For a moment Graham was silent, formulating his thoughts. Ban made no attempt to push him. The proposal was not without precedent and the circumstances were unusual. At the same time he knew that he wanted Isabelle Graham; had wanted her since the day he met her. However, physical desire was one thing; he couldn't afford to lose sight of the bigger picture. He had a duty to his family, to the souls of his murdered kin. He had to be sure.

At length Graham nodded. 'A secret betrothal it is then, for the time being.'

'The only remaining question is whether the lady will agree to the arrangement.'

'Isabelle will be ruled by me.'

Ban wasn't surprised. It was a father's responsibility to find a suitable husband for a daughter, and her duty to accede to his choice. If Graham spoke with such confidence it was because he knew Isabelle respected his judgement. Privately Ban wondered what her true feelings would be. Would she accept him willingly or would she secretly consider such a match beneath her? Beatrice had considered it beneath her. Of course, he'd been much younger then, and inexperienced, so smitten with a lovely face that he'd failed to see the character behind. That had not become apparent until he declared himself and asked for her hand…

For a moment she stared at him. Then she laughed. 'Marry you?'

At first he mistook the nature of the laughter, taking it for surprise. 'Aye, why not?'

'My father would never permit me to marry a Sassenach lord.'

'I will speak to him, talk him round.'

'It's not just that,' she replied.

'Then what? I have wealth enough.'

'But where are your lands, my lord?'

His smile faded. 'They were stolen from me.'

'And you have no prospect of regaining them.'

'I will get more.'

'How? You do not wield the kind of influence that would gain you an estate.'

His jaw tightened. 'I'll find a way.'

'That might take years, if you ever succeed. I cannot waste my life waiting on the event.'

'Would it be a waste then, Beatrice?' He paused. 'We would be together.'

'To live in the hedgerows?'

'Hardly that. I can support you in comfort.'

'But you cannot give me position.'

'Does that matter so much?'

'Of course it matters. My father is rich and powerful, the laird of fair estates. Should not my husband be the same?'

'I cannot blame you for wanting it,' he replied.
'Well then.'

'I thought... I hoped that your feelings for me were strong enough to offset that.'

Beatrice smiled coldly. 'You rate yourself too high, my lord, if you presume to think so. I am not so negligent of the duty I owe to my family and my name as to throw myself away on a mere nobody.'

Stung now, he was goaded into retort. 'The Thanes of Heslingfield are not nobodies. They come from a proud and ancient line.'

'But where are they now? They have no power, no influence. They are nothing.'

Brian pushed the memory aside. He'd been a fool and paid the price for it. The naïve and idealistic lover was long gone and in his place was a grown man who knew the world he lived in. This offer was an opportunity, one he'd little thought to have. It would provide a foundation on which much might be built—in time.

'We have an agreement then,' he said.

Graham smiled and held out his hand. 'You'll not regret it.'

Ban clasped the offered hand and hoped the words were true.

Chapter Five

Isabelle stared at her father in stunned disbelief, uncertain that she'd heard him correctly. 'A secret betrothal?'

'That's right.'

'A betrothal which will give him the rights of a husband?'

'Correct.'

Disbelief was slowly displaced by outrage. Did the Sassenach thane really imagine she would agree to this? The very fact that he had suggested it showed the kind of regard in which he held her, in which he had always held her.

'You can't mean it.'

'I was never more serious in my life.'

His expression supported the words, a circumstance that created the first stirrings of alarm.

'Marriage is one thing; this is quite another.'

'It is unusual, I'll admit, but it is not unknown.'

'This is little better than prostitution.'

'It is no such thing. Nor would I have agreed to it if I thought so.' Her father paused. 'In essence betrothal is little different from marriage. The only variation here is that it will not be made public until you are with child.'

The visualisation of what that entailed fanned her rage to red heat. How Lord Ban must have delighted in creating this little scheme. That her father should actually sanction the plan must have afforded the very greatest amusement. How much his lordship must be enjoying the thought of her reaction.

'I am not a brood mare to be covered by a Glengarron stallion!'

'It is a wife's duty to bear children and you have not done so.'

'That wasn't my fault alone.'

'I have given you the benefit of the doubt thus far, but now it's up to you to prove yourself worthy of my faith.'

'I'd gladly prove it, but not in this covert, underhanded manner.'

'You are a widow with no children and no dowry to speak of. God's blood, do I have to spell it out?' He glared at her. 'You have one chance now and this is it, unless you'd prefer the cloister.' Seeing that she remained silent he nodded. 'I didn't think so.'

She closed her eyes, trying not to give way to rising panic. Her father had spoken no more than the truth about her circumstances and her lack of religious vocation. She realised too that there was no way out of this: much as she wanted to reject this proposition a refusal to comply would leave the way open for Murdo. All he'd have to do would be to ask for her hand and it would be granted. She was under no illusions about what would happen then.

She licked dry lips. 'When is this betrothal to take place?'

'I have decided upon Thursday next.'

Her heart leapt towards her throat. Thursday was only two days away. 'That's too soon.'

'Soon or no, it's your betrothal day.'

'This haste is indecent.'

Her father's gaze grew steely. 'Your opinion is irrelevant. You'll do as you're told. The betrothal will take place in my private chamber. I shall invite Lord Ban there, ostensibly to discuss business. It will be a simple matter for you to join us unnoticed. Everyone else will be about their work and it will be quiet enough for our purposes. It won't take long.'

He was right: it wouldn't take long to join her hand with Lord Ban's and to speak the vows that would make her his. How easily a woman was disposed of. She'd had no say last time either, although then there had been a public wedding followed by lavish feasting and then the bedding ceremony, held amid ribald jests and laughter. How hollow that laughter had proved to be.

She shivered inwardly, recalling all the nights spent in Alistair Neil's bed; nights she had come to dread. *Your late husband couldn't get a cock stand.* Murdo's mocking voice echoed in her head. The words were not entirely accurate though. Alistair had, occasionally, achieved an erection but it carried a price. She swallowed hard, seeing it all in her mind's eye, her husband standing by the bed, slowly removing his belt, wrapping the buckle end around his fist…

'Take off your shift.'

'Please, my lord…'

'I said take it off.'

Trembling she complied. When she was naked he nodded.

'Lie down as I have instructed you.'

Reluctantly she obeyed, knowing what was coming and knowing it would be far worse if she tried to resist. She gasped as the belt descended across her buttocks leaving a fiery welt, her hands clawing the coverlet. At first pride kept her silent but she had quickly learned the folly of that. Since it was her cries that excited him he would continue to beat her until she did scream. When she cried out he flung down the belt and joined her, pinning her down, his knee forcing her legs apart. Then he took her from behind. It hurt, but her cries pleased him and, mercifully, that part of the procedure never lasted long, a minute or two at most before the small, probing member was withdrawn. Then he rolled off her, panting and sated. She shut her eyes, praying silently that this time she would conceive and that somehow his thin and watery seed might take root in her womb...

Isabelle had heard it said that sometimes women found pleasure in the act of intercourse but she couldn't imagine how, even if the man were not violent. Alistair had dreamed up many ways of achieving his purpose, almost all of them painful, but he took good care that the marks he left on her didn't show. Even if he had not, no one in that household would have questioned his behaviour. Nor would the law: it was a husband's right to chastise his wife if he chose. It was his right to do anything he liked, and her duty to submit.

'Are you listening to me?'

Her father's voice pulled her up abruptly. 'Yes, my lord, I'm listening.'

'It won't take long. When it's done you'll consummate the betrothal.'

Isabelle paled. 'I will not; that is not until we've got to know each other a little better.'

'Damn it, you're no blushing virgin now and this is no time for airs and graces. The union will be consummated immediately and you will give yourself to Lord Ban whenever it pleases him thereafter. Is that clear?'

She swallowed her rage. 'Very clear.'

'I hope so.'

'And just how is this arrangement to remain secret?' she demanded. 'I would not be the subject of servants' gossip.'

'There are ways and you will find them. I imagine Lord Ban will not lack invention there.'

'I am quite sure he won't.'

The sarcastic tone wasn't lost on her father. He raised an eyebrow. 'You'd do well to curb your acid tongue, my lass. No man wants a harridan for a mate.'

She lowered her gaze, quelling the urge to argue. Her father's temper was close to the edge already. If she pushed him any further he might bring the betrothal nearer still or add some further humiliating conditions to the arrangement.

'I beg your pardon. It's just that this has happened so quickly; it wasn't what I expected and it has left me unprepared.'

He looked a little mollified. 'Ah, well, I suppose it has, but you must get used to the idea.'

'Yes, Father.'

'The sooner you are with child the sooner you can live openly as husband and wife and take your rightful place in society. Remember that.'

She nodded mutely, not knowing which was worse: having to submit to the will of a stranger or, possibly, failing to conceive. All the old doubts revived. If it became evident that she was barren then she would be quietly put aside. The arrangements attending this betrothal were precisely to allow for that. She would be made to enter a nunnery; to remain there for the rest of her life, conveniently forgotten. Lord Ban would return to Glengarron and seek another wife. Either way he would emerge the winner having risked nothing. Her nails dug into her palms as impotent anger mingled with equally impotent resentment. In a man's world the only option for a woman was obedience.

Ban received the news of his imminent betrothal with outward *sang-froid*. In reality he was a little disconcerted to discover that his words had been taken so literally. He'd expected to have more time. However, Graham was obviously keen to see his daughter plighted and, given the circumstances, perhaps there was little point in delay. He listened attentively while the other man explained the details. Ban nodded. It was a good plan; one that could be implemented with the discretion they all desired.

'Afterwards, you may have the use of the chamber for an hour,' his host went on. 'I'll ensure you're no disturbed.'

Ban blinked. Whatever else he hadn't been expecting that. He'd vaguely imagined that some quiet arrangement would be made that night whereby he and Isabelle might seal their betrothal. This was something else again. If he jibbed at the thought how much more would she dislike it? Yet if he demurred now how was that going to look? After all, he'd been the one to propose this.

'I thank you for the courtesy,' he replied.

'Don't mention it.' Graham eyed him steadily. 'After this you'll be left to your own devices.'

For the first time Ban was forced to give serious thought to the possible time frame of events. A woman might conceive straightaway or it might take months. Then there were the practicalities to consider. It was easy enough for a couple to slip away and find privacy from time to time, but, equally, it would become increasingly inconvenient and the longer it went on the greater was the likelihood of discovery. That would be exceedingly awkward since it would put Isabelle's good name in jeopardy and people could not be enlightened without full revelation of the truth.

The whole business suddenly began to look a lot more complicated. Up till now most of his liaisons had been with women of a certain kind who were paid for their favours and gave them freely. Everyone benefited. A series of furtive trysts was quite different. It occurred to him that Isabelle might have reservations about the matter. Quite understandable reservations, he now decided. However, he could hardly voice the thought here.

'As you say,' he replied.

'Get her with child as soon as may be. I'd be loath to send her to a convent.'

A convent? Ban felt a twinge of guilt as it dawned on him that, if she really were barren and he had to put her aside, that would indeed be her fate. It was an unwelcome truth. However, if matters went as he hoped it wouldn't come to that. Isabelle would be his wife, openly and in all honour. Afterwards there would be plenty of time to grow closer, emotionally as well as physically.

'I'll do my best to prevent that situation,' he said.

Graham nodded. 'So will she, I'll warrant you.'

Other doubts surfaced in Ban's mind, vaguely uncomfortable doubts about why Isabelle would be submitting herself to his will. He quashed them. This was a matter of business not sentiment. Betrothals took place every day; formal marriages too in which the bride and groom had never previously met. They were wedded and bedded and there an end. Personal inclination didn't enter into it.

'Thursday it is then,' he replied.

Having left Graham, Ban went to find Isabelle. They needed to talk, although it wasn't going to be an easy conversation. However, he needed to create a right understanding between them, and honesty seemed to be the best policy there. Then she would have no false expectations. Having been married once, it was unlikely she would cherish any foolish ideas about love or romance. He hoped not anyway. Certainly he wouldn't promise what he couldn't deliver.

Isabelle was in the still room. She was tying bunches of lavender and the whole room was filled with sweet fragrance. The scent evoked old memories and for a moment he was transported back to his childhood at Heslingfield, watching the maidservants hang bunches of herbs to dry. The servants were long dead, slain when Heslingfield was destroyed.

Putting the memory aside, he stepped over the threshold and shut the door behind him. Isabelle looked up, evidently startled to see him there.

'Forgive me for disturbing you, my lady, but it is important that we should talk.'

She laid down the bunch of flowers in her hand. 'As you wish.'

Now that they were alone together it seemed rather harder to find the necessary words, to strike the right balance. If she had been less attractive it might have been easier. While betrothal was a matter of business, what followed it was going to be intensely personal. It wasn't an easy combination.

Isabelle waited with what she hoped looked like composure. However, she was keenly aware of the closed door and the sheer physical presence of the man. As he narrowed the distance between them the room seemed suddenly to shrink. With an effort she stood her ground. Ban halted a couple of feet away.

'I have just been speaking with your father.'

Her pulse quickened. 'I see.'

'He desires our betrothal to take place on Thursday and I have agreed. It's rather sooner than I expected, but perhaps that's no bad thing.'

'You mean there will be less time to discover each other's faults.'

He surveyed her steadily. 'I'm sure you have very few.'

'I hope you continue to think so.'

'There will be time to find out later. At present there are more pressing concerns.'

'As you say, my lord.'

'I want to be able to acknowledge the relationship openly as soon as may be.'

'As do I.'

'Then you will answer for your part in helping to bring this about.'

The inference was plain and it brought a pink tinge to her cheeks. 'As you will answer for yours.'

'You may depend on it.' He paused but his gaze never wavered. 'Give me an heir and you will occupy a place of honour at my side. All that you desire of worldly comfort shall be yours.'

'My lord is all kindness.'

'A husband should use his wife with kindness. You need fear no ill treatment at my hands.' He hesitated. 'It may be too that, in time, we shall grow closer in affection.'

Isabelle had no reason to doubt the first part. Ban was not as Alistair had been and that afforded considerable relief. The rest was uncertain. Could she learn how to please this man; be what he wanted in a wife? It seemed like a tall order.

'It has been known to happen,' she replied.

'So I believe, although it is not an indispensable condition for a successful marriage. When all is said and done it's a business arrangement. If there is respect on both sides it is enough.'

For no apparent reason she felt a lump form

in her throat. 'No need to muddy the waters with romance then?'

'None at all. I do not love you any more than you love me. Nor will I promise you my heart.'

'I thank you for your honesty, my lord.'

'I have no wish to lie to you.'

'I'm glad.' In a way she was; grateful too that he made no attempt to pretend what he did not feel and had let her know exactly what to expect from him.

'Then we understand each other.'

'I believe we do.' She paused. 'I will try to be a good wife to you.'

'And I a good husband to you.' He smiled faintly. 'I don't imagine that will be too difficult. May I say I look forward to our closer union.'

A rosy flush bloomed in her face. It was unwittingly becoming and he realised he had spoken the exact truth. That turned his mind in a more pleasurable direction.

'Shall we seal the bargain, my lady?'

Isabelle felt herself grow hotter. 'I… We are not yet betrothed, my lord. It would be—' She broke off awkwardly.

Ban regarded her in cool amusement. 'Improper?' As her silence confirmed it his eyes gleamed. 'I have seen you without your clothes on. It's a little late to worry about propriety.'

Her chin came up at once. 'That isn't fair and you know it.'

'Not fair? But you're going to do the same again on Thursday.'

Isabelle was reduced to speechless silence. There were many things she would like to have said but, unfortunately, denial and refusal were equally impossible. Indignation was fuelled by his evident enjoyment.

'I will do what I must, my lord.'

'Then you will seal the bargain with me now.'

The words, though quietly spoken, were uncompromising, like the arm around her waist drawing her against him. He took the kiss at leisure, ignoring resistance until resistance was abandoned and she yielded herself to the embrace. Under the scent of lavender she breathed the scent of the man, warm, heady and dangerous, arousing sensations that were unfamiliar and unexpected.

He drew back a little, looking down into her face, his expression unreadable. Breathless now, she waited, heart thumping. He was alarmingly strong. They were alone and the place private. If he chose to pursue this... However, it seemed that was not his intention because his hold slackened.

'I consider the bargain well sealed, my lady, and hold that kiss in token of many more.'

'I told you, I will do what I must.'

'Aye, and enjoy it too, I promise you.'

'A bold promise, my lord. There is little pleasure for a woman in the marriage bed.'

He strolled to the door, pausing on the threshold. 'Reserve your judgement until you have shared mine.'

With that he left her. As she listened to his retreating footsteps, Isabelle found herself trembling, though not with fear. Automatically she raised a hand to her lips where the memory of his kiss still lingered; a kiss that aroused all manner of emotion in her, but which meant only the sealing of a bargain to him. He would bed her the same way. She bit her lip. He had been honest with her about that. Theirs was a business arrangement. If it engendered warmer feelings that was good but it was by no means certain. *I do not regard it as an indispensable condition of marriage.* The only indispensable condition was that she should provide him with an heir.

Chapter Six

Ban left the building and escaped into the fresh air, away from the heady and sensual smell of lavender and the recollection of that kiss. He had no idea why he'd done that. It hadn't been his intention when first he went to speak with her. Nor had he anticipated the consequences; had not expected to feel quite so aroused or so tempted to follow his inclination. Fortunately common sense had prevailed. In two days she was his; he could be patient a little longer. The rest would follow soon enough.

He had been walking without any set destination in mind and his steps had taken him in the direction of the stables. It occurred to him that he could go and look in on Firecrest and make sure that all was well there. However, as he rounded the end of the building he checked in surprise to see a large group of men in the yard beyond. At first he thought they were all from Castlemora, but then he caught sight of Ewan and Davy in their midst. From their stance and their expressions he knew immediately that he wasn't looking at a friendly gathering.

Needing to escape from the confines of the still room Isabelle temporarily put aside her task. It afforded too much leisure to think. Fortunately there were other domestic arrangements to deal with, particularly the matter of the evening meal. With tensions running as they were she didn't want to risk incurring her father's displeasure through some perceived slight towards their guest. Therefore it behoved her to speak with the kitchen servants and soon.

She hurried along the passageway to the outer door and had just gained the courtyard when she heard the sound of men's voices. That wasn't unusual in itself, but the tone was subtly different from their typical bantering exchanges. She paused, listening. The noise originated from the area behind the stables. It was the location that raised a question in her mind for it seemed covert somehow.

For a moment or two she hesitated. It was not her part to interfere with men's affairs, and ordinarily she stayed as far away from Murdo's mercenaries as possible. Just as she was debating with herself what to do, she saw Ban. He was closer to the stables than she and evidently heading towards the source of the noise. Curiosity strove with caution. He would deal with it. She ought not to get involved. Yet somehow his being there made it harder to resist. She hesitated for a few more seconds. Then, against her better judgement, she followed him.

Rounding the end of the building she was not surprised to see a large group of men, but her heart sank for it needed none to tell her they had not met in friendship or good humour. The very air seemed charged. The focus of attention seemed to be the Glengarron retainers. The two called Jock and Ewan were standing together, their expressions tense and angry. The third, Davy, was squared up to one of the Castlemora soldiers. She recognised the man, Taggart, for he had been one of those implicated in a rape case brought before her father. The case was dismissed for lack of evidence—it came down to three men's sworn word against that of the plaintiff in the end—although Isabelle knew whom she most believed. The village girls avoided the mercenaries when possible, and with good reason.

Her gaze moved from Taggart to Murdo, standing close by. He alone seemed quite at ease, almost as though the scene afforded him quiet amusement. Isabelle frowned and hastened forwards, but Ban was before her and she heard Murdo's greeting.

'Ah, well met, my lord.'

Isabelle was both embarrassed and annoyed knowing beyond doubt that mischief was brewing here, though what the cause might be she could not tell. If Ban had detected anything amiss he gave no sign of it. She saw him acknowledge the master-at-arms with a slight inclination of the head. Then he turned his attention to his men.

Both Jock and Ewan looked flinty, Davy slightly flushed. His glance flicked from Ban to Taggart, with whom, evidently, he had been in conversation a few moments before. The latter was older than Davy by at least ten years. Of a short stocky frame he was nevertheless well built and the weathered face bore an expression both crafty and malicious. Cold grey eyes surveyed the younger man, eyes that did not reflect the smile on the mouth below.

Keeping his tone deliberately neutral Ban said, 'What's happening here?'

'A friendly conversation, my lord, no more,' replied the other.

'Indeed?' Ban glanced again towards his own men and saw their silent indignation. 'What manner of conversation?'

For a moment there was stony silence. Then Murdo spoke.

'The discussion was about swordsmanship. Isn't that right, Taggart?'

The man grinned, revealing stained and rotting teeth. 'Aye, sir.'

'What about it?' asked Ban.

''Tis just that we've all heard much about the mettle of Glengarron,' Taggart replied.

'And what have you heard?'

'That they're brave fighters, my lord—by repute anyway.' Taggart's small eyes took on a cunning gleam. 'We just wondered if it was true, didn't we, lads?'

A groundswell of agreement greeted this, the tone both challenging and mocking. Ewan and Jock exchanged eloquent glances, their hands moving to their sword hilts. Seeing it, Isabelle darted a glance at Ban but his attention was elsewhere.

'Surely you would not cast aspersions on the valour of our allies, Taggart?' said Murdo. The words sounded reproachful, ostensibly deprecating, but none present missed their underlying edge.

'I mean no disrespect, my lord.' Taggart gave Ban an unctuous smile quite at variance with the look in his eye. 'All the same, 'tis such a fine reputation that a body canna help wondering whether 'tis based on truth or exaggeration.'

Another chorus of agreement greeted the words. Isabelle watched in impotent anger, seeing whither this tended. She would have been disgusted by such an insult to any of Castlemora's guests, but in this case the ramifications were particularly worrying and especially for herself. Ban could hardly be impressed and his opinion mattered. Another minute and the situation would be out of hand. Yet how to stop it escalating without her guests losing face? She glanced once at Murdo but knew she would find no help there. On the contrary, his expression suggested keen enjoyment of the situation, an expression reflected on the faces of his men.

Before he could respond, Davy spoke out. His voice was level enough but his eyes spoke clearly of anger.

'Glengarron's reputation speaks for itself. It needs no exaggeration.'

'Is that right?' Taggart raised an eyebrow and looked round at his companions. Grins greeted his evident scepticism. 'Now I'd heard otherwise.'

'Then you heard wrong.'

'I've only your word for that, boy.'

'There is no boy here.' Davy's hand tightened round the hilt of his dirk. 'Nor no idle boasting either.'

'Shall we put that to the test?'

'Whenever you like.'

'No time like the present.'

An ironic cheer rose in reply from the bystanders. Isabelle's jaw tightened. She could not expect Davy to back down now for the insult had been thinly veiled and would be answered. However, the matter must not result in serious bloodshed. With her heart in her throat she saw Ban step forwards.

'Then let the matter be put to the test,' he said, 'in a friendly match, to be decided by first blood.'

All eyes turned his way, speculative and predatory. Isabelle was reminded of nothing so much as a pack of wolves. Ban ignored them, his attention focused on the one man he rightly divined would make the decision. Murdo met his gaze a moment and then nodded.

'An excellent notion. First blood it shall be.'

A roar of approval echoed on the still air and the men stepped back to give the two combatants room. Isabelle breathed a sigh of relief. Knowing the confrontation could not be avoided, Ban had at least prevented it from becoming fatal. He had handled the matter with tact and skill, and she could only feel gratitude for his intervention. She couldn't help but wonder what he was really thinking. Was he regretting ever coming here? Would it make him think twice about their forthcoming betrothal? She prayed it would not. Even so, the incident did not reflect well on Castlemora, and she determined that Murdo should know of her displeasure. Forgetting her usual reticence she went to confront him. He regarded her with surprise for a moment and then smiled.

'You're just in time, my lady. This promises to be interesting.'

Holding on to her temper, she kept her voice low so that only the two of them were privy to it. 'These men are guests here, Murdo. How could you have allowed this?'

'Come, my lady, it is but a friendly bout, no more.'

'If it is then it's thanks to Lord Ban.'

He was about reply when another presence drew his attention, and Isabelle saw his gaze harden. Looking round she saw Ban standing beside them and, for a brief moment, glimpsed anger in his eyes as he faced Murdo. Then it was gone and he was looking at her. The memory of that recent kiss was all too vivid and her pulse quickened.

'I didn't know you were interested in swordplay, my lady.' His tone was pleasant, his manner suggesting that this was no more than a little light amusement even though they both knew it was not. She was grateful to him, knowing how much this must be testing his self-control. It was another side to him that she had not suspected. More than ever she felt it incumbent on her to try to smooth things over.

'My lord, I deeply regret all this.'

'No cause,' he replied. 'It is but a friendly challenge, as Murdo says.'

The tone was light but she could feel the antipathy between the two men. Then her attention was drawn by movement elsewhere and Isabelle looked away, her attention on the combatants.

Both were circling with slow care, intent, never taking their eyes from their opponent's blade. It went on for some seconds. Then, almost as though by some silent mutual agreement, they launched themselves into the fray. Isabelle bit her lip, watching closely. Even her untutored eye could see that both men had been well trained for each sword seemed like an extension of the arm that held it. Both protagonists were strong, both determined. However, the younger man had the edge in terms of agility, moving out of danger with lithe impressive grace while the older relied on brute strength to force his path. The great swords carved the air, each seeking for a weakness in the other's defence, their wicked blades glinting in the hard light, the ring of steel loud in the hot still yard. Sparks flew and several times the blades came perilously close to flesh. Isabelle drew in a sharp breath and looked up at Ban.

'Isn't this supposed to be a friendly bout?' she murmured.

He smiled faintly. 'No cause for alarm, my lady.'

'No, indeed,' said another voice behind her.

Isabelle turned to see Hugh. She had been so engrossed she hadn't even noticed his arrival.

'I hope not, Brother.'

'Murdo would never let it get out of hand,' he went on.

She was deeply sceptical about that but vouch-safed no reply, for now Taggart had renewed the attack, pushing forwards, apparently driving Davy before him. She bit her lip hard to stifle a cry of dismay, but a second later realised the move had been a ruse, for the younger man whirled on heel, dodging the blow aimed at his head and leaving only empty space. Thrown off balance, Taggart staggered. It was enough. Davy's blade swung round and caught his opponent's unguarded arm. It was a shallow cut, but a bright streak of blood bloomed on the instant.

The sight was greeted with a tense silence and then grudging applause in some parts of the assembled crowd. Ewan and Jock grinned broadly but ventured no word, clearly feeling that Davy's prowess as a swordsman had just spoken much louder. Isabelle breathed a sigh of relief.

'None now can doubt the reputation of Glengarron,' she said. 'It is most clearly merited.' Her gaze flicked to Murdo and she threw him a cool look before turning back to Ban. 'Your man fought well, my lord.'

'You are gracious, my lady.'

'It is no more than the truth,' said Hugh. 'Truly it was a most excellent performance.'

Ban inclined his head in acknowledgement of the compliments. Isabelle turned to look at Murdo. His expression was like thunder. Ordinarily she would have felt apprehensive, but now the sight afforded her a strange satisfaction.

'Aren't you going to say anything, Murdo?' she asked.

A muscle jumped in his cheek but when he spoke his voice was level. 'It was a good bout and, as Lady Isabelle said, your man fought well, my lord.'

'I thought so too,' replied Ban.

'It's the truth.' Hugh glanced once at the master-at-arms. 'Taggart was completely outclassed, no question.'

Murdo's gaze hardened but he said nothing more. Ban looked at Hugh.

'If you would excuse me for a moment, I would speak with my men.'

Isabelle watched him walk away. She saw him join Jock and Ewan. Ignoring surly glances from some of the spectators, they exchanged a few

quiet words and then all three went to speak to
Davy. The young man was leaning on his sword
point to catch his breath. She saw Ban clap him
on the shoulder. Though she could not catch his
words it was clear from the younger man's expression they contained high praise and it was
merited. Davy had acquitted himself well which
was more than could be said for Castlemora. Isabelle glanced with distaste across the intervening space to where Taggart stood. He was still
holding the gash on his arm and blood dripped
through his fingers. On his face was a look of
cold malice. Without warning, he raised his
sword and rushed at Davy's unguarded back.

Isabelle cried out, 'No!'

Everyone looked round. Davy whirled and was
just in time to block the blow aimed at him. The
blades slid and locked at the hilts. Almost simul-
taneously he brought his knee up hard into his
attacker's groin. The latter grunted and doubled
up gasping, his weapon falling uselessly from
his hand. A second later the point of Davy's
blade was at his throat. For a moment the air was
charged with tension. Several hands had moved
towards sword hilts.

Hugh strode forwards and looked with contempt at the fallen man. 'Is it not bad enough
that you were bested, Taggart, without your turning backstabber?' Without waiting for a reply,

Hugh turned to Ban. 'I apologise for this cow-ardly deed, my lord. It disgraces the name of Cas-tlemora.'

'Your apology is accepted, sir. The man acted independently, and Castlemora is in no way to blame.'

He looked meaningfully at Davy. The latter paused a moment, then nodded and put up his sword. Hugh managed a tight smile in response and then looked coldly at Taggart.

'You will collect your belongings and be gone. We have no use here for such as you.' He paused and turned to the master-at-arms. 'See to it, Murdo.'

The latter inclined his head in acquiescence, his expression quite impassive. However, when she glanced his way Isabelle intercepted a look of cold fury directed towards Taggart. No doubt he would send the brute off with a few choice words. This summary banishment was a fitting punish-ment. It was a pity, she reflected, that Murdo was not leaving with him. As it was, he would doubtless be smarting from this humiliation but for the life of her she could not feel sorry for it. Rather she was proud of Hugh. In that moment he looked and sounded like the laird he would one day become. As for their guest, he had most adroitly turned the situation around.

As though he sensed her regard, Ban looked

round and met her gaze. She felt her cheeks grow red. What must he be thinking? How well she understood her brother's anger over what had occurred. The laws of hospitality were sacred, a tradition that had ever been upheld at Castlemora. Wishing to show her solidarity with Hugh and to try to calm the waters, she spoke to Ban.

'Like my brother I deeply regret what happened here, my lord.'

'Pray, do not be uneasy,' he replied. 'The incident has been dealt with and the matter is closed.'

'You are generous, my lord,' said Hugh.

'Such things happen in the heat of the moment.' Ban glanced at Taggart, who had now staggered to his feet. 'No doubt he will repent of it soon enough.'

Hugh's lip curled. 'I would say he repents of it already. The mettle of Glengarron has been proved anew.'

'It should never have been called into question,' said Isabelle.

Lord Ban bowed. 'As ever you are gracious, my lady.'

His gaze flicked towards Murdo, who stood nearby. Isabelle's followed it. Now there was no sign of emotion on the man's face and he returned the look steadily, yet she sensed the anger simmering beneath. For a moment she wondered if he too would offer an apology to their guest, but he said nothing. All around them his men were silent too, though the very air was laden with their displeasure. Once again she was made aware of how numerous they were and how powerful a force they had become. Their resentment was dangerous, and they had just been shown up. They would not forgive or forget.

On their return to the hall Hugh ordered a servant to fetch ale and then saw their guests supplied with his own hand. Having done so, he made them a formal apology. Isabelle heard him with surprise. It was the first time she had ever heard him question a decision of Murdo's, even by implication, and it pleased her greatly. Was Hugh beginning to trust his own judgement at last? It seemed he too had been much angered by what had occurred.

'I would not have a long-standing friendship broken because of the actions of a coward like Taggart,' her brother went on.

'Rest assured that it won't be,' replied Ban. 'What happened was most unfortunate but it was none of your doing, my lord.'

'None the less I am truly sorry for it.' Hugh looked at Davy as he spoke. 'I hope it has not coloured your view of our hospitality.'

Davy met his eye and held it. 'I bear Castlemora no ill will, my lord.'

'I would not have you do so for the world.'

With that Hugh moved to speak with the younger man, drawing Jock and Ewan into the conversation as well. All three had relaxed now and participated with evident goodwill. Isabella regarded her brother with pride. Once again he looked and sounded every inch the laird. It gave her real hope for the future.

'Your brother is an accomplished host,' said Ban.

'I thank you, yes.' She gave him a wry smile. 'He is right though, and I too would repeat my regret over what happened today.'

'There is not the least occasion for you to do so,' he replied. 'The matter is over and best forgotten.'

It was magnanimous and she was both relieved and grateful. The incident could so easily have resulted in the destruction of all her hopes.

'You are generous,' she said. 'Such affairs as this can cause blood feuds that last for generations.'

'I want no blood feud between Glengarron and Castlemora. As your brother says, the relationship is too valuable to jeopardise.' He surveyed her steadily. 'Rather, I intend to make the bond very much stronger.'

The allusion was plain, and once again she was reminded that their forthcoming betrothal was about business and politics. It saddened her that it should be so but it was the way of the world. In such affairs as these, men followed their heads not their hearts.

Chapter Seven

As the morning of their betrothal dawned Isabelle found it harder to maintain her composure. It was bad enough that her entire future depended on this arrangement. The manner of it made everything infinitely worse. She wouldn't even have the benefit of darkness to hide her blushes. That wouldn't trouble Ban, of course. The memory of their first meeting demonstrated as much. No doubt he would enjoy this.

Indignation came to the rescue and rallied her a little. When first the plan had been mooted it had been in her mind to dress plainly for the occasion but gradually vanity won out. She had no idea if Ban would even notice, but a fine gown would boost her morale a little, and heaven knew it needed boosting. To that end she arranged her hair into a becoming style as well.

Eventually she was as ready as she would ever be. Gathering all her courage she took a deep breath and made her way to her father's quarters.

Both men were already there when she arrived. She noted that Ban had changed his clothes for the occasion and was now wearing a tunic of dark red wool over a fine linen shirt and dark hose. A tooled leather belt was fastened about his waist. The effect was to make him look more imposing than ever.

For a moment he surveyed her in silence and then made her a formal bow. 'You look beautiful, my lady.'

'I am glad my lord approves.'

'I think the man would have to be dead who could not approve.'

Archibald Graham's craggy features assumed a faint smile. Then he gestured to the prie-dieu across the room. 'Shall we proceed?'

Ban took Isabelle's hand and led her to the small wooden altar. Then he knelt, drawing her down beside him. Her father bound their wrists loosely with a strip of cloth. It took only a short time to give their mutual consent to the betrothal and make the required promises. Then Ban slid a ring on her finger, a fine gold band set with garnets.

Archibald Graham bade them rise. 'It is done. You may kiss your betrothed.'

Ban leaned closer, his gaze holding hers for a moment. Then his lips brushed hers. It was a light and gentle caress; she might almost have said reassuring. Had he intended it thus? In truth there was very little of reassurance in the situation now.

Her father poured wine from the jug on the table and handed them each a cup before taking his own.

'Let us drink to your union. May it be long, happy and fruitful.'

Isabelle drank obediently, hoping that the wine would take the edge off her nerves. She told herself it was ridiculous to feel nervous: she was no blushing virgin. She knew what to expect and it would soon be over. Next time would be easier. She darted a glance at the man who was now, effectively, her husband. He had given his promise not to hurt her. Things could be a lot worse. All she had to be was compliant. Eventually she might even be able please him.

Ban had not missed that swift anxious glance and guessed at some of the thoughts that lay behind it. *I will do what I must*. His fair betrothed appeared to have reservations about sharing his bed, reservations he intended to banish very soon. While the situation wasn't what he'd have chosen, there was no reason why it should prove to be anything other than enjoyable for both of them.

Archibald Graham tossed back his wine and set down the cup. 'I'll leave you in peace. Just lock the door after me.'

With that he departed. With thumping heart Isabelle looked on as Ban turned the key in the lock. They were alone. For a moment or two neither of them spoke. Then he rejoined her and the room shrank around them until there was only the man and the bed. She tensed. He removed the cup from her hand and took her in his arms, his lips brushing hers, light, tentative, searching. Her heartbeat accelerated uncomfortably. Suddenly what had seemed like a mere practical detail began to assume an altogether different character. She closed her eyes, telling herself it was his right. He wanted a son; in order to get one he needed to get her with child. All she had to do was comply. She swallowed hard and a light sheen of sweat broke on her forehead. In her mind's eye she could hear Alistair Neil's voice: *Lie down on the bed as I have commanded you...* Her entire body stiffened. Hard on the heels of that response was panic. If she didn't please this man, or at least give him what he wanted, she was finished.

Ban felt her tense and drew back, sensing her unease. 'What is it, Isabelle?'

'I... Nothing. Forgive me. It's just the suddenness of it all.'

'It takes a bit of getting used to, doesn't it?' He smiled faintly. 'And you have the advantage of me since I was never betrothed before.'

'My advantage is not so great, my lord.'

'Are you referring to previous or present experience?'

'I was thinking of what went before.'

He nodded. 'This must be a marked contrast: no celebration or public feasting, no wine or toasting.'

It wasn't what she meant but wasn't able to enlighten him just then. 'Such things make little difference in the end.'

'Perhaps not and yet I think this is not what you might have expected.'

'I had no expectations before this.'

'And now?'

'I hope for the best.'

'As do I.'

He drew her closer once more. Isabelle shivered, partly in fear and partly in anticipatory dread. This man was an unknown quantity and his touch aroused sensations that were entirely foreign to her; sensations that only heightened her uneasiness. He reached for the fastenings of her girdle and, unhurriedly, began to undress her. Her girdle fell to the floor, followed shortly afterwards by her gown. He drew off the linen kirtle beneath until only her shift remained, then picked her up and carried her across to the bed. Without taking his eyes off her he divested himself of tunic and shirt revealing the hard-muscled torso beneath. Her heart began to slam against her ribs like an unlatched door in a storm wind.

He came to join her, his hands on her waist drawing her closer. She could feel their warmth through the thin fabric. He bent his head so that his lips brushed hers, gently teasing at first and then gradually becoming more persuasive. She could feel the start of his arousal against her thigh. And his face faded and became Alistair Neil's: *You'll take whatever I give you and like it...* Isabelle froze, then tore her mouth away, panting.

Ban frowned. 'What's the matter, sweetheart?'

'I can't. I thought I could but I can't.' She struggled in his hold. 'Please...'

Almost immediately she found herself free. Only too aware of the piercing blue gaze she turned away in acute embarrassment.

He frowned. 'Look at me, Isabelle.'

Slowly, reluctantly she obeyed.

'What are you afraid of? You must know I'm not going to hurt you.'

'I...I can't explain.' She swallowed hard. 'I'm so sorry.'

Ban lay back on the bed and for a moment or two he was silent. She cringed inwardly. What must he be thinking? What would he do now? To deny a man his rights was madness. It could only invite his wrath and an angry man was dangerous. She'd had her chance. Instead of seizing it she had just laid herself wide open to a beating and then rape. Had experience taught her nothing? She took a deep breath, mentally calling herself all kinds of fool.

'I'm so sorry, my lord. I don't know what came over me. A momentary panic...'

He raised an eyebrow. 'Panic? This is not the first time you have been to bed with a man.'

'Forgive me.'

'What's to forgive?'

'Opposition to your will.'

'My will? I had rather hoped it might coincide with your own, but clearly it doesn't.'

She licked dry lips. 'Your will is mine, my lord. If you still wish to...to consummate this bargain I will do whatever you command.'

'A tempting prospect, believe me. I can think of a lot of things I'd like to do with you.'

Her stomach roiled but she fought it, knowing that she had to retrieve the situation somehow, anyhow. No matter what he demanded of her now she must submit.

He sighed. 'Perhaps you're right. It is too soon; too sudden. Perhaps we need a little time to get

to know each other better, or at least for you to
become more accustomed to me.'

'My lord?' If he'd expressed a wish to fly she
could not have been more taken aback. Almost
immediately she suspected a joke at her expense
but nothing in his manner indicated that he had
intended it thus.

He smiled wryly. 'There is no need to force
the pace now.'

'But you require a son.'

'So I do and, God willing, we'll get one, but
not today I think.'

He rolled off the bed and retrieved his clothing. When he had dressed again he picked up her
discarded gown and kirtle. 'Here.'

Alarm mingled with relief. It wasn't supposed
to happen like this and yet he had just put into
words what she had been thinking. They did need
more time; at least she needed more time to come
to terms with this arrangement. She climbed off
the bed and took the proffered garments. Then,
rather self-consciously, she donned them once
more. When she had done so, he handed her the
girdle and watched her fasten it.

'That colour suits you well,' he observed. 'Of
course, any gown is helped by a lovely figure.'

She felt herself redden. 'Thank you.'

To cover her embarrassment she lowered her
gaze and smoothed a wrinkle from her skirt. Ban

smiled faintly and then turned away to pour some more wine. Then he handed her a cup.

'It's a fine vintage. It seems a shame to waste it.'

Obediently she took a sip. It steadied her a little. Then guilt replaced relief. 'I want to thank you for your forbearance. It is more than I expected.'

'And what did you expect? To be held down and raped perhaps?'

She lowered her gaze. 'Well, yes. No. I mean I don't know what I expected.'

He was dumbfounded. Her first response had been the true one and it raised some unwelcome implications. 'I have already told you that I have never forced a woman.'

'But we are betrothed so it's not the same thing. Well, not exactly.'

'Isn't it?' The blue gaze locked with hers. 'It seems uncomfortably close to me.'

Uncomfortably close indeed if she associated him with the kind of men who perpetrated crimes of violence on women. War provided the excuse. The past five years had shown him what political expediency was prepared to sanction: atrocities masquerading as justice; rape, mutilation and murder committed in the name of a king's ambition. Inevitably one became hardened in the end; learned to bury emotion. Self-preservation necessitated it. Now it appeared that emotion wasn't as deeply buried as he'd imagined.

'I will take nothing that is not freely given.'

'I will do my duty, my lord.'

'Aye, but not out of fear.'

'I see now that such fear was foolish.'

'I hope you do.'

'I'm sorry I have failed you.'

'Forget it. Let's just chalk it up to experience.'

'I will try to do much better in future.' She hesitated. 'Do you mean to tell my father about this disobedience?'

His cup stopped in mid-air. 'Of course not. Why the devil should I?'

There were several things she might have said in reply but she held her peace. Ban put down his cup and took her by the shoulders.

'This is between us now, Isabelle; no one else. I want this arrangement to work. The question is, do you?'

'Yes, my lord.'

'Good. Then we are agreed.'

'I regret giving you reason to doubt it.' She made herself look at him. 'It won't happen again.'

He nodded. 'It is well.'

In fact Ban was aware that matters were far from well. That Isabelle should be afraid to share his bed was deeply disconcerting, as was the re-

alisation of how much he wanted her. Taking
her would have been simple but the use of force
was out. The idea was distasteful in any context
but where she was concerned it was downright
repellent. Besides, it was certainly no basis on
which to build an enduring relationship. He could
only wonder what had gone before to make her
so afraid. Recalling the occasion of their first
meeting he winced inwardly. He'd hardly done
himself any favours there. Even so, she was no
virgin bride and therefore no stranger to the re-
alities of marriage. Her fears were groundless
but he'd have his work cut out to prove it. All the
same he meant to succeed. If it meant time and
patience then so be it. The prize was well worth
the winning.

After she left him Isabelle retired to the bower
to tidy her appearance and ensure that no tell-tale
signs of a tryst remained. A rumpled gown and
untidy hair would be enough to a discerning eye.
Having made the necessary adjustments she lingered awhile, needing time and space to think.
Events had gone so contrary to expectation that
even now it was hard to take in. The sense of her
folly only increased. Procrastination solved nothing: she had merely delayed the inevitable. Ban
had been forbearing this time but he'd made it
clear that he expected her compliance in future.

Surely that wouldn't be so hard: he was gentle and patient. What more could she ask for? Why on earth had she panicked like that?

The passing minutes provided no clear answers. In the meantime there were other matters requiring attention. When she had regained her composure she quit the bower and went to the hall. As she entered she saw her father speaking to one of the servants. He dismissed the man and then waited for Isabelle to approach. For a moment he surveyed her critically, his gaze quizzical.

'Is it done?'

Crossing her fingers under the folds of her skirt she nodded. 'Yes, my lord.'

'Good.' He paused. 'I pray for a happy outcome.'

'And I.'

That at least was true. It went against the grain to lie to him but there was no way to explain what had taken place with Ban, even had she felt so inclined.

'Succeed in this and your future is assured.' He squeezed her arm gently. 'I would see you safely settled and soon.'

'You will, my lord.'

'I hope so, but I suspect that time is running out.' As she opened her mouth to protest he silenced her with a finger to her lips. 'It's the truth and it must be faced. The pains in my chest occur more often now and the effects last longer. Before I die I should like to see Lord Ban your acknowledged husband.'

A lump formed in her throat making it harder to speak. 'He will be, and long before then.'

'I hope you're right.' He smiled wryly. 'Incidentally, I think him a better man than your last.'

'So do I.'

She thought there was no possible comparison; Ban was everything that Alistair Neil had never been. Her behaviour this morning had been foolish beyond belief. She vowed then and there that it would not be repeated. All she wanted now was to forget about the past and move on.

Chapter Eight

Over the next few days, Ban used some of his time to better familiarise himself with the layout of Castlemora, committing to memory the location and function of its various buildings and the immediate environs. Local knowledge was going to be essential to his plans. He also made a point of meeting regularly with his men and listening to what they had to say. They mixed more freely with the household servants and had also ventured into the village nearby, and he knew they could be relied on to keep an ear to the ground.

'Murdo and his crew are not well liked hereabouts,' said Jock. 'They've a reputation for brutality and the villagers fear them.'

'As well they should,' replied Ewan.

Inevitably the mercenaries were everywhere in evidence at Castlemora but, although they eyed the Glengarron retainers with ill-concealed dislike, they had offered no further insult.

'It seems that three of them raped a local lass and got her with child,' Jock went on, 'but when the case was brought they swore blind she'd given her consent. It was her word against theirs. When the judgement went against her, the lass killed herself and the bairn with her.'

Ban shook his head in disgust. 'Their kind has no conscience and obeys no laws but their own, or perhaps Murdo's.'

'Him they fear, my lord, and with good reason apparently.'

'So I imagine.'

'He takes good care that their more questionable deeds occur well away from Castlemora and that there are no witnesses. Any who speak out are invariably punished or else they meet with an accident.'

'I dinna much like turning my back on the scum,' said Davy.

'Their kind is better kept in plain view,' replied Jock.

Davy eyed Ban quizzically. 'Will we be staying here much longer, my lord?'

'For a while yet,' said Ban.

His men exchanged knowing grins. He returned a smile. They had guessed his interest, although not the depth of his involvement and he couldn't tell them. Much as he disliked keeping them in the dark about his intentions, he had no other option at present. The situation was too delicate to share. Although matters hadn't got off to the best start he was hopeful of amending them. If everything went as he hoped thereafter he'd be able to announce his betrothal soon enough. Then they could all go home.

'The lady is fair,' said Jock.

Ban's face remained impassive. 'Yes, she is.'

'Rumour didn't do her justice.'

'Quite so.'

'The man who wins her will be most fortunate.'

'Indeed he will.'

Realising he wasn't going to be drawn Jock let the subject drop and the conversation turned to other things.

Ban hid a smile, amused rather than annoyed by so transparent an attempt to pump him for information. In fact Isabelle had been very much on his mind. Since their betrothal the only real chance to speak with her had been when they met at table and, since the place was public, their conversation was confined to safe topics. After the disastrous episode following their betrothal she seemed a little more diffident, more eager to please. At the same time her smile had an anxious quality that he found perturbing. He didn't want her to feel anxious or uncomfortable around him; on the contrary. Furthermore it mattered rather more than he could have anticipated. Her fear was an affront to manhood: so lovely a woman ought to enjoy intimacy, not dread it, and he wanted very much to instil that idea. The setback had not abated his interest in the least. If anything it had increased. The thought of her excited him, something he had not expected to find in a potential bride. In consequence he found himself looking forward to the day when he could take her to his bed openly and as often as he pleased. When he did he wanted it to be with her willing consent.

In his exploration of Castlemora he had located an old barn which was set apart from the main buildings but close enough to afford relatively easy access. It was used to store hay and grain. Being quiet and little frequented it thus provided a convenient place for his purpose since he and Isabelle could meet there discreetly. It carried an element of risk but there was no way around that. Discovery would be extremely awkward but, if anything, the possibility lent spice to the adventure.

When he proposed the place to Isabelle she made no demur. The barn was out of the way and they were unlikely to be disturbed. Not that the fear of discovery was uppermost in her mind just then. Having had time to grow accustomed to the idea of their betrothal and to Ban's company, she just wanted to get the business of consummation over with. After the first time it would doubtless be easier.

He was waiting when she arrived. His presence seemed to dominate the space somehow and he seemed disconcertingly at ease whereas she felt as nervous as a goose at the approach of Michaelmas.

He smiled at her. 'I wondered if you would change your mind.'

'No, I haven't changed my mind.'

'I'm glad. I know this isn't easy for you.'

Her eyes widened a little. 'I think perhaps it isn't easy for either of us, my lord.'

'I'd be the first to admit that the circumstances are not ideal but you have no reason to be afraid. Nothing that happens here is going to hurt you.'

'I know.'

'Then will you trust me?'

She nodded. He drew her closer, his lips brushing hers, soft, coaxing. As she relaxed a little the kiss became more assertive, his tongue flirting lightly with hers. He tasted pleasantly of mead, a heady sweetness that mingled with the scents of hay and wool and leather. His hold tightened a little so that she was pressed against him, his hands caressing her back. Their warmth sent a tremor

along her skin. Tentatively she pressed closer.
As she did so she felt the start of his arousal. Her
pulse quickened but not entirely through apprehension.

He drew back a little, looking into her face.
'Come.'

His cloak was spread out on the hay and he
drew her down with him and then resumed where
they had left off. He took his time, kissing, caressing, using every device he knew to please
and arouse, unwilling to hurry this and lose all
the ground he had won. She was prepared to trust
him and he would ensure her trust was not mis-
placed. It was no hardship. He'd wanted her from
the first, but what he felt now went beyond the
thought of physical gratification. This woman
excited him in ways that no other ever had. For
all manner of reasons he wanted to prolong this
experience.

Gradually the caresses became bolder, explor-
ing her breast and waist and buttocks. Isabelle
tried to follow his lead, returning his kiss, sliding her hands across his shoulders and thence to
his back but the woollen tunic was a hindrance.
She paused, fumbling for the fastening of his belt.
At length she found it and unlatched the buckle.
The belt came loose and was discarded. The tunic
rode up easily, allowing access to the shirt beneath. Tugging at the fabric she managed to free

it, then let her hands slide across the warm skin beneath, feeling the play of his muscles. His kiss deepened in response, became a little more demanding.

He guided her hand to his groin and with a sense of shock she felt his erection, huge and rock hard, quite unlike anything in her experience and, for a second, deeply disconcerting. Summoning her wits she began to stroke him, heard a sharp indrawn breath in response. She felt his hand along her thigh, the touch gentle but assured. His fingers slid between her thighs and thence to her sex. She tensed; then heard his voice, quiet and reassuring.

'It's all right, sweetheart. Nothing bad is going to happen.'

Obediently she made herself relax a little, permitting the intimacy. The light stroking movement created a sensation of unexpected warmth in the core of her pelvis. That too was disconcerting but not unpleasant. She relaxed a little more as he continued. A few moments later the warmth was followed by slick wetness. For a terrible moment she thought that her flux had begun but he seemed not to find anything untoward and went on stroking her. What had been pleasant became closer to pleasurable. Her pulse quickened a little.

Ban unfastened his breeches and his erection sprang proud. She closed her hand around the shaft, wondering how on earth her body was going to accommodate him. Surely it had to hurt. Even if it did there was no turning back now. She had to go through with this, couldn't fail him a second time.

He raised her skirts higher until she was naked to the waist. She reddened, acutely aware of broad daylight and the vivid blue gaze surveying her lower body. Apparently he was not dissatisfied with what he saw because she saw him smile. A few moments later his knee parted her thighs and he slid into her, slowly, carefully, until she had the length of him. Isabelle blinked. It hadn't hurt. As she was assimilating the fact he began to move inside her. That at least was not unexpected. Recalling what her former husband had commanded of her, she put her arms around Ban and raised her knees. He thrust harder, deeper, the rhythm increasing. Isabelle moved with him, praying she might please him this time. Then he might not repent of the bargain.

The action caused an unaccustomed surge of excitement in him. However, he reined desire in hard. No matter what, possession must not become violation. Nothing that happened here today must frighten or disgust her. Consequently he held back as long as he could but eventually release became inevitable. He had to hope he'd done enough to convince her that he didn't intend to hurt her. This exercise was going to be oft repeated and when he took her in future he wanted her willing compliance.

He took his weight on his elbows and withdrew, surveying her keenly. 'Are you all right, sweetheart?'

'Yes, my lord.' She paused. 'That was…nice.'

He smiled wryly. 'Indeed it was, but it's going to get a lot better.'

'Better?'

'That's right.'

She remained silent, uncertain what he meant. Things had already gone far better than she had anticipated. Alistair Neil had never treated her with such consideration. Submission to him had felt like subjugation. Submission to this man felt quite different. Exactly why that was she couldn't have said; all she knew was the truth of it. Of course a woman could not expect to get pleasure from the act as men seemed to do, but Ban had just demonstrated that it need not be disagreeable. She had experience enough to realise that he had used restraint with her, hoping no doubt to allay her fear, and she was grateful. Such apprehension seemed foolish now.

Ban stretched out beside her, drawing her close. She smiled and closed her eyes, feeling oddly content. It would be no hardship to repeat the experience with him; quite the opposite in fact. If God allowed it they might make a child together. The possibility filled her with hope and longing. It would please her to give this man the son he longed for. It might also bring them closer. Meanwhile, she would have a baby, a small helpless being whom she could love and who would love her unconditionally. Ban had already told her that he didn't love her but perhaps, given time, they might grow closer. It wouldn't be hard to care for a man who treated her with gentleness and courtesy.

Ban too was lost in his thoughts. Things had gone better this time but there was a long way to go yet. He had been unable to arouse her as he'd hoped to. Clearly she was still too tense, too reserved for that. It was going to take a while to allay her anxiety and make her completely comfortable with him. It was a considerable challenge but he intended to meet it, to bring her to a climax with him.

When she'd experienced it once, she'd almost certainly want to do it again. Only then would she be relaxed enough for him to take things further and explore other possibilities. Imagination supplied a series of highly erotic images in which she initiated their sexual coupling. The result was a fresh wave of heat to his groin. He quashed it. It would be a mistake to force the pace. He wanted more than just to bed her again: he wanted her to enjoy it too. He wanted her to want *him*. Just where that thought had come from he couldn't have said, but he recognised the truth of it. This woman was going to be his, body and soul.

For that reason he restrained the urge to follow up their tryst too soon. Instead he let several days go by before suggesting another. If Isabelle felt pressured she would be less likely to relax and that ran counter to his plans. In the interim he used the time to talk to her on a variety of subjects, drawing her out, listening, learning more about her. The tactic paid off. She began to lose the anxious expression she had worn before and to smile more readily. Ban saw it with approval.

The next time they met at the barn she was less tense and a rather more willing participant. Again he was careful, ardent but tender, seeking by every means to increase her enjoyment. Isabelle followed his lead, clearly wanting to please him. While he wouldn't have described it as perfect sex, it was certainly an improvement.

Over the following week they built on it. The secrecy of these meetings combined with the limited time available lent them intensity and a certain excitement so that Isabelle found herself anticipating the next time they would be alone. It had become to her rather more than a business arrangement now. In spite of all former resolution her emotions had become involved too. She knew it was unwise at this stage, but somehow it had ceased to be a matter of choice. He filled her thoughts. His treatment of her was considerate and kind; she had never known such gentleness in a man. He was passionate but he never hurt her. Each time they made love it bound her more tightly to him. Except that he never actually spoke of love. She smiled ruefully at her own folly: their relationship was but new-fledged. It was far too early to be thinking in those terms. When she was carrying his child things might change. *We may grow closer in affection.* The notion resurrected all her former longing and offered glimpses of a future she had never thought to have.

She would have liked to discuss the future with Ban but it was a sensitive topic and she hesitated. Nor did he advert to it. She attributed that to his reluctance to make plans that might never come to fruition. He didn't want to make any promises. Their conversations tended to focus on past or present instead. She could understand it but deep down it hurt too. In spite of the consideration he showed her now he would put her aside if he had to.

'Is everything all right, my sweet?'

She turned her head to look at him. 'Of course. Never better.'

They were lying on his cloak on a pile of sweet-smelling hay in an old stall towards the rear of the barn. The light was muted here, the quiet broken only by the occasional cooing of a pigeon in the rafters above.

'You looked lost in thought.'

'There is much to think about. My father's health grows worse.'

'God willing he will live a while yet.'

'He doesn't think so.' She sighed. 'It seems that Hugh will be laird before too long.'

'He has all the makings of a worthy successor.'

'I believe that too. It's not Hugh who concerns me as much as Murdo.'

'Surely he will serve your brother as he served your father.'

'Murdo has too much power and he has abused it. Hugh knows that. I hope he may redress the balance.'

'That may not be easy,' said Ban. 'Men like Murdo don't readily cede what they have won.'

'If my father had enjoyed better health the situation would not have arisen but, as his condition progressed, he was glad to delegate more responsibility. Many would say too much.'

'It wouldn't be the first time such a thing has happened.' He paused. 'But, if your brother is his own man, then he will eventually take back control.'

'I hope so. Then perhaps Castlemora could go back to being the way it was. The atmosphere never used to be so tense, so…threatening.'

'Why should you feel threatened by Murdo?'

She hesitated. It was dangerous ground.

'Isabelle?'

'He aspires to my hand.' Seeing his expression she hurried on. 'There was never any chance it would be granted.'

'Did you want it to be granted?'

'Good heavens, no! I detest him and he knows it. But, as you said, he's not a man to give up easily.'

Ban's eyes narrowed a little. 'He had best give up all thought of you.'

'He is no rival to you, my lord. Indeed I hope the futility of his ambition will soon become apparent.'

'I will suffer no rivals, Isabelle. You belong to me or to no man.'

Her pulse quickened a little. 'I am betrothed to you.'

'That you are.' He rolled, pinning her beneath him. 'And it is my intention to make my claim on you very apparent very soon.'

'Is something preventing you?' It was provocative and as soon as she'd said it she was astonished at her own boldness. At the same time she knew that she wanted him to match his words to action.

His eyes glinted. 'Nothing will prevent me, my sweet. I am jealous of my rights.'

'Say you so?'

'I do say so.'

'I might refuse.'

'You might try,' he conceded.

The words were deliberately provocative in their turn and she tested his hold. It might have been steel. Ban surveyed her steadily.

'Rebellion, Isabelle?'

She regarded him speculatively. 'What if it were?'

'It would be crushed without mercy until I had complete submission.'

'Oh? And how exactly would you achieve that?'

He proceeded to show her. The method was swift and ruthless and devastatingly effective.

She relived it when she was alone in bed that night. The memory created an unwonted glow deep inside her, and once again she found herself looking forward to the day when their relationship could be declared openly. Their conversation suggested that Ban wanted that too. The mere mention of another man's interest had brought out a fiercely possessive streak that was unexpected and, on balance, more pleasing than not. It was another indication that he already thought of her as his. His subsequent actions reinforced that notion strongly. She smiled to herself in the darkness. It was impossible to think of any other man when she was with him. Not that she intended to tell him, of course. He already had too much advantage.

Ban too had reflected on their earlier conversation since it shed light on some of the things that had initially puzzled him. Murdo's attitude was one. If he entertained hopes of marrying Isabelle then his aggression towards Ban and Glengarron became more comprehensible. When Isabelle returned to Castlemora, Murdo must have seen that as a golden opportunity. Marriage to her would secure his position once and for all. He would also be gaining a very beautiful bride. The possibility that she might be barren evidently didn't bother Murdo, or he was willing to take a chance. That such an ambitious man should do so seemed suddenly significant. Of course, it might just be that he was so deeply in love that it didn't weigh with him, but, knowing what he did of Murdo, it seemed unlikely.

Ban frowned, conscious of undercurrents that he couldn't identify. Usually he was good at read-

ing men but something here eluded him. Moreover, he knew instinctively that it was important.
Nothing in Isabelle's manner caused him to think
that she secretly returned Murdo's feelings. Indeed she seemed to fear him. Either that or she
was an accomplished actress. He rejected that notion. A woman in love with another man would
have reacted very differently to their coupling.
Whatever Murdo's motivation Isabelle was already lost to him. As soon as she was pregnant
Ban intended to acknowledge her as his wife.
That would put paid to the upstart's pretensions.
It would put paid to anyone's pretensions in that
direction. No other man would touch her again.
Effectively she belonged to him now.

When they met in public he was attentive but
he also made sure that the correct forms of behaviour were observed. As his potential future
wife Isabelle deserved to be treated with the utmost respect and her father would expect no less.
He was also aware that other eyes watched them.
There must be nothing to indicate that his relationship with Isabelle was anything other than
it seemed. A prospective suitor was one thing; a
secret lover quite another.

Unexpectedly he found an ally in Hugh. The
younger man had evidently taken a liking to his
guest and lost no opportunity to speak with Ban
and to ask him about Glengarron. His questions

were intelligent and pertinent and he listened carefully to the answers.

'My father sets great store by his friendship with Iain McAlpin,' he explained.

'As my brother-in-law does with him,' replied Ban.

'I have only met him once and I was very young then. To be honest I was too overawed to speak.'

Ban grinned. 'Iain can have that effect on people.'

'I have heard many things about him.'

'What have you heard?'

'Of his prowess as a warrior, his courage, his daring, his skill as a leader.'

'All true.'

'I've also heard he's a dangerous man to cross.'

'True again.'

'Not that I have any desire to do so,' Hugh went on. 'In that respect his reputation is equally fearsome.'

'He does not look on treachery with a forgiving eye.'

'Neither should he. A man's word, when given, should hold.'

'So it should,' replied Ban.

'He would not suffer an enemy to rob or insult his kin, would he?'

'Certainly not.'

'What would he do in such a case?'

'I imagine the matter would be settled at the point of a sword. Why do you ask?'

'There is a certain matter I would have settled at the point of a sword.' Hugh's eyes were expressive of deep anger. 'When I am laird it will be.'

'Oh? May I ask who has so offended you?'

'The Neils of Dunkeld.'

Ban was instantly alert. 'Your kin by marriage, are they not?'

'Not any more. Their treatment of my sister cancels all claims to kinship. Happily she is free of them and that worthless husband of hers.'

'Worthless?'

'Aye, a swaggering fool with a handsome face and a lying tongue. The world is well rid of him.' Hugh frowned. 'The world would be well rid of all of them.'

'Perhaps it would. All the same, one must needs consider the ramifications very carefully. It is no light thing to start a blood feud.'

'I know it.'

'What does your sister think about this?'

'She is just glad to be away from the Neils and from Dunkeld.'

'Then she does not seek revenge?'

'No. Belle has spirit and courage but she does not thirst after blood. Of course, that is because she is a woman.'

'Women often show wisdom in these matters.'

'You think the insult should be swallowed?'

'By no means, but ideally it should be avenged without wholesale slaughter.'

'How?'

Ban smiled faintly. 'It is not hard to accomplish. A few whispered words in the right ears: that the Neils are treacherous; that their word means nothing; that they hold honour cheap and so forth. It would damage their social standing and tarnish their reputation irreparably.'

Hugh regarded him keenly. 'The right ears?'

'The king and the powerful members of the court around him, particularly those who have little love for the Neils anyway.'

'I have no influence with the king.'

'No,' said Ban, 'but you have staunch allies who do.'

'You mean McAlpin. Would he be prepared to act for us in that way?'

'You can ask him when you come to Glengarron, can't you?'

'I shall.'

'Good.' Ban paused. 'Such revenge is not swift but it is extremely effective.'

Hugh grinned. 'I can see that. I will think well on what you have said, my lord.'

Ban breathed a private sigh of relief. He could understand his companion's anger and admire his loyalty to his sister, but the last thing anyone needed now was for a passionate youth to plunge headlong into an ill-advised adventure that could only end in disaster. If that possibility had been averted, then it was all to the good. He would speak to Iain about it later. No doubt something could be arranged to satisfy Hugh and put the Neils' noses out of joint without them ever being able to pinpoint the cause.

Quite apart from the lad's antipathy towards his erstwhile in-laws, he had let slip some interesting detail about Isabelle's former marriage. It tended to support the idea that it hadn't been happy. In what way had Alistair Neil been worthless? Ban would have given a great deal to know.

When he met Isabelle at table, he decided to broach the subject albeit indirectly. Everyone else was engaged in conversation so they were as private as they were going to get in the circumstances.

'I spoke to your brother earlier. He is a young man with a lot of promise.'

She smiled. 'I think so too. He can be impulsive at times but his heart is in the right place.'

'He will make a good laird one day.'

'I believe he will.'

'He holds you in great affection.'

'And I him. We have always got on well.'

'As I have with my sister.' Ban paused. 'He harbours considerable resentment against the Neils on your account.'

'I know it. He has good reason to resent them but it worries me all the same. He would like to slay them all and raze Dunkeld to the ground. But for my father's intervention I think Hugh would have tried.'

'Your father shows good sense.'

'He is nothing if not shrewd.' She shook her head. 'He knows very well what the consequences would be.'

'You do not wish for revenge then?'

'What would be the point?'

'You might get your dowry back.'

'It would become blood money.' She sighed. 'I have come to regard it as the price of my freedom from that family.'

'Was your association with them so unpleasant then?'

'Not at first, but in the end…well, let's just say I'm glad it's over.'

'But surely your late husband would have sided with you, assuming sides were taken.'

'Alistair was much under the influence of his mother and she was a force to be reckoned with. He had other traits too which were not particularly attractive.' She smiled wryly. 'Of course I did not find out until after we were married.'

'I see.'

For a brief moment her expression suggested that she very much doubted that. Then it was gone. He would have liked to question her further but it was difficult ground and he didn't want to push things too far and possibly alienate her.

'Marriage is a gamble,' she went on. 'There are winners and losers. I count myself among the former since I was lucky enough to escape.'

'It's good that you can take such a positive view of things.'

'There is no point in taking any other, is there?'

'Do you not fear leaping from the cooking pot into the fire?' he asked.

'It is a risk. I should not like to be burned again.'

Beneath the words he glimpsed her vulnerability and the shadow of a former hurt. It awoke strangely protective emotions in him. He would have liked to offer the appropriate assurances but knew that he wasn't in a position yet to make any such promises.

'No one wishes to be burned,' he replied, 'and certainly not twice.'

She regarded him curiously. 'Do you speak from experience?'

'I too have known disappointment, albeit of a slightly different kind.' He paused. 'However, it was years ago and is of no consequence now.'

'And yet these things shape us, make us who we are.'

'So they do.'

'We don't forget either although we may learn to forgive.'

'Some things only God can forgive,' he replied.

'You are thinking about King William's destruction of Northumbria.'

'Amongst others.'

'He has shown himself to be a brutal tyrant. Perhaps even God will not forgive him.'

'If there is any justice the bastard will burn in hell for all eternity.' Ban paused and summoned a smile. 'But these are sombre topics for conversation, too much so for a woman's ears.'

'Do you think a woman should be shielded from the truth?'

'Women should be protected from unpleasantness as far as possible. Unfortunately it isn't always possible.'

'We are stronger than you give us credit for, my lord.'

'In some things,' he acknowledged, 'but I would wager on the power of my sword arm over yours.'

Isabelle caught the gleam in his eye and she laughed. 'So would I, every time.'

Ban surveyed her appreciatively for laughter

lit her face and made what was beautiful even more alluring. A man might feel justly proud to have such a woman at his side, to run his household and bear his children. It created a host of unwonted sensations, not least of which was to have an end to present uncertainty. Of late stability and permanence had become increasingly attractive propositions. He looked forward to the day when he could commit himself, turn his back on war and death and live in peace again. With her he might find the contentment he sought.

He reached for his cup and took a sip of wine. As he did so he became aware that he was being watched. Murdo's gaze locked with his own. The man's expression was impassive but Ban could feel hostility emanating from him. He clearly recognised and resented Ban's interest in Isabelle: what he didn't know was just how far his own hopes were blighted. That was too bad. All was fair in love and war. Ban checked himself there, mentally revising the statement. All was fair in war and in winning a bride. Love was another matter entirely.

Chapter Nine

Being so caught up in his thoughts he found sleep elusive that night. Around him other men snored and grunted. Somewhere in the darkness outside he heard an owl hoot; an ill omen according to country folk, presaging doom and death. It was a foolish notion. He forced it away and drew the blanket higher.

When sleep eventually came to him it was disturbed by troubled dreams. In them he was running through thick mist, while ever before him went the elusive figure of a woman. She had her back to him so he could not see who she was. However, he knew he must follow and find her, but whenever he drew near enough to touch her she would vanish into the mist again. Each time the sense of loss intensified until it achieved the acuteness of physical pain. Distress and loneliness increased unbearably. He knew that if he could find the woman then he would be all right, that she held the key to things he did not yet understand. He had to find her. He stumbled on in desperation and through the pale swirling vapour he heard her call his name…

'Lord Ban! Lord Ban!'

He woke in the grey dawn light to find Jock shaking him by the shoulder.

'Wake up, my lord! You must come quickly!'

'What is it?' he muttered. 'What's the matter?'

'Archibald Graham is dead.'

'What!'

Coming instantly awake, Ban stared at him in stunned surprise. 'Dead?'

'Aye, my lord. It seems he passed away in the night,' Jock went on. 'When his servant went in this morning he thought the old man was still sleeping, but the body was already cold. I had it from the steward.'

Ban leapt to his feet and began to pull on his clothing, his expression grim. This news would be a grievous blow to Isabelle. It would be a grievous blow for all concerned. Worse was the knowledge he couldn't put it right. The best he could do was to offer some poor words of comfort.

On reaching the courtyard a few minutes later it became apparent that the news of Graham's demise had spread, sending shock waves through Castlemora. Already they could hear the shrill keening of women, and groups of men stood without the hall in dismayed surprise or else exchanged huddled whispers. Gritting his teeth Ban threaded his way through them. When he reached the hall he saw Hugh there with Murdo at his side. Ignoring the latter he turned at once to the new laird.

'I have just heard the ill news, my lord. Pray accept my condolences. I know I speak for Glengarron too in this matter.'

'I thank you,' replied Hugh. From the whiteness of his cheek it was evident that he too was still in shock, and just now coming to realise the implications of his father's demise.

'On behalf of Glengarron, and on account of the deep ties between our houses, my men and I would wish to join you in paying our final respects to your honoured father.'

'I thank you for your courtesy, my lord.'

Ban inclined his head in acknowledgement to Hugh and ignored the cold stare from Murdo. If the other man objected to his presence, that was too bad. Fortunately he had no say in the matter.

'Pray offer my condolences to the Lady Isabelle.'

Hugh nodded. 'I shall do so. She keeps to her quarters at present. This news has hit her hard.'

'Of course. Your father was a great man. He will be much missed.'

'That he will, my lord. I little thought to take his place so soon. I hope I can live up to his expectations.'

'I think there is no doubt of that,' said Ban.

Hugh summoned a faint smile. 'I'll do my best.'

With that he moved on to speak to the other men gathered there. Ban drew off to one side with Jock.

'Now what, my lord?'

'We stay and pay our last respects to Archibald Graham.'

'Aye, he was a good laird by all accounts.'

'I imagine the funeral will be tomorrow.'

'Will we be leaving after?'

'Not immediately. There are matters I must attend to first.'

'As you will, my lord.'

In truth Ban had no clear idea yet how he was going to deal with the situation. He didn't know if Archibald Graham had informed Hugh of the secret betrothal. If he hadn't, it was going to make things exceedingly awkward. There must already be speculation about his extended stay at Castlemora. It was difficult to see how he could remain longer without declaring his interest. At the same time Isabelle was going to need time to come to terms with her father's loss. Ban was no stranger to grief and he knew all too well what she must be feeling now. More than ever he wanted to speak with her.

Unfortunately his wish was disappointed. He waited around for the rest of the morning hoping for a glimpse of her but she did not appear. In the end he gave it up. Probably she didn't want to speak to anyone at present. Leaving the company he took himself off, needing a little space himself to reflect and consider what he was going to do next.

He headed for the orchard. It was pleasant and private and well suited to his present mood. The place also had associations with Archibald Graham since it was here they had come to discuss Ban's betrothal to Isabelle. He smiled ruefully. The old man's intimations of impending death had been accurate after all.

Ban made his way among the trees, laden now with ripening fruit, and then checked abruptly as he realised he wasn't alone. A woman was standing by the wall. She had her back to him, apparently looking at the view beyond, but he knew her at once. Suddenly he wondered if his presence here might be intrusive; perhaps she too had wanted time apart. He hesitated.

'Isabelle?'

She turned abruptly. Her face was pale and he could see that she had been crying. In that moment she appeared younger than before and intensely vulnerable.

'I'm so sorry.' He crossed the intervening space to join her. 'This has been a terrible shock.'

'I didn't even get the chance to say goodbye to him.'

'His passing was swift and painless. Take comfort from that.'

'I do and yet I would have him back again.' Water sprang to her eyes and she looked away.

'It is hard to lose a parent, to lose any of your kin.'

'My mother died when I was young. I have only vague recollections of her. My father was always the heart of Castlemora for me.' She swallowed hard. 'We did not always see eye to eye and he was not one to show his feelings openly, but I believe he cared for me, loved me in his way.'

'I am certain of it.'

'I cannot believe he is really gone. When I sat with him it was as though he were only sleeping; that if I reached out and touched him he would wake. But he did not.'

The words ended in another flow of tears. Ban's jaw tightened. However, he said nothing just then, knowing there was nothing he could say. Instead he put his arms round her and stroked her bright hair as she wept on his shoulder. It went on for some time but he made no attempt to stop her. Grief needed an outlet.

Eventually the tears abated and she drew away a little in evident confusion, drying her face again.

'I'm sorry. I think your tunic must be as damp as my sleeve now.'

'It doesn't matter,' he replied. 'A tunic and a sleeve will dry. Sorrow takes longer to deal with.'

'You have known your fair share of sorrow, have you not?'

'Indeed, though the sight of yours hurts me too.'

The words drew a wan smile. 'I thank you for your kindness, my lord.'

Her gratitude smote him as hard as her tears. Kindness hadn't been the motivational force in his behaviour thus far. It had a distinctly exploitative quality that didn't make for comfortable viewing. Her plight had always been unenviable; today it had become a whole lot worse and for that he was partly responsible.

The funeral took place with all due solemnity. It wasn't until she stood by the open grave that her father's death achieved the status of fact in her own mind. It was still hard to imagine a world in which he didn't figure. He had always been there, ultimately a strong, protective presence even if they hadn't always been in accord. Now he was gone and, somehow, life went on.

However, it was only as she received the condolences of others that she began truly to appreciate how respected a figure her father had been, and how big were the shoes her brother must endeavour to fill. The thought of what lay ahead for him made her feel deeply anxious. Her gaze flicked once towards Murdo. His expression revealed nothing of what was passing through his mind, but with her father out of the way the master-at-arms would certainly try to increase his grip on affairs here. Would Hugh be his own man? Would he be able to keep Murdo in check? It seemed like a tall order.

Ban was a reassuring presence. He had been considerate and kind, more so than she might once have anticipated. It was an unexpected side to his character. He had shown no impatience with her tears and he had been quietly supportive of Hugh. It wasn't an easy situation but he hadn't shirked it. Nor did he neglect his public duty now.

'This is indeed a sad day, my lady. I speak for Glengarron when I say that your father will be sorely missed.'

She found her voice. 'I thank you, my lord.'

'Glengarron will always stand ready to support Castlemora. In the meantime you will let me know if there is any service I might perform.'

She thought that the greatest service he could perform for her now would be to acknowledge their betrothal, but that wasn't going to happen yet. What if it never happened? The thought of losing him filled her with momentary panic. She fought it, telling herself that all might yet be well. She must cling to that hope; it was all she had now.

Ban knew he was going to have to speak with Hugh after the funeral. It was just possible that the younger man knew about the betrothal but if not he would have to be told. Since it was not Ban's secret alone he must first consult Isabelle on the matter, and that would have to wait until the morrow.

He glanced from her to the new laird at her side. Hugh was pale but in control, no doubt trying to come to terms with the situation in which he found himself. Just a pace away from him was Murdo. The tall, dark-clad figure reminded Ban of nothing so much as a great carrion bird. Behind Murdo, at a suitably respectful distance, were ranged his men. Apart from the belt knives all men wore they were unarmed on this occasion, no doubt at his instruction. Nevertheless, their collective presence was not so much reassuring as disquieting.

However, Hugh was impressively self-possessed, then and later, overseeing all the formalities until the last of the mourners had departed. Isabelle regarded her brother with pride. Young he might be but his manner and bearing suggested that he took his new role most seriously and that gave her real hope for the future. Seated in their father's chair now, he did not look out of place.

Now that the ramifications were beginning to sink in she realised that, some time soon, he would have to be told about her betrothal. It was going to be a tricky conversation but now that he was laird it couldn't be avoided. She glanced at Ban. They needed to talk but with so many of Murdo's men present it wasn't the time or the place. Moreover, now that the day was wearing on, she could think about leaving the men to continue their drinking alone. The wake would likely continue through the night.

By now she would have expected the effect of ale and mead consumption to be making itself apparent in the men's speech and behaviour, but, oddly, none of them gave any sign of being drunk. The conversation was unusually muted too, yet underneath it the atmosphere seemed tense, almost as though they were waiting for something. Perhaps they were waiting for her to leave so that the carousing could start in earnest. She looked at Hugh. However, just then he was engaged in conversation with the master-at-arms. The two walked apart a little way, heads together, Murdo's hand resting lightly on his companion's shoulder.

Suddenly Hugh's eyes widened in an expression of shocked disbelief, his breath caught on a choking gasp. Isabelle frowned. Then Murdo stepped back and she saw the dagger plunged deep in her brother's side. For several moments Hugh hung on its point before his knees buckled and he slumped to the floor as a dark stain spread across his tunic. Isabelle screamed.

'No!'

She flew across the room, falling to her knees beside Hugh, frantically trying to discover some sign of life. He didn't move, his eyes staring up at her unseeing as blood pooled on the floor. As the realisation hit her Isabelle screamed again, a long keening howl of horror and despair.

Ban leapt to his feet and lunged at Murdo. 'You treacherous bastard!'

Before he could reach his target he was seized from behind. In spite of furious resistance he was swiftly overpowered and the edge of a blade held against his throat. He regarded Murdo with contempt.

'Why do you hesitate?' he demanded. 'You've murdered one man in cold blood. One more can make no difference to you.'

'I'm tempted, believe me, but it may serve me better to leave you alive, for now.' Murdo looked at his men. 'Take him to the small storeroom and lock him in. His men too. I'll deal with them later.'

White-faced, Isabelle looked on helplessly as Ban was dragged from the room. Then she turned to Murdo.

'Murderer! Traitor!'

He regarded her impassively for a moment, then spoke to her captor. 'Take her to the bower and post a guard on the door.'

Strong hands seized hold of her and hauled her to her feet. Isabelle shrieked and fought but to no avail. Seconds later she was lifted bodily off the floor and carried from the room.

Ban's captors dragged him to the cellar and shoved him in, locking the door behind him. It was iron-bound oak. The walls and floor were of stone, the only light source a small, barred window. Anger burned hot and for a while he paced, trying to take in the enormity of what had happened. Just then he had no fear for himself. All concern was reserved for Isabelle. With her brother slain her situation was perilous indeed. It needed no seer to tell him what Murdo intended.

He was distracted from these thoughts by the sound of footsteps. Then the door opened again and his three companions were thrust into the room. Judging from their dishevelled appearance and Ewan's cut lip they hadn't come quietly. Jock eyed Ban speculatively.

'Are you all right, my lord?'

'Aye, well enough,' he replied, 'but Lord Hugh is dead.'

'Dead? How?'

They listened in dumbfounded silence as Ban supplied the details. Jock swore softly.

'So that bastard Murdo is in charge now.'

Ban nodded. 'He'll claim Castlemora for himself, and the Lady Isabelle with it.'

'And we can do naught to prevent it. God's blood!'

Davy looked at Ban. 'Will Murdo have us killed, my lord?'

'If he intended that he'd have done it by now,' said Ban. 'I doubt he'd be so stupid. If he slays us he draws the wrath of Glengarron down on his head.'

'Aye,' said Jock, 'and even Murdo would hesitate to cross Black Iain.'

'No one in his right mind would do that,' agreed Davy, 'and yon shaven-headed villain is no one's fool.' He paused. 'So what *is* he planning to do with us?'

Ban shook his head. 'I expect we'll find out soon enough.'

Isabelle sat alone, too stunned even to cry. She had no idea how long it was until the door opened to admit Nell, whose sombre expression revealed that she knew some of what had passed. It did not take long to relate the rest. The old nurse heard her in shocked disbelief.

'Shall a usurper murder the rightful laird and steal his land and title?' she asked then.

'He has done it,' replied Isabelle. 'Nothing can stop him now.'

'What of Lord Ban and the men from Glengarron?'

'Locked up. Besides, what could four do against forty?' It had been her dread that Ban might attempt something rash in that way. Murdo already disliked him and, given sufficient reason, might well change his mind about keeping him alive.

'Even so,' Nell continued, 'you are not without friends. Murdo and his henchmen are hated by the old servants, and by the local people.'

'He will kill anyone who is caught helping me.'

Before Nell could reply the door opened again and a familiar figure appeared on the threshold.

Isabelle rose, dry-throated, darting a look at Nell. Murdo followed it, fixing the nurse with a level gaze.

'Leave us.'

The tone was quiet, but neither woman was deceived by its apparent mildness. Reluctantly Nell withdrew, closing the door behind her. With pounding heart Isabelle faced her visitor.

'What do you want, Murdo?'

'We need to talk.'

'I have nothing to say to you. Do you think I wish to speak to my brother's killer?'

'I regret the deed,' he replied, 'but Hugh was in my way.'

'You regret nothing! You killed him in cold blood.'

'The end justifies the means.'

'Nothing justifies what you have done.'

'Castlemora justifies it,' he replied. 'I have served it well these many years.'

'This deed cancels all that went before, Murdo.'

'No, Isabelle. This deed ratifies all the rest.'

'You won't get away with it.'

'And who will call me to account?' he asked.

Sick at heart she closed her eyes a moment for she knew the answer only too well. As if he read her mind Murdo nodded.

'I am Laird of Castlemora now.'

'You are a usurper, nothing more. You have no claim to the title.'

'I beg to differ. I not only claim it but will back my claim with force if need be.'

Isabelle fought to control rising terror as she recognised the truth of his words and the ramifications began to sink in.

'I am the Laird of Castlemora,' he continued, 'and you will be its lady.'

'I will never agree to that.'

'I'd prefer to have your consent but it isn't indispensable to me.'

Her hands clenched. 'How dare you?'

'There's much I'd dare to have you. I thought at one time that you were lost but then fate delivered you back to me. I only wonder that the Neils could be such fools.' He paused. 'Of course, there is still the matter of your dowry. I mean to settle the matter with them—in due course.'

'Has there not been enough killing?' she demanded.

'The Neils are thieves. They will return what they stole or pay the price for it.'

'The price is too high. Forget about the gold.'

'I shall not forget, nor will I allow them to forget.'

'It doesn't matter now.'

'I think it does.'

Her stomach churned. She had never particularly liked the Neils but she could not sanction this. It could only end one way.

'Is there nothing you wouldn't do to achieve your ambition?'

'Nothing, Isabelle.' He paused. 'Now it is almost done. Only one obstacle remains.'

She felt suddenly cold as another implication dawned. 'If you kill Lord Ban you will draw down the wrath of Glengarron.'

'Castlemora is strong enough to take on Glengarron at need. However, the Saxon thane is no threat to me now.'

'Then you will let him and his men leave unharmed?'

'They can have their lives for all I care.'

The relief occasioned by these words was partially obscured by the knowledge that Murdo might well be lying. She had to hope that he would see the good political sense of leaving Ban and his men alive. If anything happened to them on her account she could never forgive herself. At the back of her mind was the thought that, once free, they could get help.

'Glengarron is no stay to me and by the time Lord Ban gets back there my position will be fully consolidated, because by then we shall be married.'

Her stomach churned. 'I'll never agree to wed

you. I'd rather be dead than marry a traitorous upstart.'

His expression was chilling. 'Perhaps so, but the upstart will take you to his bed tomorrow anyway. In the meantime you will remain in here. Don't try any tricks, Isabelle. Your destiny is to be my wife. The sooner you accept that the better.'

'I will never accept it.'

'You have no choice, my lady.' He came closer, looking into her face. She tried to look away but a hand under her chin prevented it. 'You belong to me.'

Isabelle made no move though her cheeks were ashen. Tears welled in her eyes. Murdo saw them and his smile grew mocking.

'Ah, there now; you have no need to weep. Submit to me and your life will not be unpleasant.' The smile faded and his gaze bored into hers. 'Do anything else and I'll teach you the meaning of fear.'

That evening Ban and his men were taken from their prison under guard and escorted to the courtyard. Their horses were saddled and waiting. Hard by a dozen armed men were mounted and ready to ride. Murdo waited, looking on as the prisoners crossed the intervening space. They halted a few feet away.

'Planning to take us somewhere quiet and slit our throats?' said Ban.

Murdo smiled. 'A tempting prospect, but no, on the contrary; I'm letting you go.'

The Glengarron retainers exchanged glances, their expression suggestive of deep scepticism. It didn't pass unnoticed.

'I meant it. I'll even provide you with some food for the journey. Then you will be escorted off Castlemora land, and your weapons will be returned. After that you are free to go where you will.'

'We'll return with an armed force.'

'To what end? You cannot get back in time to prevent my marriage to Lady Isabelle, and when that is done my claim to Castlemora is complete. Nothing can change it and Black Iain will not waste time and men on what cannot be altered.'

At the mention of Isabelle's name, Ban's anger surged, along with dread for what might happen to her now. He controlled it with an effort, although the image of Hugh's body loomed large in his memory.

'If you harm her there won't be a corner of hell for you to hide in.'

'The lady will come to no harm,' replied Murdo, 'provided that you ride out of here and never return. Any attempt to wrest her from me by force might have unfortunate consequences.'

Ban's eyes blazed but he was powerless and knew it. In fuming silence he and his men mounted their horses. Murdo raised his hand in a mock salute.

'Farewell, my lord. I hope we never meet again.'

The escort closed around its prisoners and the whole cavalcade moved forwards.

Isabelle stood at her casement and, with a sinking heart, watched them go.

When the cavalcade reached the borders of the Castlemora lands, it halted. Ban exchanged glances with his men and then watched impassively while their weapons were tossed in a heap on the ground. The leader of the mercenary escort turned towards him.

'You're free to go.' His lip curled. 'If you'll take my advice you won't come back.'

With that he turned his horse's head and spoke to his companions. They smiled in derision at the Glengarron retainers and then spurred away. For a moment or two Ban watched them leave. Then he dismounted and retrieved his sword and dagger. The others followed suit in angry silence. When at length they were armed once more Jock looked at Ban.

'So what next, my lord?'

'I'm going back.'

'Right now? You're no serious?'

'Never more so. I'll not leave my w—er, Lady Isabelle to Murdo's tender mercies. I've seen what he's capable of. Besides, Glengarron is sworn to protect her.'

Jock nodded. 'Fair enough, but we need more men. Should we no go for reinforcements first?'

'We couldn't get there and back in time. Murdo was right. It's why he let us go. He thinks we're no threat.'

'Aye, and he's likely right about that too.'

'I don't ask you to come with me,' replied Ban.

'You'll no go back alone to that nest of vipers.'

'I must.'

Jock folded his arms across his chest. 'If you go, we all go.'

Ewan and Davy nodded. The younger man was pale with anger and he met Ban's eye in a level gaze.

'No one tosses me my sword and dirk and then commands me to run.'

'Damned right,' said Ewan.

Their resolution was unmistakable and Ban knew that further argument would be a waste of time. 'Very well then,' he replied. 'We all go.'

They took a circuitous route back and, unwilling to advertise their presence, tethered the horses among the trees on the hillside above Castlemora. From their vantage point Ban studied the fortified manor house. It seemed quiet with little evidence of life. Once he would have found the stillness peaceful: now it seemed ominous. He had to hope that Murdo hadn't harmed Isabelle. On balance he suspected not. The bastard's intentions there had seemed plain enough but if he thought to keep her he was much mistaken. Ban's jaw tightened.

He turned back to his men. 'I'm going down there.'

Jock raised an eyebrow. '*I?* Don't you mean *we*?'

'It's going to be dangerous.'

'Is it really? In that case ye'll be needing someone tae cover your back, won't ye?'

'I would not ask you to risk your lives in this cause.'

'Your cause is our cause,' replied Jock. 'Besides, why should we let youse have all the fun?'

The other two murmured agreement, their faces assuming expressions that Ban had come to recognise very well. He made a last-ditch attempt.

'Think of the odds, man.'

'I'd rather not,' said Jock, 'so if we're done arguing we'll just go and fetch Lady Isabelle out of there, shall we? Then we can be on our way.'

More murmurs of agreement followed this. Ban threw up his hands in a gesture of surrender.

'All right, you win. Jock, you and Ewan will come with me. Davy, be ready here with the horses. We may need to make a quick escape.'

No one remarked on the fact that one of the animals would have to carry a double burden because the lady would have no mount.

'If we're not back within the hour it'll likely mean something's gone wrong,' said Ban. 'You must get away, Davy, and see that word reaches Glengarron.'

'Aye, my lord.'

Ban clapped the lad on the shoulder and then, followed by Jock and Ewan, he made his way to the edge of the trees and thence across a space of open ground to vault the orchard wall. Once they were across it the fruit trees screened their movements and they came unopposed to the edge of the courtyard. From the direction of the hall they could hear voices and raucous laughter.

'They're at table,' murmured Ban. 'Come on.'

They ran to the rear of the women's bower, concealing themselves in the shadows by the wall. A glance round the corner revealed a guard by the door. Ewan put his head round the corner.

'Psst!'

The guard looked round at once, frowning. Ewan beckoned frantically. The man put a hand on his sword hilt and came to investigate. As he rounded the end of the building there was a stifled exclamation followed by a thud. Ban surveyed the body in grim satisfaction and then looked at his companions. Together they headed for the door.

He opened it an inch and peered inside. In the passageway beyond he made out two more men. Clearly the element of surprise was going to be short-lived. After that everything depended on being able to overpower the guards before they were able to raise the alarm.

Turning to his companions he lifted his hand, raising his fingers to indicate the number of men within and pointing in the appropriate direction. Then, quietly, he slid his sword free of the scabbard. The others followed suit. He gestured for Ewan to remain where he was. Then flinging the door open, Ban and Jock hurtled into the passageway. The first guard reached for his sword but was cut down before the blade cleared leather. The second had enough time to free his weapon and, with an ear-splitting yell, launch himself at Jock. Ban swore softly. Leaving Jock to deal with the guard he opened the inner door of the bower.

'Isabelle?'

'Ban!' She stared at him incredulously. 'You came back.'

'Did you doubt it?'

'I thought I'd never see you again.'

'I don't give up that easily.'

There came a groan from the passageway and the clash of swords ceased. Jock put his head round the door.

'I hate tae interrupt but we need to get out of here. In another two minutes this place is going to be swarming.'

Ban nodded then looked at Isabelle. 'Come with me?'

'Yes, Nell must come too. Murdo will kill her otherwise.'

He had no trouble believing it so there was only one possible answer. 'Very well, but make haste.'

Pausing only to snatch up a cloak the two women followed him into the passageway. They had just reached the outer door when they heard raised voices from the hall.

'They've heard the racket,' said Jock.

'They could've heard the racket in Dunfermline,' replied Ewan. 'What the hell were you doing?'

'Never mind.' Ban seized Isabelle's hand. 'Just run for it.'

Forgetting about stealth they fled through the orchard. Behind them the sound of voices grew louder. Once Isabelle stumbled and would have

fallen but for the strong, supporting hand round
hers. When they reached the wall Jock and Ewan
vaulted across. Then Ban swept Isabelle up and
tossed her over to them. Having done the like for
Nell he jumped over as well and then all five of
them raced for the wood. Although the distance
was relatively short it seemed to take for ever before they reached the trees where Davy waited
with the horses. Seeing the women he grinned
at his companions.

'You did it!'

'Aye, and now yon wolf pack knows we did,'
replied Ewan. 'We need to put some space between us, and fast.'

Davy led the horses forwards. Jock mounted
and reached a hand down to Nell. 'Ride pillion
behind me, mistress.'

Breathless now, Nell could only nod. When
she was safely ensconced, Ban turned to Isabelle, tossing her up on to his own horse. Then
he mounted behind her, locking an arm about her
waist. In the distance they could hear more shouting. Turning the horses' heads the little group
rode away through the trees and thence up the
track to the top of the hill, retracing their earlier
route. The path was clear even in the summer
half-light and the horses made good speed. When
they reined at the top of the hill Ban glanced
back. Even at that distance he could see a flurry

of activity below and then the clatter of horses' hooves on stone. Pursuit was imminent. He knew they would never outrun it when two of their horses carried extra weight. Moreover he guessed that Murdo would split his force to pick up their trail. In that they would be assisted by the light of the rising moon.

After several miles at a breakneck pace the fugitives came at length to a stand of trees and the men slowed, reining in beneath the sheltering canopy. For a moment or two they listened. In the distance they heard the muffled thud of hooves.

'We must find somewhere tae lie low, my lord, or we're dead meat,' said Jock.

'Aye, but where?' asked Ewan.

Isabelle took a deep breath. 'There is a cave in the wood beyond the next hill. It's big enough to take men and horses.'

'How far, my lady?' demanded Ban.

'Two miles perhaps.'

'Tell me the way.'

Under her instruction he headed into the trees and thence along the right-hand fork of the trail. The horses were blowing hard, their necks and flanks streaked with sweat and flecked with lather. At this rate they would soon be spent. Isabelle thanked her lucky stars that she had ridden this country for the majority of her life and

knew it well. She had found the cave by chance
while out on one of her illicit solo rides. It was in
a rocky outcrop set back off the trail and its en-
trance was not visible from the track below. Nor
was there any sign of it ever having been inhab-
ited, save perhaps by wild beasts. It might give
them a chance, if they could reach it in time; if
Murdo's men didn't know about it. Otherwise she
and all her companions would be caught in a trap.
The thought brought cold sweat to her forehead.

The horses plunged on, across a small stream
and up the slope, their breathing laboured now.
Relentlessly the riders spurred them forwards.
Behind them the echo of hoofbeats grew louder;
a sinister rhythmic drumming that struck terror
into the heart like a pronouncement of impending
doom. When she glanced back Isabelle could see
a line of fire bright against the darkening land.
Torches! Murdo's men would use their light to
follow the trail. It seemed to be taking for ever
to reach the top of the hill. It had not seemed so
large before. Eventually they reached the summit
and then began the hazardous descent, the horses
plunging and sliding down the trail, bushes slashing at their legs and flanks. Then they were into
the trees again and the pace slowed a little.

By the time they reached the rocky outcrop
it was clear the horses couldn't go on much further, burdened as they were. With unspeakable

relief she recognised the narrow path that led up
to the cave. The dark mouth yawned before them.
Dismounting hurriedly, Ewan threw his horse's
reins at Davy.

'Take him. I'll go and wipe our tracks as far
as I can.'

He seized a fallen branch and raced away leaving the others to enter the cave. Ban dismounted
and then lifted Isabelle down. His hands lingered
a moment on her waist.

'Are you all right?' he asked.

She nodded, aware of him to her very finger-
tips. 'Aye, my lord.'

'We may outwit them yet. Take Nell and get
as far into the cave as you can.'

Without argument the two women obeyed.
Presently Isabelle felt the cold stone wall at the
rear of the cavern and turned with her back to it,
clutching Nell's arm. As her eyes adjusted to the
gloom she could just make out the dark mass of
the horses, just catch the sound of their breathing.
The blood pounded in her ears. It was echoed by
another rhythm: the drumming beat of galloping
hooves drawing nearer. Hardly daring to breathe
she listened as the sound increased. Then she
heard men's voices and caught through the trees
below the flicker of torchlight. Isabelle shut her
eyes and swallowed hard, praying. A noise in the
cave mouth made her start. Then she realised it

was Ewan returning. Had he been able to erase their tracks in time?

The drumming changed tempo, slowed and then stopped altogether. The searchers had slowed their horses to a walk. She could visualise the leading riders, grim faced, hard-eyed, looking for the trail by the light of the torches. Her overwrought imagination heard the chink of harness, the creak of saddle leather. These were men battle-hardened, accustomed to the outdoors, well used to tracking and guided almost by the scent of fear. They would relish this chase. When they ran their prey to ground they would flush it by whatever means necessary and, having it fast, would destroy it. Ban and the rest would be slain where they stood, she and Nell dragged back to Murdo. Almost she could see the cold ruthless gaze, the pitiless eye that would delight in her fear and seek to enhance her humiliation. He would make her watch the deaths of her companions before he carried her by force back to Castlemora. Then… The very thought was enough to freeze the blood. There was no hope of effective resistance. Murdo had the power to do with her whatever he wished. Isabelle trembled, feeling sick with revulsion. Before she would permit that to happen she would make an end of her life at the point of a dagger.

She waited, nerves stretched to screaming

point, as the voices came closer and she could make out individual words.

'…lost the trail…might have doubled back… fan out…'

She heard hoof falls on dry earth and the clink of an iron shoe on stone. They must be right below the hiding place. If they looked up they would see only trees and undergrowth and then the rock wall. If you didn't know the path was there you would miss it. She had only found it by chance. *Please, God, let them be deceived.* Hardly daring to breathe she clutched Nell's arm more tightly. Seconds crawled by like hours. Then the voices moved away and the flickering lights with them. Silence formed and grew and became oppressive. Then the hoofbeats sounded again but they too gradually faded into the distance.

'They've gone,' she breathed.

Nell squeezed her arm murmuring, 'Thank heaven.'

No one moved for several minutes more; then she heard Ban's voice, soft through the gloom.

'They've ridden on.'

Isabelle felt weak with relief. 'Will they return, my lord?'

'Possibly, but I think it unlikely they will find this place. You chose well, my lady.'

She could make out only his outline, dark

against the lighter gloom at the cave mouth, but his presence was solid and reassuring.

'We will remain here tonight and move at first light,' he went on. 'The horses are tired and it's too dangerous to go on anyway.'

Again she realised just how much he was risking for her sake. Instinctively she reached out a hand and let it rest on his sleeve.

'Thank you.' Even as she said the words they sounded woefully inadequate to her ears.

'Did you think I would leave you behind?'

'In truth I have not been able to think at all.'

'That is hardly to be wondered at in the circumstances.' His hand closed over hers. 'I am only sorry that I did not guess the extent of Murdo's treachery.'

'No one could have guessed it.'

'He will pay for what he has done this day, Isabelle, I swear it.'

A lump formed in her throat and it was impossible to speak. Correctly interpreting her silence he squeezed her hand gently.

'Try to get some rest. It will be a long hard day tomorrow and we are still far from safety.'

He left her then to go and speak with his men. Feeling utterly bereft she watched him go; then turned back to her companion. They found a level space at the rear of the cave and lay down, rolled in their cloaks, huddled together for com-

fort. The earthen floor was hard and the night
air cold now and Isabelle shivered. For a long
time sleep eluded her and her ears strained to
catch every sound in the still night. Her eyes had
grown accustomed to the darkness and she could
make out the shapes of the men some yards off.
Despite the reassurance their presence afforded
it could not dispel the chill of realisation that in
the broader scheme of things she was alone. With
father and brother dead her situation was dire
indeed. However, even that did not match the
desolation she felt at their loss. Her father had at
least lived to the full. It was his time to go. Hugh
should have had his whole life ahead of him; not
been cut down in first flush of manhood. Grief
mingled with loathing for his killer.

She might have escaped for the time being
but knew full well the danger was far from over.
Murdo was single-minded in the pursuit of his
goals and patient too. He would stop at nothing
to find her. The thought of that eventuality made
her feel sick. Death would be preferable. The only
glimmer of light in all the present gloom was that
Ban had come back for her. She had never been
more thankful for anything in her life, but for the
first time it occurred to her that he might have
other motives than rescuing her from Murdo's
clutches. With Hugh's death she was no longer a
widow with a meagre dowry; she was heiress to

Castlemora. Had that been part of Ban's calculations when he rescued her?

At some point amid these thoughts she eventually fell into an uneasy sleep and woke at dawn, feeling stiff and cold, aching from the ride and the hard ground. However, not for the world would she have complained. Raising herself on to one elbow she looked around. Beside her Nell was still asleep. The men were stirring though. Further off she saw Ban speaking to Jock and Davy. Their voices were soft and she could not hear the words, only a murmur of conversation. The young man called Ewan stood on guard at the cave mouth, surveying the quiet woodland.

Isabelle rose slowly and straightened her dishevelled garments. Then she fastened her cloak about her shoulders for the air was cool yet. For a moment or two she hesitated and then moved towards the others. Sensing her approach Ban looked round.

'Good morning. I hope you managed to get some sleep.'

The tone was courteous but his expression was hard to read. It did nothing to alleviate her confusion. The knowledge of what she owed him was counterbalanced by her doubts about his real motives.

'I did, my lord.'

'Are you hungry?' he asked.

In that moment she realised that she was, having eaten nothing since the previous day and precious little then. She watched him take a small bundle from the saddlebag. He handed her a small portion of bread and cheese.

'Scant fare, I'm afraid,' he said, 'but it will stave off hunger the while.'

'Thank you.'

'Take some for your companion too.'

As she took the offering his fingers brushed hers, unintentionally perhaps, but the touch sent a charge along her skin. His hands were strong and capable; hands that could wield a sword or dagger or hold a woman close. When she recalled some of their other qualities it brought a tinge of colour to her cheeks, and in confusion she addressed herself to the food. Thankfully he had turned away to supply his men, thus failing to see her discomfiture.

She found a convenient rock to sit on and ate her portion. Having done so, she took the other to Nell. The older woman groaned and roused herself with difficulty, for the night spent on hard ground had taken its toll, but she said no word of complaint. Instead she smiled at Isabelle and took the food gratefully.

At length the horses were saddled and the fugitives remounted, leaving the shelter of the cave and descending the narrow path into the wood. Wreaths of mist lingered in the hollows and wound about the grey trunks of the trees where, hidden from view, birds sang. Progress was slow at first, for Ban had no wish to stumble unawares on an enemy camp or a chance patrol.

Isabelle, riding pillion now, watched the undergrowth closely for any sign of movement that might suggest an ambush. Nothing stirred. Even so they spoke soft for sound carried in the still air.

'When we get out of the trees we'll pick up the pace,' he told her.

'How far are we from Glengarron?'

'About a day and a half,' he replied, 'as near as I can estimate.'

Her heart sank. 'Still so far?'

'Far enough,' he conceded, 'but we'll get there.'

'Will we?' She paused. 'Forgive me, I did not mean to doubt you. It's just that I cannot help feeling afraid.'

'I can understand that, given the nature of the enemy, but he won't take you back.'

She experienced a twinge of guilt. He had risked much for her sake, was still risking much, when he could have abandoned her and saved his own skin. And still so many perils lay ahead. On the other hand she was now a considerable prize; valuable enough to be worth the risk involved.

Their betrothal had only ever been a business arrangement but now the stakes had increased dramatically. When he came back for her he knew she would go with him because there was no alternative.

Riding so close to him she was at leisure to observe without being seen. Her eyes followed the strong line of his back to the broad shoulders and the tawny hair that curled over the collar of his tunic, and thence to the hollow of his neck, the familiar planes of cheek and jaw, the curve of his mouth. If he turned round their lips would be close enough to kiss. She blinked back tears as desire competed with suspicion.

Once clear of the trees Ban picked up the pace to a steady canter that covered the ground without tiring the horses too much. The time might yet come when they would need every bit of speed the animals could summon. As they rode they kept sharp watch, looking for any evidence of their pursuers, but the landscape was empty and they advanced unchallenged. Guessing the road would be the first place that Murdo's men would watch, Ban chose a cross-country route using sheep tracks and narrow ways, avoiding the crests of the hills where they would be on view for miles around and using the natural features of the landscape to hide their progress.

* * *

At noon they stopped to water the horses and to rest awhile. The men took it in turns to keep watch.

Seeing the women refreshing themselves at the stream Ban took his companions aside for a quiet word.

'We make good progress,' he said, 'but we're not home yet and Murdo is not the type to give up his prey easily.'

'Would that we might get word tae Glengarron,' said Ewan. 'Reinforcements would be welcome just now.'

'Aye, they would,' agreed Davy. 'I'm ne'er one to run from a fight, but odds of ten to one are no so good.'

Ban glanced towards the two women feeling all the weight of his responsibility. Isabelle's vulnerability seemed all the more pointed. Somehow he must get her to safety. There would be time enough to think after that. Since their escape from Castlemora her manner to him had been different somehow; it was courteous but at the same time a little more aloof as though something preyed on her mind. Given what had happened in the last few days it wasn't surprising. Her father's death had been bad enough but with Hugh's murder on top of that… Ban vowed silently that he would keep his promise. Murdo would answer for his crime. In the interim Isabelle needed time to grieve. When they reached Glengarron he could give her that at least.

Only once in the course of that day did they see evidence of the enemy, a small patrol of a dozen men, but they were fully half a mile away and moving south, parallel to the fugitives' present course. Ban reined in.

'Will they see us?' asked Isabelle.

'No, they're not even looking in our direction.' He frowned as an unpleasant thought occurred to him. After a moment he found Jock alongside. The craggy face was grim.

'Are ye thinking what I'm thinking?' he asked.

'Probably,' replied Ban.

Ewan looked from one to the other. 'What is it, my lord?'

For answer Ban nodded in the direction of the distant riders now drawing away, evidently riding fast. 'Look yonder.'

Ewan frowned. 'What are they doing?'

'Murdo has moved his men ahead of us. It's why we haven't seen hide or hair of them since last night. He knows he can move much faster than we and he's planning to throw a cordon of patrols across our way.'

Ewan frowned. 'Cut us off from Glengarron, ye mean?'

'Precisely.'

A tense silence followed.

Jock threw Ban a wry glance. 'What now?'

'We have to get word to Glengarron. It's our only chance. One of us must go on ahead and find a way through Murdo's patrols.'

'Aye, you're right. Will I get going then?'

'No, not you: Ewan must go. He was born hereabouts and knows this region better than anyone.'

The younger man nodded. 'I ken every rock, bush and sheep track for twenty miles.'

To Isabelle's surprise he didn't look remotely concerned by the thought of danger or possible capture. As if in answer to the thought Ban turned in the saddle and met her eye.

'If anyone can get through he will.'

'I'll get through, my lady,' Ewan replied. 'I swear it.'

'Ye'd better,' said Jock. Then, jerking his head in the general direction of home, he added, 'Away with ye then, lad, and keep your eyes open.'

'I'll mind the advice.'

With that Ewan turned his horse aside and rode away in the wake of the enemy patrol. The others watched until he was lost to view among the rocks and trees. Isabelle sent a silent prayer along with him. Nell eyed her shrewdly.

'He'll get through all right,' she said.

'But will it be in time?' replied Isabelle.

'Have no fear, my lady,' said Jock. 'He will get through and Lord Iain will send aid.'

Beside him, Davy nodded. 'Aye, that's right, and then yon mercenary scum will see if Glengarron's reputation has been exaggerated or no.'

Ban's answering smile belied his inner concern. The foe was ruthless and dangerous. If this had involved just himself and his men, that would have been one thing. The presence of the women was quite another for their safety must be his top priority. Even so, the thought of the coming conflict filled him with savage anticipation. It would be good to come face to face with Murdo instead of all this running and hiding. When he did he would take pleasure in killing him. And then…what?

For the first time he did let his thoughts run on a little. Even with the immediate threat removed, Isabelle would still be vulnerable until their betrothal was made public. She had just become an heiress and thus a considerable prize. It might be that the king himself would take a hand in the matter once he heard of it, and he would hear. Castlemora was a rich estate. Loyalty could be bought thus and alliances too. Since Malcolm had paid homage to King William might not closer ties be sought, ties of marriage between Norman and Scot? It was an unwelcome possibility. On the other hand it could be removed by the declaration of his betrothal. In many ways that was a highly desirable solution but it still left one critical problem outstanding. Ban's jaw tensed. The future was growing more complicated by the hour.

Although he suspected they would not stumble across any of the enemy patrols as yet, he never relaxed his vigilance all through the remainder of that day, nor at night when they made camp. They dared not light a fire for fear of attracting unwelcome attention, and that evening they ate the last of the food. With more supplies they would have had the option of staying put and waiting for help; as it was they had no choice now but to go on. He calculated they were perhaps ten miles from home. It should have been an easy ride in the morning. Now he knew it would be anything but. With every step they would be riding ever closer to danger. All Murdo had to do was let them come.

Chapter Ten

Isabelle rolled herself in her cloak and lay down beside Nell, trying to sleep. However, the hard ground and the evening chill held sleep at bay and presently she gave it up. Taking care not to disturb the others she moved apart and sat down in the lee of a boulder, resting her back against the stone. Above her the stars burned in the deepening vault of the sky, and the moon, almost at the full, was mounting the heavens. All the country round was bathed in its soft silvery light.

'Beautiful, isn't it?' said a quiet voice beside her.

With a start she looked up to see Ban. She had not heard him approach or even been aware of his presence until that moment. It astonished her that such a large man could move so silently, or with

such feline grace. The thought also occurred that
he must have been watching her, unseen.

'Aye, it is,' she replied.

Not knowing what to say to him she fell silent
again, fixing her gaze on the stars, glad of the
darkness that concealed her expression. If he was
aware of any awkwardness he gave no sign, and
casually sat down nearby. Aware of him to the
last fibre of her being, she waited.

'When we reach Glengarron,' he said, 'I hope
to offer you better entertainment than this rough
living.'

She didn't tell him that rough living wasn't her
main concern. She could have borne any amount
of that if he was near; if he had truly cared for her.

'I think you will be glad to see the place
again,' she said.

'Indeed.'

'Your sister will be pleased to see you safe.'

'Ashlynn, aye. I'm sure she will also be happy
to meet you.'

Isabelle hoped it might be so but her experiences at Dunkeld made her wonder. Blood was
thicker than water and if it ever came to taking
sides Lady Ashlynn would not support a stranger
over a beloved brother.

'I look forward to it,' she lied. Would he tell
his sister what had passed during his stay at

Castlemora? She supposed them to be close so it seemed possible. Her spirits sank further.

'She is expecting another child very soon,' he went on.

'Another? My goodness.' A lump formed in her throat. 'You will be an uncle thrice over.'

'Aye, I will. It's beginning to make me feel old.'

'I find that hard to believe.'

'Why so?'

'You seem tireless in all things.'

He grinned. 'I'd defy anyone to remain tireless after being in the company of my nephews for more than half an hour. The very thought of a third is exhausting.'

'It might be a niece this time.'

He considered it. 'A little girl? That might be nice.'

Alive to every inflexion of his voice she heard the wistfulness behind the words. 'You are fond of children, I think.'

'Children are relatively uncomplicated,' he replied. 'And they give us hope for the future.'

Although the tone was casual she knew that the sentiment was not. Getting heirs was a matter of prime importance, and especially to this man. It was also dangerous ground and she was reluctant to linger there when he had been speak-

ing more freely. There were so many things she
wanted to know.

'How did your sister meet Lord Iain?'

'It was during the Harrying. He pulled her out
of a freezing river.'

'How romantic.'

'She didn't think so at first.' He smiled faintly.
'Nor did she wish to come north with him.'

'He must have been very persuasive.'

'He didn't give her a choice although, as it
turned out, he had good reasons for that.'

'Where were you at the time?'

'Unconscious and then out of my head with
fever. When Heslingfield was sacked I was
wounded in the fighting and left for dead. Iain's
men found me among the slain.'

Isabelle tried to imagine her feelings if Castlemora had been overrun and burned by Norman thugs and her own family slaughtered. A
brother's murder gave an insight into the horror
but she guessed even that fell far short of what
Ban had experienced. How did a person recover
from such events?

'They patched me up as best they could,' he
continued, 'put me in a wagon and took me with
them. When I eventually came round I was at
Dark Mount. I had no idea that Ashlynn had been
saved until Iain brought her to see me one day.'

'That must have been a very special moment.'

'It was. We had always been close and when I discovered that she was alive and well…let's just say that the world seemed a little less bleak.'

She recognised the understatement and sensed the emotion he did not articulate. She could only guess at his state of mind at that time. Yet, in spite of everything he hadn't given up; he had survived and carved out a new life for himself.

'And you've been at Dark Mount ever since.'

'That's right.' He didn't add that there was nowhere else to go. 'Iain offered me a place among his men and I was glad to accept it. I've never regretted the decision.'

'He is a man who commands respect. My father always said as much and he did not give his praise readily.'

'Your father was right.'

'Well, I look forward to meeting Lady Ashlynn and your nephews.'

'You will be able to do so very soon.'

The thought occurred to her that if Ewan did not get through then the chance of any of them seeing Glengarron was remote. Perhaps Lady Ashlynn would wait in vain for her brother to return. Isabelle swallowed hard. The thought of his death was chilling, like the thought of a world without him. Yet he had obviously weighed the risk and found it worthwhile. Suspicion resurfaced and with it an urge to confront the matter head on. Whatever the truth it was better than doubt.

'Why did you come back for me?' she asked.

'No man takes what is mine and gets away with it. And, as I told you, I would not leave you with Murdo.'

She licked dry lips. 'Is that the only reason? After all, Castlemora is a considerable prize.'

He didn't pretend to misunderstand. 'Aye, it is and, God willing, we shall return and reclaim it very soon.'

'You mean *you* will claim it. You will be laird.'

'I shall, and you its lady, if events fall out as we hope.'

If. She shivered inwardly. So much hung on that one little word. 'And if they do not?'

'Come what may,' he replied, 'I shall claim Castlemora.'

'What?'

'It is a rich and valuable estate and the king would rather see it in the hands of an ally than an enemy.'

'And so at a stroke you regain all that you once lost.'

'That's right.'

For a moment she was speechless. No matter what happened he would emerge a winner whereas her position remained precarious. She dreaded to ask the next question but knew she had to now.

'Will you acknowledge our betrothal *if*…when we reach Glengarron?'

'When circumstances make that possible.' He paused, surveying her steadily. 'Nothing has changed. The arrangement still stands.'

'I see.' She lowered her gaze. He had been brutally frank but now at least every last trace of doubt was gone. Formerly she had been glad of his honesty and in a way still was, but this time it hurt too. His affections were not engaged; to him she was a means to an end. *I do not love you any more than you love me.* Tears pricked behind her eyelids and she blinked them away, sickened by her own folly. Her ability to please this man was limited to sharing his bed, or wherever else he chose to take her. It occurred to her then that Glengarron was both haven and fortress. She might have escaped from Murdo but, in doing so, she had put herself into hands that were more powerful and, in their way, more dangerous. This man had the power to hurt her in ways that Murdo never could.

'First though,' said Ban, 'we have to reach Glengarron.'

'One more thing I would ask, my lord.'

'Which is?'

Isabelle met his gaze. 'If we are not rescued

in time, I beg that you will not let Murdo take me alive.'

For a moment he was silent as he tried to read her expression. 'The situation will not arise.'

'It might, and I would rather be dead than submit to him.'

'I promise you will never again be in his power.'

'Thank you.'

He squeezed her arm lightly. 'Don't be afraid. All will yet be well.'

Feeling the warmth of that touch Isabelle's heart constricted. How was it possible for a man to be such a mass of contradictions? How did one reconcile gentleness and courtesy with ruthlessness and ambition? How could a man who was so ardent in bed have a heart sheathed in ice?

'I pray you are right,' she replied.

His hand fell to his side. 'You should try to get some sleep, my lady. We have another long day ahead.'

She nodded, not trusting herself to speak further. Seeing her about to rise, Ban stood up first and offered his hand. There was a fleeting hesitation before she took it and as he drew her to her feet he felt her tremble. For a moment they remained thus facing each other. Then, with a tremulous smile, she withdrew her fingers from his.

'Goodnight, my lord.'

* * *

He watched her walk away, conscious of conflicting emotions. It hadn't been an easy conversation but he hadn't wanted to lie to her either. Only a fool would let slip an opportunity like the one he now had. Castlemora was going to be his. When that happened he wanted Isabelle at his side and he wanted to keep her there. He couldn't imagine any other woman in that role. It wasn't just her beauty that drew him now; she possessed intelligence, honesty and courage as well. Together they were a heady combination. Her company was agreeable too and, unlike that of most other women, it didn't pall. When he left her she lingered in his thoughts; with her he found himself speaking of things he didn't discuss with anyone else. She could be disturbingly perceptive at times, but she also had a way of seeing straight to the heart of a matter. It would be pointless to lie to her, she would know at once. Besides, he had no wish to because if he did she would think less of him. He sighed, wondering then what she did think. Probably her opinion of him was not high. Nor could he blame her for it. If they lived to reach Glengarron he would try and make it up to her.

For all his confident words earlier he couldn't deny to himself how serious their situation was. Everything depended on Ewan now. If he got through they had a chance. If not… Ban tried not to think of the alternative.

The rest of the night passed uneventfully and at dawn they rose and saddled the horses. There was no more food and already Ban could feel hunger pangs clawing his stomach. He knew the others must feel the same. It was hard enough on a man never mind a woman, yet he heard no word of complaint. Instead Isabelle greeted him with a brave smile. It touched him more than any tears could have done and his esteem increased. In spite of her youth and her vulnerability she could face a difficult situation with courage and he admired that.

Gathering the reins he mounted the big chestnut and waited while Davy lifted Isabelle up behind him. He felt her settle herself on the crupper and then the light, familiar clasp of her hands on his waist. He smiled wryly. The best he could say of present circumstances was that they offered the perfect excuse to keep her close.

When Nell was safely perched behind Jock, the little group set out. The pace was slower now and they rode with caution, their eyes watching for any sign of movement in the landscape. For some time it was open and afforded little cover but Ban knew that presently it gave way to stunted trees and rocky outcrops, the very places for an ambush. He had no intention of falling into one if he could help it.

'The bastards are there somewhere,' muttered Jock. 'I can feel it like an itch I canna reach.'

'Aye.' Ban scanned the terrain ahead. 'Even so we've no option now but to go on.'

'Ewan should have reached Glengarron by now.'

'Aye, he should.'

'That being so, help is on its way.'

Neither of them mentioned any of the possible ifs attaching to that statement. In spite of the sunlight Isabelle shivered inwardly. Safety was so tantalisingly near, a matter of a few miles, but it might as well have been a hundred. Her eyes scanned the surrounding land for any sign of movement. Like Jock, she could sense that the enemy was close. Perhaps Murdo was watching them even now. Her stomach knotted. She could almost see his gloating smile. He meant to play with them like a cat at a mouse hole.

In the event it was the flash of sunlight on steel that revealed the presence of the enemy behind the boulders on the hillside half a mile away. Ban reined in his horse. He had no sooner pointed out the location to his companions than there was an answering flash from a hillside opposite. He cursed softly.

'They're strung out in groups and who knows

how far?' said Jock. 'We canna ride round them, and if we try tae go through they'll close in and encircle us.'

'Even if we got past this lot there'd likely be another group beyond,' replied Ban.

'They've seen us at any rate. What do ye want to do?'

'Let them come to us.' Ban glanced around. 'We'll take a position up there on yonder hillside. See where the land levels off a little under that outcrop? The rock face will protect our rear, those boulders our flanks, so they can only come at us from the front and a few at a time.'

'You mean to try to hold them until reinforcements arrive?'

'There's no other choice.'

He touched the chestnut with his heel and, with the others following, headed for the place in question. Isabelle half-expected armed men to rise up out of the ground and bar their progress, but they reached their goal unhindered. Ban dismounted and spoke to his men.

'Loose the horses. They'll only be in the way here.' As they moved to obey he turned back to Isabelle and lifted her down. 'Do you and Nell take shelter among the rocks, my lady.'

More than anything now she wanted to remain within the sheltering circle of his arm but could only nod in mute obedience. Could he not

hear her heart beating from where he stood? For
a moment more he looked into her face and his
own expression grew serious. Letting his arm fall
from her waist he drew the dagger from his belt
and, reversing the blade, handed it to her.

'Take this. It's little enough, but it offers you
some protection.' He did not add that it also offered a choice if things should go amiss.

Isabelle understood him well enough and took
the knife without hesitation. His sacrifice today
was like to be the greatest any man could ever
make. Hers could be no less.

'I will use this rather than go with Murdo.'

His hand closed over hers and squeezed it. 'Be
of good courage, my lady. All may yet be well.'

'God be with you,'

'God be with us all,' he replied.

Movement among the rocks below revealed
the enemy closing in. Isabelle counted a dozen
men but knew there were many more. It was just
a matter of time before the rest arrived. The situation was hopeless. Oddly that knowledge filled
her with resolve and her hand tightened round
the hilt of the dagger as she hastened to join Nell.
Behind her Ban and his men drew their swords
and waited.

The approaching horsemen grew larger by
the moment, looming out of the landscape like
so many spectres of evil. Now it was possible

to make out the details of their horses and their arms, then their faces. Grim, eager for the coming fight, they drew rein at the bottom of the slope. When they saw the three men there they grinned, evidently considering this to be no contest. Then they dismounted. There followed the chilling sound of metal scraping wood and oiled leather as blades were drawn from scabbards. With expressions of keen anticipation the mercenary force advanced.

Ban had chosen his spot well. The ascent was not only steep but the limited access meant that, at most, only two or three men at a time could approach the sheltering fugitives. Nothing loath the first of them began their approach.

'Well, here they come.' Jock's hand tightened round the hilt of his sword.

'There's an awful lot of them,' replied Davy.

'Aye, and it's only part of their force. It willna take the others long tae join them.'

'If Ewan's bringing those reinforcements, now would be a good time.'

'That it would, lad, but while we're waiting let's kill as many of the bastards as we can, eh?'

The first three mercenaries reached the level shelf below the crag and raced forwards to meet them. The air rang with the clash of metal. Ban lunged for his opponent's breast, a deadly stroke turned aside just in time. It was returned in kind.

Ban parried it and cut again and again, the blade
an arc of light so fierce was his attack. His opponent, forced back, stumbled on the uneven
ground. Ban's foot swung up and caught the man
hard in the groin. He heard the grunt of pain.
Without giving his opponent time to recover he
sped him with a thrust to the gut. Out of the corner of his eyes he saw Jock and Davy in fierce en-
gagement with their own opponents. He heard a
cry but could not investigate for the next man was
on him. However, though big, he was no match
for Ban with a blade and was brought low with
a thrust to the shoulder. No sooner had he fallen
than another rushed to take his place. There followed more cries and curses as Jock and Davy
accounted for their own. Even as these fell more
men rushed forwards but with no more success.
Gradually the rocks and sparse turf grew dark
and stained with blood. All smiles had vanished
from the faces of the mercenaries now and were
replaced with grim intent to cut down the defenders and avenge their own.

Ban glanced at the bodies around and then at
the advancing tide and he knew it was just a matter of time before they were overpowered. Sweat-
ing now, he could feel the strain in his sword
arm. Beside him, Jock and Davy fought on. He
glimpsed blood on Jock's neck and chest, but
since the man fought unimpeded he assumed it

was someone else's. Davy appeared unhurt, fighting with single-minded concentration and zeal. As his foe fell beneath his sword there came a pause and for a moment no more men came forwards to challenge the waiting three.

Breathing hard they saw a familiar figure approaching.

'Murdo,' murmured Ban. He turned briefly to his companions. 'This one's mine, lads.'

The oncoming warrior was flanked by a dozen more. Pausing near the top of the slope he scanned the scene swiftly, taking in the pile of corpses and then the three defenders beyond.

'Surrender yourselves! You're heavily outnumbered and pinned down. You cannot win. Give up the Lady Isabelle and I'll spare your lives.'

'Aye, right,' muttered Jock.

'If you want her you'll have to come and get her,' replied Ban, 'but to do it you must come past me.'

The thought of Isabelle in Murdo's clutches was anathema. Ban tightened his grip on the sword. It wasn't going to happen; not now, not ever.

'It'll be a pleasure.' Murdo drew his sword. Then, with a curt gesture to his men, he began to advance. Reaching the top of the slope he halted a few yards from Ban.

'It will afford me much satisfaction to cut your

throat,' he said then. His cold gaze flicked to where Isabelle stood with Nell. 'Did you really think to take what was mine?'

'I was never yours, Murdo,' she retorted, 'nor ever will be.'

'You are mistaken, Isabelle, as you will soon discover. When this is done perhaps I'll take you here in front of your champion, before I run him through.'

Isabelle paled, but Ban's lips curled in a sardonic smile. 'Come, braggart, you must catch the bear ere you skin it.'

Murdo half-turned and signalled to his men. Then they advanced. Ban hefted his sword, flanked by Jock and Davy.

'Get ready,' he murmured.

Jock eyed the approaching men with a jaundiced expression. 'We're ready. If we can just hold them off awhile longer…'

No one replied for even as he spoke they heard the distant thunder of hoofbeats, and saw in the middle distance a rolling cloud of dust that marked the approach of many men. The defenders exchanged glances, their expressions grim.

'The rest of the mercenary force,' muttered Jock. 'This is about to get interesting.'

'Very interesting and very busy,' replied Davy.

Murdo glanced at the distant riders and smiled. 'Get ready to die, you Saxon dog.'

Ban made no reply. He had time only for a fleeting regret that he had failed Isabelle, and then Murdo was upon him. The great blades clashed with bone-jarring force. The warlord was skilled and strong and, as yet, fresh to the fight. With each shuddering blow Ban felt his aching muscles protest, but he could afford no respite. He fought instinctively now, slashing and parrying in return, seeking a weakness in the other man's play. It needed but one unguarded moment. However, Murdo was fit and agile; each time it seemed as though Ban's blade must break through his guard the edge was turned. Beginning to tire now, he knew mounting desperation for, with each moment, the sound of advancing horsemen grew louder. He dared not risk a look to see how close they were. His opponent too had heard the sound and his expression of triumph spoke louder than words.

Redoubling his attack he forced Ban to give ground. Unable to see where he was putting his feet the younger man stumbled. Though swift to regain his balance, Ban caught a glancing blow and felt the sword open a gash across his ribs. He drew a sharp breath, gritting his teeth against the pain. Warm blood flowed down his side. Seeing the spreading red stain, Murdo smiled.

'Next time it'll be your heart.'

Breathing hard, Ban vouchsafed no reply. He

had no breath to waste in idle banter and swung once more into the attack. A bloody slash appeared on Murdo's arm and he swore. Ban gave him no time to recover. Sheer agility saved Murdo from the blow aimed at his ribs and he countered swiftly. He wasn't laughing now and his play became a shade more cautious.

Ban could feel his strength ebbing. Blood pounded in his ears. It grew louder and louder and then, with sinking heart, he realised it was the sound of horses' hooves. The rest of Murdo's force had arrived.

From her place among the rocks Isabelle watched the conflict in mounting horror. She could see that Ban was tiring, weakened from his earlier exertions and now loss of blood. Yet somehow he fought on. The defenders had put up a magnificent fight but they could never win. Her fingers tightened on the hilt of the dagger. It seemed they would all die here today.

Suddenly Nell gripped hold of Isabelle's arm. 'Dear God!'

Isabelle followed the older woman's gaze. In the distance she could see the roiling cloud of dust as another group of horsemen approached.

'The rest of Murdo's force,' she murmured. 'It's over.'

Unable to tear their eyes away they watched

the riders draw nearer. They were many, fifty at least, mounted on swift horses, the sun glinting on spur and harness. The riders were clad in stout leather tunics and all were armed with sword and shield. In the vanguard was borne the banner that proclaimed their proud identity: a great bird of prey in flight with curving talons outstretched.

'Wait!' Nell's hand trembled and a tremulous smile hovered on her lips. 'Not Murdo's men. Merciful heavens, it's Glengarron.'

Hardly daring to hope, Isabelle strained to see. 'Are you sure?'

'Look at the banner. Does it not bear the device of a red kite?'

'On my life I think it does.' Isabelle clutched her companion's sleeve. 'Oh, Nell. Ewan must have succeeded.'

The sound of hooves grew louder. By now the mercenaries lower down the hill had also seen the threat for warning shouts echoed across the slope. Sunlight glinted on steel. Murdo frowned and glanced that way. It was for a split second only but that moment's inattention was enough and the edge of Ban's sword caught him in the side. Murdo gasped and disengaged, falling back a pace or two, his free hand clutching the wound. Blood seeped through his fingers. He looked around in cold fury and, assessing the situation at once, he began to retreat, shouting at his men to do likewise.

As he stumbled away down the hill two of his men stepped out from among the rocks to cover his retreat. Seeing the bows in their hands Isabelle cried out. It mingled with Ban's warning shout. Davy flung himself flat but Jock was too slow. Before their horrified gaze he stood motionless a moment and then his legs buckled and he fell, the feathered shaft buried in his breast. Ban uttered a great shout of rage. Raising his sword he flung the blade with all his might. The archer shrieked and fell. The second man lifted his bow and let fly the shaft. Ban felt a savage, fiery pain deep in his shoulder. His assailant turned and fled down the hill. For another second or two Ban looked on. Then he toppled sideways into darkness.

'Ban!' Isabelle ran to him and fell on her knees at his side, her hand seeking his. 'Ban! Look at me, I beg you.'

No reply was forthcoming. He was quite still, his face pale, the turf around stained with blood. Struggling with a rising sense of dread she sought for some sign of life; a breath, a movement, anything that would show he lived. She discovered none.

'Dear God, no. Please, no.'

Below them the tide of battle was turning and

already many of the mercenary force were dead. The rest were in full retreat. Some had already broken away and were riding hard for the hills, a detachment from Glengarron in hot pursuit. The rest of the arriving force was heading towards the crag. In the lead was a man on a big dapple-grey horse.

The mercenaries who had been on the slope with Murdo were now trapped. Aware of the danger they broke and ran for cover among the rocks. Undeterred the riders dismounted and moved forwards in pursuit. Isabelle watched in stricken silence. What should have been deliverance had become something from nightmare. Ban was dead and Jock too. They had given their lives for her and in that moment she wished with all her heart that it had been she who had died.

Running feet announced another arrival and looking up she saw Ewan. He reached the top of the slope and checked, his horrified gaze taking in the scene of carnage. Then he saw the bodies of his fallen companions and his cheeks grew ashen.

'Holy Mother.' His gaze met Davy's and held it. 'I've come too late.'

Davy, pale too, clasped his shoulder. 'It's no your fault.'

Ewan shook his head and looked miserably at Isabelle. 'I'm sorry, my lady.'

Before she could reply they were joined by another man, a tall, dark-haired warrior carrying a great sword. As her gaze took in the details of that imposing figure she realised who he was.

The Lord of Glengarron paused, his dark gaze resting on her a long moment. 'Lady Isabelle?'

As she nodded his image splintered through her tears. He glanced at Davy and Ewan now standing grim-faced with Nell, and then looked down at the still form beside Isabelle. Recognition and shock registered in his face and with a muffled oath he hastened forwards.

'Ban!' Swiftly sheathing his sword Lord Iain knelt and drew off his gauntlets, his fingers searching Ban's neck. For a moment his expression was grim. Then he drew in a deep breath. 'There's a pulse but it's weak.'

Isabelle's heart lurched. 'Oh, thank God!'

'We must get him back to Dark Mount as soon as may be.' He turned to Davy and Ewan. 'Get some help to carry him and Jock down to the horses.'

As they hurried away to do his bidding, Iain turned back to Isabelle.

'You are not hurt, my lady?'

'No, my lord; thanks to you and Lord Ban.'

'Would that we had arrived sooner,' he said.

Just then one of the Glengarron captains appeared. 'Beg pardon, my lord, but the remnant of the mercenary force has fled; some ten or a dozen men in all. Do you want us to go in pursuit?'

'Aye, and bring me their leader, that or his body.'

'Murdo was wounded,' said Isabelle, 'but not badly enough, I fear.'

Lord Iain turned to the captain. 'If they are carrying a wounded man it will slow their progress. Search thoroughly. We need to find him.'

The man nodded and hastened away. Isabelle shivered as the implications hit her. Correctly interpreting that expression Lord Iain's tone grew gentler.

'Have no fear, my lady. We'll find him eventually, dead or alive.'

They made their way down the slope to the horses. Isabelle looked in horror at the carnage all around her. The air stank of blood and slaughter. Horror was followed by guilt and remorse. All these men had died because of her. Ban was critically wounded. Reaction set in then and she trembled, feeling sick to the core of her being.

Iain surveyed her critically. 'Can you ride, my lady?'

She nodded, unable to speak now.

'Come then,' he said.

Chapter Eleven

Afterwards Isabelle had only the haziest recollection of the ride to Dark Mount and then, on arrival, a confused impression of men and horses and shouted orders as the injured were taken indoors. She craned her neck to try to see Ban but caught only a brief glimpse of him as the men bore him away. Then she was conducted to the great hall. Servants bustled around in obedience to Lord Iain's commands. Isabelle stood to one side, trying not to get in the way. In spite of Nell's presence, she had never felt more alone in her life.

Then a different woman appeared, a very beautiful woman with tawny hair and deep-blue eyes. She was in the advanced stages of pregnancy. In spite of this and her small stature she had about her an aura of natural authority. Isabelle quailed inwardly, knowing this must be

Lady Ashlynn. She looked pale and no wonder. Ban had said they were close. How would she receive the woman for whose sake he had been so critically hurt?

Seeing his wife approach, Lord Iain stepped forwards to meet her. 'We have a guest, my love. Lady Isabelle of Castlemora.'

Heart hammering, Isabelle curtsied. Ashlynn inclined her head in acknowledgement.

'You are welcome, Lady Isabelle. You need not be afraid; here you are among friends.'

The tone was unexpectedly kind and it brought a lump into Isabelle's throat. Somehow she murmured an appropriate response.

'You've had a terrible experience,' Ashlynn went on. 'You must be exhausted.'

'Do not be concerned about me, my lady.'

'I cannot be anything else since I know what it is to be hunted by those who intend only harm.'

Knowing something of the woman's history Isabelle recognised the words for truth. She also knew it must have taken enormous courage to face such perils alone. Just thinking about it engendered respect.

'Had it not been for Lord Ban I would never have escaped at all.' Her eyes met Ashlynn's. 'Is he… Will he be all right?'

'The healers are with him now.'

'I see.'

'When you are rested we will talk again. In the meantime a chamber has been prepared for you. Morag will show you.'

The chamber was spacious and well appointed and its window afforded a fine view of the glen. However, Isabelle barely took it in. Nell regarded her in concern.

'You need to rest. You look exhausted.' She paused. 'It will not help matters if you fall ill yourself.'

'I know. It's just that it seems wrong to sleep while Ban is in danger.'

'He's in good hands. The healers at Dark Mount are famed for their skill.'

'I fear for him all the same. He's lost so much blood.'

'He's a fighter in every way. He'll not give up the ghost just yet I think.'

'I pray you're right.'

'I've seen a good many fighting men in my time. I know a survivor when I see one.'

The words chimed with what Isabelle already knew of Ban's past. The result was a small flicker of hope.

'He has survived other wounds,' she replied.

'Worse ones, I'll wager.'

'It may be so. If only he doesn't get a fever.'

'We'll worry about that if it happens,' said Nell. 'In the meantime you should get some rest.'

Wearily Isabelle nodded. Then she removed her cloak and lay down on the bed. 'You will wake me at once if there's any news?'

'Of course.'

Isabelle closed her eyes and said a silent prayer. Within minutes she was asleep.

It was evening before she woke. The rest had refreshed her and when she had bathed her face and combed her hair she began to feel a little more like her old self. Her gown was in a sorry state after the adventures of the past two days, but there was nothing much to be done about it. Somewhat self-consciously she ran her hands over the front of the creased and dusty skirt, not liking to appear before her hosts so unsuitably attired. Under the circumstances perhaps they would forgive her. What mattered now was to have news of Ban.

On reaching the hall she found Lord Iain there with his wife and several others whom she did not know. Feeling suddenly awkward she hesitated in the doorway. However, Ashlynn turned at that moment and saw her there.

'Lady Isabelle. Pray come and sit down.'

She crossed the room aware of the curious stares directed her way. What must they think of her? By now the whole of Dark Mount would know who she was and how she came to be there. Furthermore they knew Lord Ban had been grievously hurt in her cause.

Sensing her nervousness Ashlynn smiled. 'You look a little better, though you are still too pale.'

'I am quite well,' replied Isabelle, 'but what of Lord Ban?'

'Meg has drawn the arrow and stanched the wound. His other hurts are not so deep but he has lost a lot of blood one way and another. What he needs now is rest and time to heal.'

'He will be all right, won't he?'

'I pray God he will.'

Isabelle drew in a ragged breath. 'He has been so kind, done so much to help me.' Tears welled in the hazel eyes. 'Now he may die and if he does it will be my fault.'

'I am sure it cannot be your fault,' replied Ashlynn.

'But it is. If it weren't for me he would have returned home unscathed. By rights he should have.'

'Won't you tell me what happened?'

Tactfully she led Isabelle aside and sat her down on the other side of the hearth before drawing up a chair for herself.

'Now you may speak freely.'

She listened with close attention as Isabelle

spoke of her father's death, and offered her condolences. When her companion went on to speak
of Hugh's murder and the events following, Ashlynn was shocked and horrified.

'Truly this Murdo is a most evil man.'

'I think him capable of any outrage,' replied
Isabelle.

Of the origins of her relationship with Ban,
she said nothing, being too ashamed to confess it.
Nor did she mention their subsequent betrothal.
Ban had wished the matter kept secret and she
would not break faith with him, no matter how
hard it was to remain silent. If Ashlynn guessed
she was not being told the whole, she evidently
knew better than to try to force a confidence. Isabelle was grateful for it, and for the kind attempt
to offer what reassurance she could.

'My brother has a strong constitution and an
even stronger will. Once before, when first we
came to Dark Mount, he was nigh unto death but
he fought it and won.'

'He mentioned that he had been injured at that
time.'

'He has a taste for dangerous odds.'

Isabelle's heart swelled. 'I never saw a braver
man, or a more skilful fighter.'

'I know of only one man who could best him.'

'Who is that?'

'My husband.'

Glancing across the room at Lord Iain, Isabelle could not doubt the words. Despite his courtesy towards her she held him in considerable awe. A more powerful and charismatic figure would be hard to find, except for Ban of course. Thinking of how much she owed him, owed to both of them, only intensified her guilt. Somehow she had to try to make amends or, if not, to make herself useful at least.

'Ban is going to need careful nursing for a while,' she said. 'I would be glad to help in any way that I can.'

Ashlynn smiled at her. 'That is a kind offer and I am grateful. Meg and her assistants have several patients to look after at present and another pair of hands would certainly ease their load.'

'I'd be glad to do it.'

'Being so near my time makes me feel of limited use. I tire much more quickly than I did.'

Isabelle managed a wan smile. Her companion's swollen belly was a mocking reminder of failure and humiliation. 'That's quite understandable. Just let me know what you need me to do.'

'Bless you. Your help will be much appreciated.'

'It's the least I can do after all that Glengarron has done for me.'

It was a partial truth only. The real reason for

her offer was not just about gratitude, though she certainly felt that. Rather it was the need to be with Ban, even if he was unaware of the fact.

After the arrow was drawn Ban had remained unconscious for some time, being weakened by loss of blood. Meg came daily to check the dressings and look at the wound which, mercifully, remained free of infection, and to administer draughts of poppy and wine to take the edge off pain.

'Sleep is the best thing for him just now,' she said. 'Rest will help the wounds to knit.'

'How long will it take do you think?' asked Isabelle.

'Two weeks, maybe three. Several more after that until he's fully fit again. All the same he was lucky. Another inch and the arrow would have pierced his lung.'

Isabelle shivered inwardly. 'Yes, he was lucky.'

'If there's any change in his condition call me.'

'I will.'

Meg left the room, closing the door behind her. Isabelle surveyed the sleeping figure with misgivings. His flesh was still pale beneath the stubble of his beard, his eyes sunken and shadowed, cheek bones jutting in sharp relief. Bandages swathed his shoulder and torso.

'Don't die,' she whispered. 'Please don't die.'

She no longer felt afraid for herself, only of a future where he was not.

It was another week before he came to full consciousness. Rising slowly from a well of darkness he looked about in surprise. The room was vaguely familiar yet how he came to be there he could not imagine. In his memory was a confused mass of images: a hill and sky and fighting men. He stirred and then winced as pain lanced through his shoulder.

'Don't try to move yet. You will tear the wound afresh.'

With an effort he turned towards the voice and saw Ashlynn. He managed a faint smile and received an answering smile in return.

'God be thanked,' she said then. 'You have frightened us all, Brother.'

'How long have I been here?'

When she told him his brows drew together as tried to make sense of the information.

'You were unconscious most of that time.'

'How did I—?' He broke off aware of the dull throbbing in his shoulder, and glanced down at the bandages round it. Other bits of memory began to come back. He frowned and his hand clenched on the coverlet.

'Isabelle! Where is she? What happened to her?'

Ashlynn, fearing to see him agitated, was swift to give reassurance. 'She is here, Brother, safe within these walls.'

'Is she well?'

'Very well.'

'I'm glad. There were moments when I feared—' He broke off as other recollections stirred. 'Jock is dead.'

'Yes. I'm sorry.'

'What of his family?'

'Iain has already been to see his wife. She will be taken care of and the children too.'

'Even so they will miss Jock sorely. So will I. He was a loyal friend and a brave warrior.'

'Yes, he was.'

Ban's jaw tightened. 'His death will be avenged, I swear it.' He frowned as another unpleasant thought occurred to him. 'Davy and Ewan? Are they...?'

'They are both well.'

'Thank heaven for that.' He paused. 'What of the traitor, Murdo?'

'Iain had his men conduct a thorough search, but they have found no trace of him.'

'Damnation. As long as the swine's alive he'll remain a threat.'

'His force is decimated and he is injured,' said Ashlynn. 'Surely he can pose little danger now.'

'You don't know him, Ash. He's single-minded

in following his purpose, and cares not how he achieves it. He wants Isabelle, and she may yet be in danger.'

There were many questions she would have liked to ask him about that, but knew it was too soon. Already he looked exhausted.

'Isabelle is safe for the present,' she said. 'No harm shall come to her here. Meanwhile, you should try to sleep a little.'

It was testimony to his fragile state that he did not argue. 'Will you come back later?'

'Try keeping me away.'

The door closed softly behind her. Ban shut his eyes. Unbidden Isabelle's image drifted into his mind. She was safe. That was something at least. *She is here...within these walls.* The knowledge filled him with conflicting emotions: relief, hope, pain. For her he had risked and lost the life of a friend. Or rather he had risked and lost a friend for the sake of his own ambition, his own desires. Ashlynn hadn't mentioned his betrothal and he felt sure she would have done so if she had known of it. Therefore it seemed Isabelle had kept silent. That gave him pause since it would have been very much in her interest to declare it. Why hadn't she? Most other women would. He knew she hadn't enjoyed the clandestine aspect of their relationship yet he had followed his inclination regardless. Looking back he experienced a twinge of guilt and shame.

He could well imagine Ashlynn's reaction to his behaviour; she would take him roundly to task over it and demand he acknowledge Isabelle properly. Continuing the relationship in the same covert manner would not be something his sister would ever sanction, not even, he suspected, for the sake of an heir. After her experiences during the Harrying, Ashlynn was nothing if not protective of those she considered vulnerable. And Isabelle was desperately vulnerable. *Nothing has changed. The arrangement still stands.* How glib those words seemed now. Suddenly a great deal had changed and made everything far more complex than even he had imagined. Even his feelings were complicated: emotions that were unaccustomed and disquieting. He had no experience to call on, nothing that might help him find his way. The knowledge did little to raise his spirits.

Chapter Twelve

The next time he woke he felt rather better, his mind sharper. Turning his head he saw a woman standing by the window. She had her back to him, her form silhouetted against the late afternoon light. However, her gown was familiar.

'Ashlynn? Could I have some water?'

At the sound of his voice the woman turned quickly and his heart performed a painful manoeuvre as he recognised her.

'Isabelle. What are you doing here?'

'Lady Ashlynn is resting so I've been sitting with you awhile.'

'I see.'

For a moment or two they surveyed each other in silence. He realised she was wearing one of his sister's gowns. The forest-green one. Ashlynn must have lent it to her. He thought the colour suited her well.

She looked away. 'I'll fetch you that drink.'

He watched her cross to the table and pour water from the jug into a horn cup. Then she returned. Sitting carefully on the edge of the bed she leaned towards him. As she did so he caught a subtle trace of lavender scent from her gown. It was as unexpected and disconcerting as her presence. She held the cup to his lips. To cover his inner confusion he drank some of the water. It gave him a little space in which to gather his thoughts.

'Thank you.'

She straightened and moved away, replacing the cup on the table. 'You look a little better today.'

He frowned. 'Today? Have you been here before then?'

'Several times.'

The thought that she had been with him, watching him sleep, was strangely unsettling though not displeasing.

'I wanted to help,' she went on, 'and it seemed little enough to do—in the circumstances.'

'I thank you for your care.'

'It is I who should be thanking you,' she replied.

'I don't want your gratitude, Isabelle.'

The tone was unintentionally abrasive and she looked away. Ban mentally cursed his tactlessness.

'What I meant was you owe me nothing.'

'That isn't true and we both know it. But for me none of this would have happened.'

'You have no reason to feel guilt. The responsibility lies with Murdo.'

The name fell between them, bitter and unsavoury, evoking unpleasant memories. Isabelle grimaced.

'I hope to heaven that he has died of his wound by now. If so my brother is justly avenged.'

'Aye, he is, although I'd hoped to kill Murdo myself.'

'The sooner he's dead the better. Otherwise you would have a blood feud on your hands into the bargain.'

'A blood feud?'

'He intended to get my dowry back from the Neils.'

'Ah.'

'Since they would rather die than yield up a penny of it there would have been slaughter on a grand scale.'

'That there would.'

She shook her head. 'I would not have anyone die for such a reason, not even Alistair Neil.'

He frowned, uncertain he'd heard aright. 'Forgive me, but I'm not sure I follow.'

'The truth is that there was no love lost between us.'

It wasn't in the least what he'd expected to hear and it caused a rapid revision of some earlier assumptions. 'That might have changed, with time.'

'No amount of time would have made any difference. My late husband was a brute. So, while I would not have sought his death, I cannot wish him back either.'

He was silent for a moment or two, letting the implications sink in. Then he recalled another conversation. *There is no pleasure for a woman in the marriage bed.* Suddenly a whole lot of other ramifications occurred to him. Was that part of her reluctance for their betrothal? Had she been afraid he would hurt her? The idea was abhorrent. He needed to find out more.

'But your father couldn't have known that when he agreed to the marriage?'

'No, I truly believe he did not.' She sighed. 'It seemed to be a glittering match in every way. I must take my share of the blame since I also took it on face value.'

'You are not the first to have made that mistake and I imagine you won't be the last.'

'Are you speaking in general or specific terms?'

He hesitated. 'I once fell for a beautiful face, but it didn't take me long to discover the shallowness behind.' He smiled in self-mockery. 'I was a lot younger then.'

'What was her name?'

'Beatrice.'

He shifted position a little and winced at the answering stab of pain in his shoulder. It carried him back four years to a patch of muddy ground and four men whose fists and feet hammered home the penalty for presumption.

Isabelle surveyed him steadily. 'She hurt you, didn't she?'

It was not the pain he remembered. Flesh healed after a while; humiliation never did. At best it could be buried.

'It was many years ago and it has long since ceased to matter.'

'If you say so.'

He averted his gaze. 'If you don't mind I'd like to sleep awhile.'

'Of course.'

'You need not stay. I'm sure you have better things to do than play nursemaid to me.'

With that he shut his eyes, bringing the conversation to a definitive end. Isabelle made no attempt to alter that. He heard her move away and then the door opened and closed. He was alone. It should have come as a relief but what he felt just then was bereft.

Isabelle didn't return to her room but took the stairs to the top of the tower instead. At the end of the passageway a small door led out on to a terrace which overlooked the glen and the hills beyond. It was a private place, found by accident not long after her arrival at Dark Mount, and just now the solitude was welcome. She leaned disconsolately against the warm stone trying not to think about Ban. After all he'd just made it very clear that he didn't want her company. Considering what she knew of marital relationships she ought to have been better prepared for rejection. As it was, it hurt more than any beating in her experience.

She sighed. How was it that some women seemed to possess an innate understanding of how to please a man, while she had none? Her mirror told her that she was not ill-looking, but physical beauty wasn't enough. Alistair Neil had found her attractive but she had never been able to please him in any of the ways that mattered. Ban had found her attractive enough to seek a betrothal, and to bed her of course, even to rescue her, but he didn't love her. She was a possession, like his horse and his sword. *No man takes what is mine.* He'd been injured and lost a friend on her account. Small wonder if he blamed her. Far from pleasing him as she had hoped, this alliance had left an indelible memory for all the wrong reasons. The one consolation in this sorry mess was that he was on the road to recovery, and if she'd helped towards that the effort had been worthwhile. He was out of danger so he wouldn't need the intensive nursing he'd had hitherto. There was no point in her returning to the sick room again. For both their sakes it was better to stay away.

For the next three days Ban's heart leapt every time the door opened, and each time it sank when he saw that the visitor wasn't Isabelle. He realised then that she had taken his words to heart and wouldn't be coming back. Ashlynn, who visited regularly, watched him in concern. His injuries were healing well and he was able to sit up and take nourishment again, but his spirits seemed low. His temper was uncharacteristically short too. At first she attributed it to pain but when she asked if his wounds were hurting he denied it.

'I hate to see you like this, Ban. Won't you tell me what's wrong?'

'Nothing's wrong.'

'Then why are you behaving like a bear with a sore head?'

His jaw tightened. 'I'm just tired of lying abed, that's all.'

'It won't be long before you're up and about again.'

'It can't come too soon as far as I'm concerned.'

'It can't come too soon for the rest of us either,' she replied.

It drew a self-deprecating sigh. 'I'm sorry, Ash. I don't mean to be ungrateful—or bearish. It's just having too much time on my hands and not enough to do.'

'Good try, Brother. If I didn't know you better that might have convinced me.'

'All right, I've had things on my mind as well.'

'Would one of them be Lady Isabelle by any chance?'

He looked up sharply. 'Why should you think that?'

'Well, let me see… She no longer comes to this room. You're in a foul humour and she looks utterly despondent.' She paused. 'Am I getting close?'

He heaved another sigh. 'It was my fault. I spoke more harshly than I'd intended and I hurt her feelings.'

'Then perhaps you should apologise.'

'It's not that simple.'

'Well, it would be a good start.'

'Damn it, Ash. Do you think I don't know that?'

'So the difficulty is…?'

'I fear she won't want to listen.'

'Perhaps you should give her the benefit of the doubt.'

Their conversation remained much on his mind and the more he dwelt on it the more irksome his invalid status became. He knew he was going to have to talk to Isabelle and that was going to be impossible while he was confined to bed. After four more days he could stand it no longer and announced his intention of getting up.

Ashlynn sighed. 'I suppose it wouldn't be of any use to tell you to wait a little longer?'

'No use at all,' he replied.

In fact his shoulder pained him very little as long as he didn't try to use his arm, and the gash along his ribs was now mending to a vivid scar.

'I'll help you into your shirt then, shall I?'

'I need to shave as well.'

'Why can't you just grow a beard like other men?'

'Because it itches and drives me mad.'

'You're already mad, Brother. The beard has nothing to do with it.'

He returned a quelling look. Ashlynn grinned.

It took a while to accomplish both tasks but eventually it was done. Ban thanked her and then turned towards the door. As he reached the threshold he hesitated. Dark Mount was quite large and there were innumerable places a person might be. He didn't think his strength equal yet to an exhaustive search.

'Where?'

'I'm not entirely sure, but you could try the roof terrace.'

It wasn't far and he reached the door a few minutes later. Taking a deep breath he opened it and went out. The terrace was empty. He was aware of disappointment but at the same time it felt good to be outdoors again, to breathe the free air and feel the sun on his face. He strolled to the parapet and looked out across the glen, thinking of the men who would never look upon it again. As soon as he could mount a horse he would go and see Jock's wife. He owed her that courtesy.

It was the sound of a creaking hinge that drew him back and he glanced round. His heartbeat quickened a little as Isabelle stepped out on to the terrace. She didn't notice his presence at first, but, having closed the door behind her, looked up and then stopped in her tracks.

'Ban.' The word was accompanied by a spontaneous smile. Then it faded into something closer to quiet consternation. 'I…I thought you still abed.'

'I found it increasingly tedious.'

'Well, I am glad to see you so far recovered.'

'I have had good care though I fear I was not always a good patient.'

'Nell says that fighting men rarely are.'

'She's right. By nature we do not take kindly to being shut up for any length of time.'

'Then I'll leave you to enjoy your new-found freedom.' She turned towards the door.

'Isabelle, don't go.' The tone was midway between a command and a plea but it checked her long enough for him to close the gap between them. 'I must speak with you.'

With an effort she faced him. 'My lord?'

'What I'm trying say is that I'm sorry for my churlish behaviour the other day.'

It clearly took her by surprise, he noted with wry amusement, but then it would, given his previous manner towards her.

'You were not yourself,' she replied.

'No, but that isn't a good enough excuse.' He paused. 'I would have apologised sooner but you did not return.'

'I thought you would not welcome my company.'

'I can understand why you might have thought so, but still I hoped that you would come.'

'Did you?'

'Very much so.'

'Oh.' She paused. 'I thought…'

'Thought what?'

'That you would still be angry.'

'I was not angry with you. It's just that what we spoke of then is something I have preferred to forget, and I over-reacted.'

'I did not mean to open old wounds.'

'I know.' He sighed. 'The past has a habit of returning to haunt us.'

'I think I will never be free of it. Not of the memories or of Murdo.'

'He will be held to account by and by for the wrongs he has done you.'

'The greatest wrong he did me was when he injured you.'

He blinked. While he knew she was grateful for her recent deliverance, this implied a rather deeper feeling than gratitude. It was disturbing on many levels, like the way she was looking at him now. Of course it would be easy to read more into it than she'd intended. He probed a little further.

'Would it have grieved you then, if I had been killed along with Jock?'

'How can you ask that?'

'If I had been you would be free.'

She looked into his face. 'I could not forget you so easily.'

'I'm flattered.'

'It wasn't flattery. I am your wife, Ban. What hurts you also hurts me.'

Her words suddenly swept him into much deeper water and they filled him with disquiet. He had hoped that, if they were eventually able to put their relationship on a regular footing, she might one day come to care for him, but it wasn't supposed to happen yet.

'I am honoured, truly.'

'I did not know it until I thought you might die; that I might lose you for good.'

The look in her eyes was more eloquent than words and his heart lurched. She was standing very close to him. The urge to take her in his arms was almost overpowering; his entire being craved the touch and taste and scent of her, but if he followed his inclination it wasn't going to end with a kiss. And even a kiss was too dangerous. A kiss now meant emotional reciprocation and he couldn't give in to the temptation. It would be no better than a false promise, an earnest of something he might not be able to give.

'I am doubly honoured, my lady.'

It was courteous and, he realised, quite sincere, but he knew it fell far short of what she wanted to hear from him. Her expression registered a variety of emotions, one of which was hurt. It cut him like a blade. He had no wish to be the cause of hurt but this was the lesser of two evils: better a little pain now rather than a great deal more later on.

Isabelle was quick to recover her composure. 'Of late I have had leisure to think about the current situation.'

'I also.'

'Then perhaps you have come to the same conclusions.'

'Which are?'

'That the previous arrangement will not suffice at Dark Mount. I want us to live openly as man and wife. I have thought it over and it seems to me that there is little reason now not to acknowledge our betrothal.' She hesitated. 'If I do not conceive you can still put me aside and the law will support you. You have nothing to lose.'

She might have added that he had never had anything to lose but she did not. She might also have wept or begged. Whatever emotion lay under the surface it was now firmly under control, her manner cool and business-like. It engendered both admiration and respect. He surveyed her steadily, weighing the words in his mind. She had stated the case succinctly and accurately and, he decided, with considerable courage since it pointed up her vulnerability. Not only that, her words had echoed his own conclusions about the best way forwards now. In this at least he could grant her what she wanted.

He nodded. 'Very well. Let our betrothal be acknowledged.'

'Thank you. It will be a relief to dispense with secrecy.'

'I'm inclined to agree.' He paused, regarding her with curiosity. 'It must have been a considerable temptation to reveal the matter, and yet you kept silent. Why did you?'

'It was a secret, and one you had not authorised me to reveal.'

'Even though to keep silent was detrimental to your interests?'

The hazel eyes met his gaze steadily. 'My interests are bound up with yours, my lord. I also made certain promises that I would keep faith with you, and I will honour them.' She paused. 'In every way that I can.'

He felt strangely humbled by the declaration. Underlying that were other feelings that he couldn't afford to examine. Instead he took her hand and carried it to his lips.

'I will go and speak to my brother-in-law directly.' He bowed and turned away, heading for the door. However, on reaching it he stopped for a moment and looked back. 'Incidentally, you were mistaken when you said I had nothing to lose. From where I stand it looks like a great deal.'

Chapter Thirteen

Isabelle watched the door close behind him and then slumped against the stone parapet, trying to order the chaos of her thoughts. That he should so readily agree to acknowledge her was an enormous relief. The thought of trying to carry on a clandestine relationship at Dark Mount had filled her with dread; it would only have been a matter of time before the matter was discovered, and the consequences were too dire to contemplate. Now at least that particular cloud had been lifted. Others remained.

She had declared her feelings as boldly as she dared but it was very clear that they were not returned. That Ban desired her and wanted to keep her was not in doubt. His decision just now reinforced that. In the final analysis it was only common sense. In any case it cost him nothing to grant her that much. She knew enough about him now to know he would not mistreat her, that all she desired of material possessions would be hers. What he would never give her was his heart.

Iain regarded his brother-in-law with undisguised surprise. 'Betrothed? Since when?'

'A few weeks ago.'

'God's blood, man, you must have moved fast.'

'When I see what I want I go after it.'

'Quite right. Besides, your lady is fair.'

'So she is.'

'All the same, I wish you'd told us before.'

'Let's just say that circumstances got in the way.'

Iain's eyes narrowed a little, his expression speculative. 'Why do I have the feeling I'm not being told the whole story?'

'Because you aren't,' replied Ban, 'but it's all you're going to get for the moment.'

'Fair enough. It's your affair after all.'

'As you say.'

'When you went to Castlemora I didn't expect matters to turn out half so well,' replied Iain. 'A lovely bride is an enviable prize but now you've a rich estate to boot.'

'The estate isn't mine yet.'

'No, but it will be, and soon, I promise you

that.' Iain clapped him on the shoulder. 'The usurper's days are numbered.'

'Aye, they are. I mean to have his head mounted on my spear.'

'Good. We shall discuss this further by and by. In the meantime I think your sister should be told the news, don't you?'

Ashlynn heard it with incredulity and delight. Then she sent a servant to fetch a jug of the best wine and demanded that her brother should go and fetch Isabelle.

'For this news should be celebrated properly.'

Realising that argument would be futile, Ban retraced his steps. However, he had only half completed the journey when he encountered the object of his errand coming the other way.

'Well met,' he said. 'I was coming to look for you. Your presence is required in the hall.'

'You've told them?'

He nodded, then seeing her anxious expression, smiled faintly. 'Don't worry. The news has been well received.'

'I'm glad.'

He held out his hand. 'Shall we?'

Rather shyly she put her fingers in his and allowed herself to be led down to the hall. Ashlynn embraced her warmly.

'I am so pleased that we are to be sisters.'

'As am I, my lady.'

'Let us dispense with formality. You must call me Ashlynn. You're part of the family now.'

'And a most welcome addition too,' said Iain. He kissed Isabelle's cheek and smiled. 'His taste is far better than I imagined.'

'Yes, it is,' replied Ashlynn. 'Although I thought he would never find the right woman.'

Ban raised an eyebrow. 'I told you; I'm hard to please.'

'I can vouch for the truth of that.' Ashlynn laughed. 'I've been trying to marry him off for years.'

Isabelle felt herself redden. She was unused to being the centre of approving attention, but their expressions of welcome seemed quite genuine and that raised her spirits. She glanced at Ban. Even knowing the reasons it was still hard to believe that he was prepared to commit himself in this way; to acknowledge himself her husband. It might only be a business arrangement but it filled her with pride none the less.

'When is the wedding to take place?' asked Iain.

Isabelle's heart turned over. She had assumed that the matter would stop here, that given the knowledge of their betrothal, the rest would be tacitly assumed. It had never occurred to her that others might see it differently. In silent consternation she looked at Ban but, far from appearing thrown by the question, he looked quite remarkably calm.

'As soon as may be,' he replied, 'and with a minimum of fuss.'

Ashlynn sighed. 'And I was hoping for a splendid feast with hundreds of guests.'

'We appreciate the thought but need not such magnificence.'

'So be it.' She looked across at her husband.

'Three days hence you shall go to the kirk,' he said. 'That will give us time to prepare a feast in celebration.' Then, seeing Ban's expression, he added, 'A small feast, ye ken.'

'And time to find something suitable for the bride to wear,' said Ashlynn.

To cover her confusion Isabelle swallowed a mouthful of wine. It was dark and potent, as dangerous in its way as the events in which she was now ensnared. It didn't help to know that she was a most willing participant.

It wasn't until later that she was able to take Ban aside and ask the question uppermost in her mind.

'Did you anticipate this?'

'Of course. Didn't you?'

'Well, no. I thought that betrothal was virtually the same thing.'

He regarded her with quiet amusement. 'There's little difference. This is merely the seal of official approval. Not easy to obtain, I may say, for all my sister's jesting.'

'It is not surprising. You are her only brother. I should have felt the same if Hugh had ever...' Her voice trailed off as realisation struck with the force of a hammer blow. 'But he won't, will he?'

Ban's amusement faded and he made no reply but his silence spoke louder than words. Isabelle looked away quickly as water welled in her eyes.

'He'll never find a bride and bring her back to Castlemora; never watch his children grow up.'

'Isabelle, don't, sweetheart.'

The concern in his voice caused her chest to constrict as though a suffocating weight were pressed there. She tried to draw breath but it emerged as a choking sob. Then the tears spilled over. Mortified, she tried unsuccessfully to stop them.

'I'm s-sorry...'

He shook his head. 'You don't have to apologise. I know very well how it feels to lose your family and your home.'

That quiet empathy was her undoing and the dam burst. Across the hall the buzz of conversation faded, and curious looks came their way. Ashlynn rose from her seat, meeting her brother's gaze with a questioning look. Seeing her about to start across the room he held up a warning hand and shook his head. Then, gently and firmly, he guided Isabelle away.

When they reached her chamber she collapsed on the bed. She seemed almost unaware of him now, entirely lost to her grief, her entire body shaken by racking sobs. He made no attempt to check them, knowing that this was long overdue. Instead he covered her with a blanket and then left her alone, closing the door quietly behind him.

He was in no mood to return to the hall and face the questions that would inevitably follow so he went out on to the roof terrace. Dusk was settling over the glen now and the air was cool and fragrant with the scent of heather. He leaned against the parapet and breathed it gratefully. Isabelle's grief had touched a chord in him that resonated deeply. It also hurt in a way that he could never have anticipated.

The morning was far advanced before she put in an appearance next day. Ban had been speaking with Ashlynn but he broke off the conversation as Isabelle entered, and he went to meet her. She looked pale and there were dark shadows under her eyes. The lids were still a little swollen and tinged with pink but otherwise she looked composed.

'Come and sit down.' He led her to a chair, regarding her in concern. 'Are you hungry? I'll have one of the servants fetch food.' He caught Ashlynn's eye and saw her nod.

'No, I thank you.' She met his gaze. 'I just wanted to say that I'm sorry about what happened yesterday. I must have embarrassed you.'

'You have no need to apologise and I wasn't embarrassed; only worried.'

'I didn't mean to make such a spectacle.'

'Grief comes when it will,' he replied, 'and it must find an outlet.'

'Well, it definitely did that.'

'Aye. My tunic is still very damp.'

She managed a wan smile. 'I shall try not to ruin any more of them.'

'It'll survive.' He glanced up as a servant appeared with a platter of food and a jug of ale. 'Which is more than you will if you don't eat something.' He poured a cup of ale and handed it to her, then set about slicing bread and a little meat. 'Here.'

She ate it to please him rather than because she wanted to but, having done so, began to feel slightly better.

'Would you like to get out for a while?' he asked. 'Some fresh air might do you good.'

'All right.' As she said it she knew it wasn't on

account of fresh air, no matter how beneficial. It was because she wanted to be in his company.

'There's a new foal in the stables. Would you like to see it?'

'Very much.'

The children looked up from their game. Then Robert piped up. 'Can we come too, Uncle Ban?'

'Aye, why not?'

They let out a cheer and ran to join him. Isabelle watched in quiet amusement. It was another side to him, one that not so long ago she would never have suspected. Yet it was evident that he held his young nephews in affection, and they him.

He gestured towards the door. 'Shall we go, Lady Isabelle?'

They reached the stables a short time later. The foal and her dam were in a loosebox at the far end. Looking at the new arrival Isabelle couldn't help but smile. It was a filly. With her spindly legs and woolly coat and absurd little tail she was thoroughly engaging. As yet she was still shy, staying close to the mare, but curious too, regarding the visitors with huge liquid brown eyes.

'Beautiful, isn't she?' said Ban.

Isabelle nodded. 'I think she's wonderful.'

'She was born last night.'

'What colour do you think she'll be eventually?'

'My guess is bay like her dam. She'll likely make the same size too, or a little more.'

Robert looked up at his uncle. 'Can we ride her soon?'

Ban shook his head. 'Not for some time yet. Not until she's grown bigger and is strong enough to carry a rider.' Seeing the child's disappointment he added, 'You'll be a lot bigger yourself by then.'

'Will I be big enough to learn swordcraft?'

'Aye, you will.'

Robert beamed. Then Jamie drew his attention and the two fell into their own conversation. Isabelle surveyed them for a moment or two and smiled sadly, thinking that Ashlynn was fortunate indeed.

'Now that I'm on the mend we must go out for a ride,' said Ban. 'I'd like to show you the rest of Glengarron.'

'I'd like to see it, but not until your shoulder is up to it. I'd hate to be responsible for your suffering a relapse.'

'It's improving all the time. Exercise can only do it good.' He surveyed her speculatively. 'Of course, the pace might have to be slower than you're used to, for a while at least.'

She laughed. 'Ouch. I suppose I deserved that.'

'Let's just say that your predilection for speed is…memorable.'

'I shall not indulge it just yet.' She let her hand rest a moment over the site of the injury. 'The healers might take a terrible revenge otherwise.'

Her touch was light and fleeting but his pulse quickened a little in response.

'It might be unwise to cross them,' he replied. 'They have a formidable collection of medicines at their disposal.'

'I shall heed the advice.'

They left the stables and, while the children ran on ahead, strolled back towards the tower.

'Are you feeling a little better now?' he asked.

'Much better, I thank you.'

'You've had a bad time, and then been up-rooted as well. I realise it hasn't been easy for you.'

'No, but everyone has been most kind.'

'I remember I felt like a fish out of water when I first came here.' He smiled ruefully. 'I had made up my mind to leave and seek service with the king, but then Iain invited me to stay and ride with him instead.'

'You have never regretted it, I imagine.'

'Never. He's a man I esteem very highly.'

'His reputation doesn't exactly tally with the man I've met,' she replied.

'Marriage has mellowed him somewhat, but

don't be fooled. There's still an iron hand in the velvet glove.'

She smiled. 'Your sister is a remarkable woman nevertheless.'

'Yes, she is. And so are you.' They reached the tower doorway and he paused at the bottom of the stairs. 'Kindred spirits, I'd say.'

His words produced a golden glow deep inside. Nor could she fail to be aware of his nearness now or their relative isolation. Would he kiss her? It was painful to realise how much she wanted him to, how much she had missed close physical contact with him in the past few weeks.

For a moment or two he didn't move and her heart sank. Then, slowly, he reached for her waist, drawing her to him. His lips brushed hers, tentative, searching; then gradually becoming more insistent. Isabelle swayed towards him, closing her eyes, yielding to the embrace, her need keen, revelling in the familiar taste of him, in the musky scent of his skin. Pressing her hips against his she let her tongue probe his mouth, no longer caring if her manner appeared bold, knowing only that she wanted him, demanding his response.

It was instant. He crushed her closer and the kiss grew passionate. Deep inside a small spark flickered into life and created its own pool of warmth. And then she was kissing him back with equal abandon, avid, hungry, her hands clasping his buttocks, pulling him nearer. Almost immediately she felt him grow hard. Lifting her feet off the floor he carried her across the passageway and into the small storeroom beyond, heeling the door shut behind them before tipping her backwards on to a pile of filled sacks and following her down.

He drew up her skirt and slid a hand between her thighs, a touch that set every nerve alight. The spark became flame and its warmth expanded, forming a coil of tension. It elicited a faint unexpected ripple of sensation that was shocking and wonderful. Wanting more she relaxed her thighs a little to facilitate him. His fingers found the nub they sought and teased gently. She drew in a sharp breath as a wave of warmth flared in her abdomen. At its heart was the growing coil of tension. It tightened further sending a tremor through her. As the delicious stroking continued the sensation increased and then rippled outwards in a wave of pleasure. She gasped, her eyes widening with astonishment.

'Holy God!'

He smiled and continued. Her body shook as successive shock waves hit her.

'Ban, please…'

The words were involuntary since she had no real idea of what she was asking him for, only that he held the key to something just out of reach. Something elusive and magical. Isabelle writhed, her body bucking beneath his hand.

He shifted his weight, pressing her down, parting her legs wide. Then he thrust into her. Excitement intensified, her body quivering in response as he began to move inside her, with long slow strokes. Impatient now she closed her legs around him, pulling him deeper but he refused to be hurried, making her wait, letting the rhythm build gradually. Isabelle writhed beneath him, feeling the core of tension expand and rise, carrying her with it. She had no idea what it was carrying her to, only knew that she wanted this more than anything in her life before.

'My lord, I beg you…'

The rhythm increased, lifting her higher, carrying her towards the edge of a precipice. He thrust deeper and she cried out in ecstasy, arching against him. An answering fire flared in him, searing, hot and possessive. Still he controlled it, carrying her with him to the brink. Then he let go of all restraint and then they went over together in a rush of pleasure so intense she thought she might die.

'Dear God!'

Ban closed his eyes, breathing hard, his skin sheened with sweat. It had never taken much for her to inflame him but this was different again. Nothing had prepared him for the sheer heart-stopping delight he'd just experienced. He looked into her face and saw her smile at him, her lovely eyes dark with passion. The effect was sultry and powerfully erotic holding a promise of things to come. The implications created a thrill of anticipation. Unwilling to let her go just yet he remained inside her, holding her there at his pleasure. Most definitely at his pleasure.

He grinned. 'That was incredible.'

'Yes, it was.' Privately she thought that incredible didn't begin to describe the experience. Her entire being thrilled with it. Every last expectation had just been turned on its head. In that moment she understood exactly how lacking her former marriage had been, how barren in every sense of the word. Tears pricked her eyelids. 'Thank you.'

He kissed her gently. 'You're welcome.'

Chapter Fourteen

The revelation of that marvellous impromptu tryst refused to go away. It was as though she had awoken after a long sleep and found herself in a different world; a world she was desperate to explore further. Nor could she help thinking about the man who had taken her there. He filled her thoughts and her heart. Only now, in retrospect, did she understand the extent of his skill and his patience. *It's going to get a lot better.* At the time she'd had no idea what he meant, a depth of ignorance that was scarcely creditable now. Had Alistair Neil lived she might never have made the discovery at all, would likely never have met Ban. Her heart constricted. The idea of being without him was unbearable. He had given her life meaning. One day she hoped that she might come to mean more to him, that one day his love-making might be motivated by more than just physical desire.

Later she joined Ashlynn and the two of them spent an enjoyable hour examining gowns, eventually settling on one in deep-blue velvet. Fortunately they were much of a size, so it would be a simple matter of letting down the hem to allow for the fact that Isabelle was taller.

'It is kind of you to do this,' she said. 'I can't tell you how much I appreciate it.'

'I'm glad to help. I know what it's like to lose everything.'

'It still has an air of unreality about it.'

Ashlynn nodded. 'It was the most terrifying period of my life. To be cast into the world without family, friends, money or help is unspeakable. I still have nightmares about it sometimes.'

'I don't wonder at it.'

'There were times when I thought… Well, you know what it's like. I don't have to tell you.' Ashlynn squeezed her companion's arm gently. 'It means so much to know that my brother has found the right woman at last; that I'm gaining a sister with whom I shall have so much in common.'

Isabelle summoned a bright smile. She wasn't about to disillusion Ashlynn by telling her the real reasons for her brother's choice of wife.

'I'm glad too.'

'In spite of having a good and loving husband I have missed female companionship.'

'I can understand that. Men don't seem to see the world in the same way somehow.'

Ashlynn grinned. 'You're right there. Sometimes I think they might be a different species altogether.'

'It isn't just me then.'

'I do my best to exert what influence I can, but my sons are clearly cast in the same mould as their father.' Ashlynn laid a hand on her belly. 'I wouldn't mind at all if this child were a girl, just to even the sides a little.'

Isabelle tried not to feel envious. 'I hope soon to follow your example and give my husband a son.' She paused. 'Many sons.'

'Of course. Why should you not?'

There was no easy way to answer that so Isabelle didn't try. 'Did you… Was it very long after marriage before you conceived your first child?'

'Not so long. A few months only.'

The words created a feeling of cautious optimism. 'I pray that I will be so fortunate.'

'I'm sure you need have no worries on that score.'

Isabelle hoped with all her heart that she was right.

* * *

The wedding took place two days later, as planned. For Isabelle it was bittersweet. She had the acknowledgement she sought but not the one thing she would have prized above all else. When she looked at Ban her heart filled with pride and longing but, she reflected sadly, this was as much as he was prepared to grant. It did at least show that she had his respect and, perhaps, liking, and that was better than nothing. More than ever she was grateful for being able to look the part. She could only hope that Ban would approve.

In fact Ban found himself staring. Dressed in a deep-blue gown embroidered at neck and sleeve, with her auburn hair held by a circlet of flowers, she looked at that moment more like a goddess than a mere mortal. As he took her hand Isabelle looked up and met his gaze, returning his smile. Very gently he squeezed her fingers. Then they knelt and made their vows before the priest. When it was done he drew her close and kissed her, a lingering and passionate embrace that held in it a promise of the night to come.

Then there followed all the usual congratulations from friends and well-wishers before they returned to the great hall for the wedding feast. The hall had been swept and decked with flowers and leafy boughs. For all her sister-in-law's assurances about a small-scale celebration, it seemed that all of Glengarron was present. More than one of the assembled crowd commented on the beauty of the bride, whose happiness was plain to see. And the groom too looked remarkably well, seemingly unable to take his eyes off her. Throughout the meal he plied her with food and drink, serving her with his own hand. In truth Isabelle ate little, being too caught up the excitement and the suddenness of it all and too aware that she might have been Murdo's bride. The thought was chilling.

'What is it, sweetheart?' Ban's blue eyes registered concern for he had seen that fleeting shudder.

'It was nothing.' She smiled, meeting his anxious gaze. 'A bad memory.'

'Nothing shall harm you now, Isabelle. You can let go of the past.'

'I know it.'

He carried her hand to his lips. 'We will build a future you and I.'

In his eyes she read both promise and passion. It sent a *frisson* down her spine. He was her lord now. Later he would take her to his bed. Thereafter, she must give herself to him whenever he wished it. The thought filled her with eager anticipation. Her love-making with Ban had stripped away all her earlier suppositions and revealed her naivety at the same time. In a way it had empowered her too. She did have the ability to attract a man and to arouse him and to please him, even if it was only in bed.

Across the hall the musicians struck up a tune and Ban smiled. 'Will you dance with me, my lady?'

'Gladly.'

He took her hand and led her to the floor amid cheers of approbation. The measure was slow and intricate; a courtly dance that kept the couple close yet permitted only the meeting of hands. Yet every touch, every look thrilled, for her at least. Envious looks came their way from men and women alike but she paid no heed, having eyes only for Ban. She had not expected him to dance so well or to move with such effortless grace.

'Where did you learn to do this?' she asked.

'Heslingfield mostly, though Iain has had some input too.'

Isabelle was genuinely astonished. 'Lord Iain?'

'He underwent his knightly training in France, where I understand the gentler arts were taught most rigorously. He has since filled in the gaps in my education.'

'He has done a good job then.'

'So I think.'

'The man is full of surprises, isn't he?'

'You have no idea.'

She laughed. 'It's something else you two have in common.'

'What else?' he asked.

'You are both handsome, both warriors, both brave…'

'I could listen to this all night but if I allow you to continue I fear it will turn my head permanently.'

'I cannot think your head would be so easily turned.'

'You have the power to turn heads, my lady.'

Her eyes sparkled. 'Now who is the flatterer?'

'It wasn't flattery.' He shot a glance around the room. 'Every man here would like to be in my shoes right now.'

Her cheeks flushed a little, her heart beating faster for his praise. 'There is only one man here who interests me.'

Ban's gaze locked with hers. 'I shall endeavour to retain your interest by every means in my power.'

The dancing went on into the night. Isabelle's hand was solicited by various partners and she accompanied them to the floor for each new measure, prepared to engage in polite conversation and show a pleasant manner, but her smiles she kept for Ban alone. Many a man cast appraising looks her way but if she noticed it she gave no sign. He saw it with approval. It pleased him that other men admired his wife and he was content to let them look. However, that was all they would ever do. Isabelle was his. He hadn't realised until he met her that he possessed such a jealous streak. His mind ran on ahead to the hour when they would retire. It had felt like an age since she had shared his bed but far from quenching desire their former love-making had only increased it, and he found himself impatient to be alone with her and resume where they had left off. Just thinking of the possibilities caused his body to respond. Yet it was more than physical attraction now, he acknowledged. His feelings for her had strengthened with time and grown complex and multi-layered, albeit harder to identify. All he knew for sure was that he wanted to build a future with her; sire children with her if heaven permitted it. That part still carried an element of risk but he couldn't regret taking it now.

Much later, after the feasting and the dancing, when the hour grew late and night replaced blue dusk, she retired to the chamber she was to share with her husband. There Nell had helped her to undress and comb out her hair. Across the room the great bed waited, dressed now in fresh linen and strewn with sweet herbs and flowers. The night was soft and warm and through the

casement she could see the moon, already high
in the heavens where a thousand stars shone. It
was beautiful, a night made for romance, for love.
Isabelle bit her lip. Ban had never used that word
and never would. He had told her that long ago.
She had to hope now that she had enough love
for two. He had been patient with her in so many
ways; had put his life on the line for her and he
had given her the acknowledgement she longed
for. It was time to give something back, to do all
in her power to make this marriage work. Her
first had been a disaster but at least Alistair Neil
had taught her a few things on the way. Perhaps
past experience could be turned to good account.

The ensuing thoughts were positively sinful.
She smiled to herself, realising then that there
had been a shift in her thinking and it had happened without her being aware of it. This was
no longer just about being able to please him in
general by seeing to his household and his comfort and being what the world would consider a
dutiful wife: it was much more specific. It was
about wanting to reach the man; about touching his heart. It would be no easy feat. What she
sought was protected by emotional armour that
had been forged by grief and loss and years of
war. Even so, she had to believe it could be done,
that she could somehow find a way…

She was roused from her thought by the sound

of men's voices raised in jesting and laughter. The noise came nearer and footsteps sounded in the passage outside. Her heart leapt. The men were bringing her bridegroom. Suddenly the door was flung wide and he was carried in shoulder high. They deposited him at the foot of the bed with much lively banter and raucous laughter, ogling his bride the while.

Ban bore it all good-humouredly but had no intention of being kept longer from his wife. Thus his companions were firmly shown the door. It took several minutes before the last of them was ejected and the door shut and barred behind them. He turned then to Isabelle, letting his eyes drink in each detail. Apparently what they found was pleasing for his gaze warmed.

She remained quite still and waited, aware of nothing but the man. Her heart was thumping so hard she was certain he must hear it. His gaze never left her as he slowly divested himself of his clothing to reveal the hard-muscled body beneath. Her heart swelled with pride to think that the world knew that this man was her husband. She saw him smile and the blue eyes met and held hers.

'You are so beautiful.'

Then he reached for her, drawing her against him, his mouth on hers in a soft and lingering kiss. His hands slid beneath her hair, lifting its weight off her neck and shoulders, letting its silkiness slide through his fingers, breathing its subtle scent. His tongue ran lightly over her lower lip, suggestive, exciting. Of its own volition her mouth opened to him, her tongue flirting with his. She leaned closer and felt his arms tighten around her as the kiss grew more intimate. Yet for all that it was unhurried and infinitely persuasive sending warmth the length of her body.

He smiled. 'I've been dreaming about this all evening.'

'So have I.'

'Oh?' His lips gently nibbled her ear lobe. 'And what did you dream?'

Isabelle shivered at the touch. 'I am too embarrassed to tell you, my lord.'

'That sounds deeply shocking.' His tongue probed her ear.

The shiver became a tremor. 'Verging on sinful.'

'Better and better,' he murmured.

His fingers tugged gently at the fastening of her shift. It slid lower leaving her upper body naked. His tongue travelled down her neck to the peak of her breast. Her breath caught in her throat. Then she was kissing him back, her lips finding the warm hollow where neck met shoulder. She felt his hands on her waist, gentle and warm, and then the garment slipped over her hips and fell to the floor.

Ban's eyes darkened with passion. The moonlight lent her flesh a faint iridescence like soft pearl. For a moment or two he drank in her soft curves, feeling his body respond. And then her mouth travelled lower, pressing soft kisses to his neck and breast, setting every nerve alight. Unhurriedly she sank to her knees in front of him, her hands brushing his waist and hips. Ban almost forgot to breathe as the implication hit him. Isabelle glanced up, a seductive and naughty expression that caused his pulse to quicken. Her mouth closed round him, her tongue teasing gently. He drew in a deep breath as every muscle in his belly grew taut and the familiar coil of tension formed in his loins. The exquisite sucking motion increased until it seemed his blood had turned to flame. Heart hammering, he slid his fingers through her hair, his hand cupping the back of her head, drawing her closer. Desire grew hotter and with it need. The tension tightened. With an effort he controlled it, letting the sensation build, carrying him to the brink. Somehow he found his voice.

'Enough, my sweet, or I'm going to lose control completely.'

She drew back a little. He raised her and led her two paces to the bed, tipping her backwards and then following her down, pinning her there with his weight. She would have twined her arms about his neck but he prevented it, clamping her wrists beneath his hands, his mouth on hers, searing, demanding. Excitement soared. He pressed her thighs apart and thrust deep and repeatedly, his need overtaking him now.

Isabelle burned, every fibre of her body resonating from the feel of him, revelling in this fierce possession. The heat in her pelvis expanded in a ripple of pleasure, every muscle taut with it. She moaned softly. The thrusts intensified, harder, utterly dominant now, pushing her relentlessly to the edge. Isabelle screamed, half-swooning, her body bucking beneath him, carried on a cresting wave of pleasure. He came quickly then, unable to help himself, crying out, his body shuddering with glorious sensation. Ruthless, he held her there, in thrall to his will. Isabelle closed her eyes in total surrender, loving every second of that delicious tyranny.

Eventually he drew back a little, breathing hard, caught between astonishment and delight.

'Dear heaven, that was beyond words.'

She thought that words couldn't begin to explain or describe what she felt then. Once she would never have dreamed such delight existed. How could one be so completely subject to a man's will and yet enjoy every moment of it? How was it possible to want a man so much? She smiled and gave him a sideways look. It was unwittingly sultry and vaguely mischievous. Ban saw it and grinned.

'Have a care, vixen. Such an expression can only elicit one kind of response.'

'Oh? And what is that, my lord?'

'I mean to show you presently.'

And he did, then and later.

When Isabelle eventually woke next day the sun was already high. She stretched luxuriously and then turned her head to find Ban propped on one elbow watching her. As her eyes met his he smiled.

'Good morrow, Wife.'

'Good morrow, Husband.' Idly she traced a finger along his arm, her gaze taking in the silvery lines of old scars on his skin. The finger traced the course of the livid gash along his ribs and then continued upwards to his shoulder, to the site of the arrow wound. Close to it was another familiar scar, a long deep cut that ran from shoulder to breast, evidently the result of a savage downward slash from a sword. It had healed cleanly but she had seen enough injuries to know it must have been life-threatening. She had never asked him about it but now curiosity stirred.

'How did you get this?'

'It is the legacy of a Norman blade.'

She looked thoughtful. 'From the time you told me about? At Heslingfield?'

'Aye. It would have done for me too, but for Iain and his men.'

'Then I owe him and them a debt of gratitude.'

'I also.'

Isabelle pressed closer and kissed the scar. Ban's arms tightened about her and she grinned, regarding him speculatively.

'The sun is high, Husband.'

The innocent tone brought forth an answering grin. 'So it is, Wife.'

'Is it not time we were up?'

'I already am.'

Glancing down she saw irrefutable proof of this and raised an eyebrow. 'Was last night not enough to sate your lust, my lord?'

'Not nearly enough, as you are going to discover.'

Before she had time to say more he rolled, pinning her beneath him. Then his lips were on hers in a long and deep embrace. She could feel his arousal against her thigh and the answering heat in her pelvis. Recollections of the previous night only intensified it and she returned his kiss with equal ardour.

Ban looked down into her face, his eyes dark with passion. 'You play with fire, my sweet.'

'Is that dangerous?'

'Most assuredly.'

'How so?'

He proceeded to show her and in considerable detail. The sun was much higher before they eventually left the sanctuary of the bedchamber.

Afterwards they walked together in the glen, following a steep track that led up the hillside. From the top the panorama of hills was spectacular and Isabelle surveyed it with awe.

'It's magnificent.'

'Isn't it?'

They sat down on a convenient rock to get their breath back. Although she continued to gaze at the view every fibre of her body was aware of the man beside her.

'I found it by chance,' he went on, 'not long after I came to Glengarron. I've come here often since, whenever I've needed a little time apart.'

She nodded. 'I can understand that.'

'I needed quite a lot at first, to try to come to terms with what had happened at Heslingfield. Iain knew that and he left me alone.'

'He reads men well. It's what makes him a good leader.'

He regarded her in surprise. 'That's a very astute observation.'

She smiled. 'Not mine, my father's.'

'Ah, but then he had many of the same qualities as Iain.'

'He didn't read Alistair Neil very well,' she replied. 'If he had he'd never have permitted the match to go ahead.'

'He told me that your husband was often from home. It seems to me that he must take his share of the blame if you did not conceive a child.'

'Even when he was there marital relations were...difficult.'

'Difficult? How?' As soon as he'd said it he winced inwardly. 'I beg your pardon. That was a very impertinent question.'

'It cannot be avoided any longer.'

'You don't have to tell me.'

'I think I do.' She reddened a little but, having committed herself thus far, knew she had to go on. 'Alistair could not always perform his marital duties. When he did...well, he needed...he needed the stimulation of violence.'

Ban frowned. 'Violence? What sort of violence?'

She drew another deep breath. 'He liked to beat me. When I cried out it excited him, you see.'

He did see. Suddenly a whole lot of things had just become clear and he was sickened. That any man should hurt a woman was beyond all bounds of acceptable behaviour. 'I'm so sorry.' Even as he said it he realised how trite the words must sound to her.

'In a year of marriage I did not once conceive,' she went on. 'It was the reason the Neils wanted me gone.'

'Why should they put all the blame on you?'

'In such cases the woman is always to blame.'

Ban had the uneasy feeling she might be right. Had he not listened to the voice of doubt without even speaking to her? There were always two sides at least to every story. Moreover, this account had major implications.

'That's in the past now, my sweet.'

'Is it?' Her anguished gaze met his. 'What if it wasn't just him? What if it *was* me?'

'From what you've said I feel pretty sure that it wasn't.'

'You may still have married a barren woman.'

'Isabelle, I suspect these fears are groundless.'

'You don't know how much I pray for that. I want to bear your children, Ban, not have you put me aside one day.'

His jaw tightened. 'I have no wish to put you aside.'

'You might have no choice. You need direct male heirs.'

'We'll have them, I'm certain of it.'

'That's what Murdo said.'

Ban's eyes glinted. 'Oh, did he?'

'Ironically, he was the only person at the time who took my part.'

'He must have had good reason.'

'Murdo was ever well informed. It seems that some of his information came from whores who had lain with Alistair Neil. They said he couldn't—' She broke off, feeling her face redden.

Ban regarded her keenly and then he laughed out loud. Isabelle grew hotter.

'It's no laughing matter.'

'Forgive me, but surely you know what this this means.' When she continued to stare at him he grinned broadly. 'Your former husband was impotent, my sweet.'

Isabelle's heart gave a painful lurch. 'Then… it wasn't me?'

'If Murdo is right it most certainly wasn't you.'

'Oh, Ban.'

'It would also explain why he had no qualms at all about wishing to take you to wife.'

Just then she didn't know quite whether to laugh or cry. 'I hate Murdo more than any other living man, but I hope with all my heart that he was right about this.'

The very thought that it might be so lightened her spirits dramatically.

It seemed also to have affected Ban. At table that evening he was attentive and courteous as usual but he seemed more relaxed than he had erewhile. He laughed more, and took a larger part in the discussion. It gladdened her to see it. If this development could please him so much, how much more would he be pleased when she was with child? She allowed herself to use *when* now, rather than *if.* Smiling to herself she took a sip of wine and relaxed a little, allowing herself to be drawn by the convivial atmosphere.

Ban and Lord Iain began to relate the tale of a distant exploit, of a cattle raid that had become a mud-splattered stampede in an unexpected thunderstorm. With impeccable timing one would interject with more details, piling one absurdity on another until their listeners were crying with laughter. Isabelle laughed too. The story lent another dimension to these men who, it seemed, were not infallible despite clever planning and could make themselves the butt of a joke. It only made them more attractive in her eyes. It occurred to her then that laughter bound men as effectively as shared adventures and success in battle, and guessed that their shared history was colourful, chequered and, at times, hilarious.

She gave the conversation her full attention, absorbing every detail about Ban's background so that she could flesh out what she already knew. Understanding of the past would provide added insight into his mental processes now. The survival instinct was strong in him and it had coloured his thinking for years, teaching him to separate emotion from events. And yet he was not incapable of feeling, of loving. With Ashlynn and with his young nephews the barriers came down. Might they one day do the same for his wife?

Chapter Fifteen

Now that his shoulder was growing stronger Ban had begun to exercise gently and, eventually, to ride again. His first trip was to visit Jock's wife. As he had anticipated it wasn't an easy meeting for either of them but it was necessary and, ultimately, he was glad he'd done it.

'Jock would have been pleased,' said Isabelle when they met later.

'It was the least I could do,' he replied. 'Maggie and the children will be taken care of in the material sense, but they're utterly bereft and nothing can change that.'

'You miss him too, don't you?'

'He was a brave man and a good friend.'

'I regret his loss more than I can say.'

'You have no need to feel guilt, Isabelle. He would not want you to.'

'All the same I do feel it, and keenly too.'

'Then it's time to take your mind off it for a while.' He paused. 'Would you care to ride out with me tomorrow?'

'I'd like that.'

'The glen is pretty at this season. You might like to see more of it.'

'Yes, I would. Very much.'

They kept the horses to a steady pace. Apart from her concern over Ban's current level of fitness, Isabelle wanted to be able to take in the details around her. Glengarron was certainly beautiful at this season with the purple heather on the hills and the clouds high in a late summer sky, dappling the hills with light and shadow.

'I can understand why you have grown fond of this place,' she observed.

Ban nodded. Not so long ago he had thought he wouldn't live to see it again, never mind see it with the company he would most have sought.

'It has become a second home; one I little thought to have.'

'In that respect at least you were fortunate.'

'More than I can say.'

She smiled wryly. 'Life never turns out as we expect, does it?'

'Not very often,' he agreed. 'But then we live in uncertain times.'

'I used to think that marriage would place me out of harm's way; that somehow a home and husband would make me invincible.'

'No one is invincible.'

'True. It's just that we don't expect harm to come from those closest to us. It seems like the worst kind of betrayal.'

'It is.'

'You speak from experience.'

'Very much so.'

'Beatrice?' She stopped herself there, mentally cursing her tactlessness. 'Forgive me, I shouldn't have said that.'

'Forget it.'

'I speak without thinking too often. I didn't mean to resurrect a demon.'

'No demon, at least not now. I have long seen her for what she was.'

'It's good that you have.'

'She was part of a dream I once wove. It had no basis in anything other than wishful thinking and eventually I had a rude awakening.'

She hesitated, but his manner now seemed more relaxed than before. It encouraged her to test the water a little further. 'Did she love someone else?'

'I believe she loved only herself. I merely entertained her for a while.'

'I'm sorry to hear it.'

'She completely neglected to mention that, even while she was seeing me, she was betrothed to an earl.'

'What!'

'I could scarce believe it either.' He shrugged. 'She only broke with me because the wedding was imminent.'

'Good heavens. That must have been unspeakably hurtful.'

'It was, but not nearly as hurtful as what followed.'

Isabelle regarded him keenly but remained silent, content to let him take his time. He drew a deep breath.

'I should have kept my temper but I didn't and we quarrelled. Beatrice screamed and the servants came running. I was taken before her father. She accused me of having pursued her against her wishes and of having forced my attentions on her.'

'How could she do such a thing?'

'I think there wasn't much she wouldn't have done just then to make herself out to be the injured party.'

'Her father believed her?'

'He believed her all right. After all, she was betrothed to an earl, one of the richest and most powerful men in the land. Why should she deign to look at a landless Saxon thane?'

Isabelle stared at him, appalled. 'What did he do?'

'He had four of his henchmen give me a beating for presumption. They were very thorough.'

'You might have been killed.'

'They stopped short of that; it would have invited serious trouble from Glengarron. Instead I was thrown on my horse and ejected from the premises.' He smiled wryly. 'Hardly a tale of high romance, is it?'

'I could not think of anything less so, or of anything more unjust.'

'I have never spoken of it until now, but I should not like you to think that Beatrice was an object of affection.'

Her throat tightened. 'I am glad you told me. I shall honour the confidence.'

'I know.'

His look and tone were entirely earnest and that created a variety of emotions in her. She knew it could not have been easy to speak of such things, especially after so long a silence. That he should have trusted her with the truth made her feel honoured and deeply moved. It also induced an uncomfortable reappraisal of her own response to his status as a dispossessed Sassenach thane. She was ashamed to think of it now. A man's character did not derive from how rich he was or how much he owned. If wealth and land were indicators of goodness and worth Alistair Neil should have been among the foremost in all of Scotland. It was a lesson learned late but learned thoroughly.

The path they had been following climbed steadily until it levelled out again at the top of the hill. The position afforded an uninterrupted view down the glen and for a little while they paused to admire it. Isabelle thought then that they might turn back but somewhat to her surprise Ban turned his horse's head away from Glengarron.

'There's a pretty little lochan among those trees yonder. It's not above a mile distant. I thought you might like to see it.'

'Of course.'

They rode on quietly for some way across a stretch of open heath. As they continued the track passed close to an ancient ring of standing stones, as tall as a man and all lichened and weathered. Isabelle surveyed them curiously.

'What do think they were for?'

'Worship of the gods perhaps, or some other form of ceremonial.'

'The place certainly has an atmosphere about it.'

'I once saw Iain settle a score here with an enemy.'

Her eyes widened a little. 'He killed a man here?'

'Aye, he did. A Norman knight called Fitzurse; an evil swine and no mistake. He tried to stab Iain in the back.'

'Then he was justly paid out for it.'

'That he was,' said Ban. 'My only regret is that the brute didn't die at my hand.'

'Why so?'

'It was he and his mercenaries who burned Heslingfield and slew my kin.'

'Then surely you had the right to face him in combat?'

Ban shook his head. 'Iain's claim was older than mine. He'd been seeking Fitzurse for years before I came on the scene, and with good cause. I yielded to his right on condition that he avenged us both for past wrongs, which he duly did.'

'This Fitzurse sounds like a truly evil man.'

'He was. The world is well rid of him.'

Isabelle shivered inwardly. The stones had doubtless witnessed much bloodshed and no doubt would witness much more. In this land only the strong survived. Men like Iain and Ban.

'Does the lochan have a bloody history too?' she asked.

He laughed. 'Not as far as I'm aware.'

In fact the lake was, as he had as said, a pretty place. It was situated in a natural bowl of the land, its rocky shore screened by birch and rowan trees, its clear waters sunlit and still. Isabelle reined in at the edge of the trees and looked around.

'It's a pleasant spot,' she observed.

'I hoped you'd think so. I've always liked it. I come here from time to time.'

'I can see why.'

'Would you like to stop for a while?'

'Why not?'

They dismounted and tethered the horses to a bush, then strolled to the water's edge. Isabelle smiled, enjoying the warm sunshine and peaceful green beauty of the place, more than ever aware of the man beside her. It had been in such a place that she'd first met him, a memory that caused a different kind of heat deep inside.

By tacit consent they walked a little way and then he spread his cloak in a sheltered turfy hollow among the rocks and they sat together in companionable silence, leaning against the warm stone. Isabelle eyed the lochan speculatively.

'Do you suppose the water is warm?'

His eyes gleamed. 'Why? Were you planning to swim?'

She reddened a little. 'I'm not sure that would be wise.'

'It would be most unwise. The lochan is freezing.'

'You speak from experience.'

'That's right.' He paused. 'Of course, you don't have to take my word for it. In fact I'd be very happy for you to put it to the test. I'll sit here and watch.'

'You'll do no such thing.'

He sighed heavily and they both laughed. Then her gaze met his and laughter faded and became something more intense. He leaned closer, his face only inches from hers. She met it in a light and gentle kiss. Ban shifted a little, sliding his arms around her for a more lingering embrace. It set every nerve alight. His hold tightened and the kiss became deeper, his tongue teasing and flirting with hers. Isabelle slid her fingers through his hair. It was thick and tawny as a lion's mane and, unlike most men, he kept it clean. It slipped easily through her fingers, the feel of it subtly sensual. Gently she caressed the back of his neck. The kiss became passionate.

Shifting just a little she slipped a hand between them and stroked. There followed a sharp intake of breath and in moments she felt swelling hardness beneath her fingers. The suddenness of it astonished and encouraged at the same time. She heard him groan.

'You're playing with fire again, my sweet.'

She said nothing, only continued to stroke him. Ban drew another sharp breath, his expression taut and ecstatic. She could see resolve crumbling and bit back a smile.

'Have you no mercy, woman?'

She reached for the fastenings of his hose and tugged gently. Freed from the confining cloth his erection stood proud. Even though she had witnessed it before it still had the power to astonish and, now, to excite. Stronger was the desire to have him inside her. She realised then that this wasn't just about conceiving a child any more: it was about a different kind of need; needing him, wanting him, wanting this.

Shifting position she lifted the hem of her gown and straddled him, lowering herself slowly, letting him slide into her. It felt quite astoundingly good. His hands slid behind her buttocks pulling her closer. She began to rock slowly. She heard another sharp intake of breath and continued. He thrust deeper. Isabelle bit her lip to stop herself crying out. Ban frowned.

'Am I hurting you, sweetheart? Do you want me to stop?'

'No, you're not hurting me, and don't you dare stop.'

He laughed softly. She felt him thrust again, and then repeat the action, more strongly each time. Her body moved with him, feeling the rhythm build. She watched him carefully, noting what pleased him and repeating it. His breathing grew ragged and he pulled her hips down harder. Involuntarily she clenched her muscles round him and heard him gasp. His whole body shuddered. She did it again. He groaned, thrusting deeper, harder, until his body spasmed and she felt the hot rush of his release.

She smiled, breathing hard now, heart hammering. 'That was amazing.'

'You're amazing,' he replied. 'That was incredible.'

'I'm glad.'

Mingled with that was relief that she had pleased him. It astonished her to discover how easily she could arouse him.

'Rest with me awhile, sweetheart.'

Isabelle lay down beside him, filled with a sense of well-being and contentment, basking in the sunshine and in the feeling of his arms around her. She had never imagined that intercourse could be so enjoyable or a man so considerate. It created feelings of rightness and belonging, of wanting to please him even more. Alistair had forced her to do things that she loathed; the thought of doing them with Ban filled her with excitement and anticipation. She smiled to herself. All in good time.

At some point amid these musings she must have dozed because she was brought back to full consciousness by a man's thumb gently brushing across the peak of her breast. It created a sensation so delicious it was hard to breathe. Opening her eyes she saw Ban looking down at her. She saw him smile. The gentle brushing motion continued creating a ripple of pleasure. He bent and kissed her softly.

'You have been more than generous in pleasing me. Now it's my turn to please you.'

'You did please me, my lord.'

'Not as much as I hope to,' he replied.

Her pulse quickened a little. Before she had a chance to speculate any further she felt him tugging gently at her gown.

'Take it off, Isabelle.'

For a moment she wondered if he was serious, but nothing in his expression gave her to think otherwise. Slowly she got to her knees and, somewhat uncertainly, complied. Ban nodded approval.

'The shift as well.'

The quiet command sent a wave of heat through her entire body. 'It's broad daylight, Ban.'

'So it is.'

'There are no locks on the doors either.'

'That'll add a little zest to the occasion.'

In spite of their earlier history this was still shocking. She ought to refuse. She didn't want to refuse. She wanted whatever was going to happen next. With slightly unsteady hands she unfastened the shift and drew it off.

'Unbind your hair.'

She drew the braid over her shoulder and untied the ribbon, aware of his gaze following her every move. Slowly she undid the heavy plait and shook her hair free. It flowed over her back and shoulders like auburn fire. Ban unlatched his belt and laid it aside, then pulled off his tunic and shirt. She could see the new scars on his shoulder and ribs, livid in the sunlight. Unhurriedly he unfastened his breeks…

Later they lay together in sated stillness, drowsy and utterly content. Through half-closed eyes he studied her carefully, drinking in every detail of her face, the soft hollow of her neck and shoulder, the swelling breasts and delicate pink nipples. Her skin was smooth and pale as alabaster. His gaze travelled lower to her waist and the curve of her hip and triangle of hair that covered her sex, the same shade as the fiery auburn tresses now carelessly spread across his cloak, and then lingered a moment on her belly. Perhaps his seed had already taken root in her. Perhaps even now she was carrying his child.

Isabelle's eyes fluttered open and she smiled. 'A penny for them.'

'I was just thinking that it would be good to

create life instead of taking it. That I've seen enough of bloodshed and war.'

'You've seen your share. Heslingfield…'

He sighed. 'Heslingfield was just the start. Since then I've fought my way across fields of slaughter where the corpses were piled high and the blood ankle deep. And for what? Scotland has become a vassal state in spite of it.'

'You did what you had to, Ban, according to the dictates of conscience.'

'No, I fought because I wished to slay Normans, and because I enjoyed it.' His smile grew bitter. 'God knows how many men have died at the point of my sword.'

'You took as much risk as they.'

'Hatred helps a man to stay alive. Rage lends strength to his arm. Eventually it becomes cold and more terrible until the only thing that brings joy is killing.'

'But it's not the only thing that brought you joy. You must have felt that when you discovered Ashlynn was still alive.'

'It was the one bright spot in all the darkness.'

'You love your nephews too. I've seen you with them.'

'It's easy to love innocence, to want to protect it.'

'You will be a good father, I know it.'

His smile lost the bitter edge. 'I hope so.'

'I think Hugh would have been too. Now I am the last hope of our house.'

'Castlemora will be regained, Isabelle, I swear it, and our children will grow up there. But before any of that can happen I must first deal with Murdo.'

'I wish there was some other way but I know very well that there isn't.' She took a deep breath. 'If anything were to happen to you...'

'It won't. I have more to lose than he.'

'Castlemora means a great deal to you, doesn't it?'

'I wasn't talking about Castlemora.' His gaze held hers. 'I was talking about the future I want with you. And such a future is worth fighting for.'

Her heart gave a peculiar little leap. That he was speaking of the long term indicated a shift in his thinking that gladdened her immensely. More important still was the suggestion of an emotional bond. If so, it might strengthen. One day it might even become love.

She smiled. 'Yes, that's worth fighting for.'

Chapter Sixteen

It seemed that he was not alone in considering the problem of Castlemora, and on his return Iain sought him out. For a moment or two he surveyed his brother-in-law appraisingly. Ban exuded energy and rude health once more and there was a glow in his eyes that hadn't been there until recently. Iain grinned.

'Marriage suits you.'

'I think it does. Besides, I've wanted Isabelle since the day I set eyes on her.'

'And she is not indifferent to you, I think.'

Recalling their recent tryst by the lochan, Ban grinned. 'No, fortunately.'

Iain regarded him shrewdly. 'Even married to you Isabelle is still vulnerable. She always will be while Murdo lives.'

'This was in my mind also.'

'He must be dealt with, Brother. He has been robbed of a prize and his is not a forgiving nature.'

'Nor is mine, or not where he's concerned anyway.'

'We should seek him out while his power is weakened. He lost many men in that last fight, but he will recruit more and that soon enough.'

'He attracts human scum like dung attracts flies.'

'We should act within the month. He must be crushed before he can turn his force against Glengarron because, make no mistake, he will.'

'Then let's do it.'

'We're agreed then.'

'Aye, we're agreed.'

With preparation in train Ban was kept busy and thus spent less time with Isabelle. She understood it, even though she missed his company. Sometimes, from a discreet distance, she watched the men training. They practised for several hours each day, honing the skills that would keep them alive in the coming battle. Yet she knew that, inevitably, some of them would not return. It was an occupational hazard and one that every fighting man accepted, but now she was emotionally involved with Glengarron and its people. Jock's death had sealed that.

She wondered how her own people were faring under Murdo's governance, and she feared the worst. Now that her father's restraining hand was gone there would be nothing to stop him. Archibald Graham had always held that power and privilege went hand in hand with responsibility and obligation. Murdo had no such moral compass: to him power was an end in itself to be wielded as he saw fit and without any consideration for those weaker than himself. At Castlemora he was the law. All she could do was to pity those under his sway and look forward to the day when his rule was over.

Isabelle's nineteenth birthday was fast approaching and Ban had commanded a feast in celebration. However, he also had a surprise up his sleeve. Leading her down to the courtyard he gave commands to the grooms to bring forth their mounts.

'Will you ride with me, my lady?'

'Gladly.'

Isabelle watched as the grooms led Firecrest out. He was followed by another man leading a pretty bay mare with a flowing mane and tail. Immediately Isabelle moved forwards to stroke the horse's nose.

'I haven't seen this one before. How beautiful she is!'

'You like her?'

'Of course.'

'She's yours.'

Isabelle turned towards him, her eyes shining. 'Ban, she's wonderful. Thank you so much.' She raised herself on tiptoe to kiss him. Never in a hundred years had she expected so generous a gift.

'Since you cannot ride your own mount I must supply another.' He smiled. 'Do you want to try her?'

Isabelle laughed. 'You know I do.'

They rode out together and Isabelle put the horse through her paces. The mare was fleet of foot and soft of mouth, responding to the lightest touch of the rein. Such a fine animal must have cost a fortune. That Ban should have thought to surprise her thus filled her heart with joy. There could be no doubting his regard for her. It was evident in his every look and touch. She responded to it like a flower to sun. Having been so long starved of affection she hungered for it now, exerting herself to please him in every way, longing for the time when affection might deepen into love, praying for the event which would bring that about.

* * *

When they stopped to let the animals rest a little he took her in his arms, looking down into her face. 'Are you happy, Isabelle?'

The question caught her unawares. 'Of course. Why should you doubt it?'

He smiled gently though his expression was no less earnest. 'I want you to be happy. I want you to forget what went before as though it were no more than an evil dream.'

'That is exactly what it seems now.'

'I'm glad.'

'I wish that you had been my husband from the beginning, that I'd never set eyes on Alistair Neil or his cold-hearted clan.'

'So do I.' He did not add that her father would never have considered him a suitable match for her then. Archibald Graham had only ever seen him as a last resort. The knowledge saddened him but he no longer felt bitter or angry. In the end he was the winner.

Isabelle sighed. 'My only regret is that Hugh will never know about this.'

Ban dropped a kiss on her hair. 'Perhaps he does know.'

'Do you believe the priests are right; that the dead really watch over the living?'

'I like to think so.'

'It is a comforting thought.'

'We all need those,' he replied.

* * *

A few weeks after Isabelle's birthday cele-
brations, Ashlynn was delivered of her baby, a
healthy girl who had her mother's blue eyes. Iain
was clearly delighted and Ban too since his sister
had come through the birth safe and well. Isabelle looked at the tiny baby and a lump formed
in her throat. Envy was unworthy but she couldn't
entirely banish it. How wonderful it must be to
bring new life into the world. How wonderful to
watch it thrive and grow and to have the uncriti-
cal love of a completely dependent being. Her
breast ached with longing. From the corner of
her eye she glanced at her husband. Perhaps one
day they too might have a child of their own, as
healthy and as beautiful as this. Then truly they
could lay the past to rest.

Ban had no trouble interpreting that look and
knew he was more than willing to do his part in
bringing about the desired event. However, in
the background remained the shadow of a conflict. Before he and Isabelle could ever live secure an enemy had to be faced. Unwilling to spoil
the mood he had put off saying anything, but
now that his sister had been safely delivered of
her child he knew that Iain's mind would turn to
other things.

In that he was right. Leaving the women to
admire the new baby he took Ban aside.

'Tomorrow I begin my preparations for an assault on Castlemora.'

'When do we ride?'

'As soon as the harvest is in. The men cannot be spared before then.'

Ban nodded. The grain was almost ready for cutting now, aided by the warm sunshine and unusually dry summer months. 'So be it.'

'This matter cannot be delayed any longer. The sooner Murdo is dealt with the better.' Iain grinned. 'Castlemora is about to have a new laird.'

'Aye.'

Seeing Ban's thoughtful expression Iain's eyes narrowed a little. 'Is something wrong?'

'It's just hard to take in, that's all. After so many years of dispossession it seems incredible to think of being a landed nobleman again.'

'That's understandable. In your place I imagine I'd feel the same.' Iain paused. 'But this is the moment and we must act. Only then can you regain your rightful place in the world.'

'I shall regain it, never fear.'

'How is the shoulder now?'

'Not yet as strong as it was, but I'm exercising a little more every day. I'll be fit enough when the time comes.'

'Good. I need you with me, Brother.'

'I'll be there, never fear.' He paused, eyeing

his companion steadily. 'Just one thing though. When we do meet Murdo, the bastard's mine.'

Iain nodded. 'So be it.'

Back in the bed chamber the two little boys stared at the cradle wide-eyed. Then Robert looked at their mother.

'A girl?' The tone suggested bemusement and curiosity. It was echoed in his expression. Clearly the concept was entirely strange to him.

Ashlynn smiled. 'That's right. You have a little sister.'

He looked at the baby again. 'That's good… I suppose. All the same, she's very small, isn't she?'

'All babies are small,' said Ashlynn, 'but she'll grow soon enough.'

'She's not going to be much use at tag for a while.'

'No, not for a while.'

Isabelle caught Ashlynn's eye and smiled. Then, leaving her to speak to the children, she left the room and returned to the chamber she shared with Ban. He was conspicuous by his absence but Nell was there, folding clothes. She looked up as Isabelle entered.

'Have you seen the wee mite then?'

'I have, and she's beautiful. Perfect in every way.'

'Well, that's good. I trust Lady Ashlynn is well.'

'She is.'

'I'm glad to hear it. Childbed is hard on a woman.'

Isabelle thought she'd gladly endure any amount of pain if it meant she could have a child, if she could give her husband the son he longed for. Sons perhaps. Daughters too. She smiled to herself. Ban was lusty enough to sire a dynasty and he did not neglect his responsibility. Since their marriage very few nights had gone by without him claiming his rights and that was no hardship to her: the thought of him was enough to make her feel weak at the knees. Ban was inventive, sometimes demanding, but he never hurt her. In his arms she had only experienced uninterrupted delight.

Suddenly she was very still as the implications of that began to dawn. The natural interruption hadn't occurred. It had been weeks since her last flux. Mentally she began counting backwards. Her breathing quickened and instinctively one hand went to her belly. She shut her eyes for a moment, fighting a rising tide of excitement, and made herself count again. The answer was the same. She ought to have bled three weeks ago. The ache in her breast might not be due to envy after all. Her heart thumped harder. Dear God, was it possible?

'Are you all right, my lady?'

Nell's voice brought her back to earth with a start. 'What? Oh, yes. Perfectly.'

'Are you sure? You look a little pale.'

'It's nothing, really.'

'Maybe you should sit by the window and get some air.'

Isabelle knew she was far too excited to sit. 'I think I'll just go outside for a while.'

Before she could be questioned further she hurried out of the room. Once in the passageway she paused, wanting to avoid company for the time being, and then headed for the roof terrace. As she'd hoped it was empty and she could have the place to herself. For a while she paced up and down, fighting to contain her excitement, trying to collect her thoughts, uncertain whether to laugh or cry. In the end she did both.

When she was a little calmer she began to think more rationally. It was early days yet, too soon to say anything to anyone. She needed to be sure. In another week or so her flux was due again. If she missed that as well… The hope was almost painful. She glanced down at herself again. Could she really be carrying Ban's child? If so she must have conceived very quickly. Her heart swelled with joy until she thought it might burst. She tried to imagine his expression when she told him. He would be thrilled. The future they both wanted was within their reach. She clasped trembling hands.

'Please, God, let it be.'

She remained on the terrace until she was reasonably certain of being able to control her emotions in front of others, and especially in front of Ban. Whatever happened she would not raise his hopes until she was absolutely certain.

In spite of her best intentions she could not entirely conceal her secret. It manifested itself in quiet smiles and a strange suppressed excitement. The next week seemed to crawl by but at its end there was still no sign of her flux. Moreover her breasts were larger and slightly sore too. Then, one morning, she was sick for no apparent reason. Despite the queasiness in her stomach she was utterly elated.

Ban had left the chamber a little earlier so she was alone. The impending confrontation with Murdo meant that he had even more duties to undertake, and he was assiduous in carrying them out. The harvest was imminent and all the men would be required to help. He also spent a part of each day in exercising the muscles in his shoulder to build up their strength. It would be a while before she saw him but Isabelle could hardly wait until they were alone to tell him her news. She smiled to herself. Then another wave of queasiness rose like a tide and she rushed for the bucket once more.

Just then the door opened and Nell came in. She took in the scene at a glance, her brow creased with concern.

'Good heavens. You are unwell, my lady.'

Isabelle straightened and wiped her mouth. 'No, I was never better.'

'I don't quite…'

'I'm pregnant, Nell.'

The older woman stared at her and then her face was wreathed in an incredulous smile. 'May God and all the saints be praised! That's wonderful news.'

'Isn't it?'

'How far along are you?'

'About two months, as near as I can tell.'

'Does he know?'

'Not yet.'

'He'll be thrilled, I'm sure of it. What husband is not on hearing such news?'

'It's a dream come true. I can't wait to tell him.' Isabelle sat down on the edge of the bed, waiting for her stomach to quieten. 'We've both been hoping for this. I had no idea it might happen so soon.'

Nell squeezed her arm. 'I'm happy for you, my lady.'

'I was so afraid I might never conceive; that what happened before was my fault. This is such a vindication.'

'Forget what went before. Just think about what is.'

'I shall. I want nothing more than to put the past behind me. If I could expunge every memory of Alistair Neil I would.'

'He'd dead, God rest his soul. Lord Ban has given you what Neil never could.' Nell grinned. 'The first of many I have no doubt.'

'I truly hope so.' Isabelle laughed shakily. 'I want a dozen children at least.'

'Well, there's no reason why not, is there?'

'Not any more.'

Later, when she had washed and dressed and made herself presentable Isabelle left the chamber and went in search of Ban. When the hall and the courtyard revealed no sign of him she enquired of a servant and was informed that he was currently closeted in private discussion with Lord Iain. Stifling disappointment she realised her news was going to have to wait. In the meantime there was a pile of mending awaiting attention. It occurred to her then that there would also be baby clothes to sew now as well. Smiling to herself she re-traced her steps to the tower.

In the event it was evening before she saw Ban again. The hours out of doors had evidently agreed with him. In the past few weeks the pal-lor of illness had been replaced by a healthy tan that banished the shadows beneath his eyes and enhanced the strong lines of his face. With his mane of tawny hair and lean athletic frame he looked every inch the warrior he was. As he took his place beside her at table her heart constricted with love and desire and she longed for the hour when they would be alone.

The conversation was mostly about the forth-coming harvest and Isabelle was content to let the men talk, letting their banter and laughter wash around her. Her thoughts drifted to Castlemora. It would be harvest time there too; a harvest that would be used to feed Murdo and a horde of mer-cenary troops. Her father and brother must be turning in their graves. Hopefully though, not for much longer. With an effort she put the thought aside. This was no time for sad or gloomy re-flections.

'Are you all right, sweetheart?'

She looked up to see Ban regarding her closely. 'Oh, yes, of course.'

'Only you looked miles away.'

'I was thinking of Castlemora and harvest time there. It was always such a joyful occasion. I used to love watching the grain brought in, knowing the lean months had come to an end.'

'You'll see it again, I promise, and with a feast such as has never been seen.'

'I'll hold you to that.'

'It should be a season of plenty this year,' he said. 'Let's just hope this fine weather holds a little longer.'

'Yes, let's hope so.'

She seemed momentarily downcast and, guessing at some of the thoughts passing through her mind just then, he changed the subject. 'I missed your company today.'

Isabelle shook her head. 'I believe you were too busy to spare any thoughts of me.'

'You're wrong. You were often in my mind.'

'Oh? And what were you thinking, my lord?'

He leaned closer and whispered in her ear. Isabelle's cheeks turned a deep shade of pink. He saw it and grinned appreciatively. 'You really are most attractive when you blush.'

She darted a look around but everyone else was engaged in conversation and seemed not to have noticed. Even so she lowered her voice. 'You are incorrigible.'

'Where you are concerned I am.' He paused.

'Dare I hope that you thought of me in my absence?'

'I may have done, once or twice.'

'Only once or twice? I must try to make it harder for you to forget me.'

She regarded him speculatively. 'And how do you mean to do that, my lord?'

'I'll show you later, when we're alone.'

Her skin tingled. When they were alone, she would tell him her news. She smiled quietly, hugging the secret to herself a little longer. Ban eyed her curiously, sensing something different about her this evening but not being able to define it precisely. These sudden changes of mood were strange. Nevertheless, the mysterious smile was beguiling and seductive, and he began to feel impatient to have her to himself again.

Rising from the table he held out a hand. 'Shall we?'

They bade the company goodnight and took their leave. A crowd of grinning faces watched their departure. Ban ignored them, leading her firmly by the hand. He didn't stop until they reached their chamber. Drawing her inside he shut and barred the door, then took her in his arms for a lingering kiss that set every nerve aflame.

'I've been waiting to do that all evening.'

She smiled. 'Only that?'

'That was just the start, my sweet.'

He stepped back just long enough to remove her clothing and his own and lead her to the bed. Then he made love to her, a hot and passionate coupling that drove all else from her mind and there were only the two of them carried on a rising tide of pleasure. Afterwards they lay together in sated quiet. Isabelle snuggled closer, her head on his breast, listening to the steady rhythm of his heartbeat, breathing the familiar musky scent of his skin. Her whole body felt deliciously weary now, every fibre alive to his nearness. She glanced up and saw him smile. She knew then that the fire was not out, it was only banked. The knowledge created a thrill of anticipation. It seemed almost indecent to enjoy physical union as much as this: the church would certainly regard it as a sin. Yet it didn't feel like a sin to lie with Ban. It felt like paradise, another undoubtedly blasphemous notion. Marriage was for the procreation of children, not for carnal pleasure. That thought brought her back to the matter that had been uppermost in mind until he took her to bed, and she smiled.

Ban squinted down at her. 'What?'

'I was just thinking about pleasure.'

He grinned. 'All in good time, sweetheart.'

'That's not what I meant.'

'Oh?' He regarded her curiously now. 'Then what did you mean?'

'That some would find such bliss sinful.'

'They are fools then. If we were not intended to enjoy this God would not have given us the means to do so.' He traced a finger lightly over her shoulder. 'Enjoyment is a celebration of his gifts.'

'Speaking of gifts…'

'It seems to me that you have many,' he replied.

'One more now, for you.'

'What gift, sweetheart?'

'The greatest gift: a child.'

His hand stopped abruptly and he stared at her, unsure he had understood. 'A child? You mean you're…'

She nodded. 'I'm going to have a baby.'

For a moment or two he was utterly incredulous but the look in her eyes spoke louder than words. His heart seemed to miss several beats before lurching violently back to life. As he tried to assimilate the news he felt almost light-headed. His dearest wish had been granted. She was going to have a child; their child. His line would continue and the memory of his dead kin would live on. His throat tightened.

'Darling, that's wonderful. Are you quite certain?'

For a second she lost track of her thoughts. What had he just called her?

'Isabelle?'

'Oh, yes, quite certain, now.' She smiled tremulously. 'I've suspected for a while but I didn't want to speak until I was sure.'

'When? When is the baby due?'

'In the spring.'

He let out a crow of delighted laughter. 'I'm going to be a father.'

'Yes.'

'That's marvellous. The most marvellous thing I ever heard.' He laid a hand on her belly. 'I never expected it would happen so soon.'

'Well, you've certainly done your part to bring it about,' she replied.

His smile faded a little as another thought occurred to him. 'You should have spoken sooner, sweetheart. If I'd known I would not have…'

Her gaze met his. 'Ban, it's all right. I won't crumble to dust.'

'Even so, I should not have been so rough. Did I hurt you?'

'No, of course not.' She kissed him gently. 'There's nothing to worry about.'

He lay back on the pillows trying to take it in, his mind a whirl of different emotions. Never in a thousand years had he expected to hear such news so quickly. The implications of it left him breathless. He was going to be a father. The knowledge thrilled and terrified him at the same time. He took her hand and raised it to his lips.

'Thank you.'

Her throat tightened. 'I have dreamed of this for so long.'

'I know.'

She hesitated. 'I pray that I will give you a son but…'

'That will be as God wills. The point is we are going to have a child.'

'Many children I hope.'

'Well then, what need to worry whether the first is a boy or a girl?' He put his arms round her and drew her close. 'It is a blessing I once thought never to have.'

'And I.'

'You have nothing to reproach yourself for.'

'It means so much to know that it wasn't my fault.'

In that moment he glimpsed the extent of her pain and her fear and they moved him deeply. So too did the knowledge that, for a while at least, he had contributed to that, allowing doubt to govern his behaviour. It shamed him to think of it. *The woman is always to blame.* His jaw tightened as the words came back to haunt him.

'I'm so sorry, sweetheart.'

She looked up quickly. 'For what?'

'For my former behaviour towards you. I cannot think of it without disgust.'

'You have not ill used me.'

'Not in the ways you are thinking of perhaps, but in all others.'

'Not so.'

'It is so, starting with my near rape of you beside that river, and ending with a series of clandestine trysts in a hay barn.' He shook his head. 'It could not be considered knightly behaviour, by any stretch of the imagination.'

'You took a chance that most men would have shunned.'

'I took advantage.'

'It has worked out in the end.'

'That doesn't make me feel any better about it.'

'Let's not dwell on the past, Ban. We have so much to look forward to.'

He kissed her gently. Before they could truly look forward the present menace must be dealt with. Her revelation tonight only made it more pressing. Their child would have its inheritance no matter what. After that he would devote himself to being a better husband.

Chapter Seventeen

Work began on the harvest, and most of the inhabitants of Glengarron, saving only the very young and the very old, were busy in the fields, the men cutting the grain, the women binding and stacking sheaves. As each field was cleared the gleaners moved in, collecting what had been dropped or missed, so that nothing was wasted. Even the children helped. Gradually the granaries began to fill. People smiled as they worked, knowing that the year ahead would be a year of plenty.

Isabelle would have volunteered her services to help but Ban refused to hear of it. 'You are with child. Heavy work is out of the question.'

'Other women do it.'

'You are not other women. You are my wife. Besides, harvesting is no work for a lady.'

'And yet I have done it in the past.'

'Maybe so, but you're not doing it now.'

'Very well. If you feel so strongly, then I won't.'

His gaze locked with hers. 'I know you won't.'

'Arrogance hasn't entirely deserted you, has it?'

Ban bit back a smile, enjoying her. He knew he ought not to push this any further but the temptation was suddenly irresistible.

'I am your husband and I will be obeyed.'

Isabelle folded her arms. 'I will obey, in this case, because I can see your reasoning.'

His eyes glinted. 'You will obey in every case whether you see my reasoning or not.'

'Or?'

'Take the consequences.'

'Why, you arrogant, overbearing…'

'Arrogant? Overbearing? Then I'd best do what I'm accused of.'

Before she had a chance to anticipate him he seized hold of her, drawing her hard against him in a fierce embrace. His mouth, slanting across her, was hard, demanding, forcing her head back in a searing kiss that left her breathless. Isabelle struggled ineffectually, her hands against his chest making no more impression than a sparrow's wings. Though still annoyed she could not be indifferent to him. His passion now was deliberately provoking but it excited her as well. She burned in the embrace even while she fought it. He held her until she capitulated. Panting she could only stare at the face looking over hers.

'Let me go, Ban.'

'No.'

'Let go, villain.'

'I detect unwifely defiance here which must be answered.'

Without warning he swung her off the ground and into his arms before striding back the way they had come. Isabelle's struggles made not the slightest impression. She was taken to their chamber with the utmost ease. Then he kicked the door shut behind them and carried her to the bed, depositing her on it and following her down. Understanding his intent, Isabelle struggled harder as annoyance vied with desire. In moments her wrists were pinned, her body pressed down into the coverlets by his. Then his mouth was on hers again, gently this time, though no less insistent. Familiar warmth kindled along her skin and her body gradually relaxed beneath him as she returned the kiss. Then he drew back a little, looking into her face.

'That's better.'

She was about to deliver a blistering retort when she saw his grin. Her eyes narrowed as realisation dawned. 'You did that on purpose, didn't you?'

'That's right.'

'And I rose to the bait.'

'Beautifully.'

It drew a reluctant laugh. 'I should know better by now.'

'Aye, you should.'

For a second or two they surveyed each other in silence. Then she tested his hold. It didn't budge.

'Ban?'

'Isabelle?'

'Are you going to let me go or not?'

'Not,' he replied.

Having been refused permission to help with the harvest Isabelle turned her attention to sewing clothes for her baby and assisting Ashlynn with household chores. She enjoyed the other woman's company and valued their developing friendship. After being so long without sympathetic female companionship it was precious. In spite of keeping herself occupied, Isabelle could not overcome a sense of foreboding as harvest drew to a close. When it was done the men would ride for Castlemora.

Ashlynn too was unwontedly sombre. 'No

matter how many times I see Iain ride off to fight I always feel nervous.'

'Damn Murdo. I wish the murdering brute would drop dead of heart failure or fall from his horse and break his neck or choke at table.'

'Any one of those would be an ideal solution.'

'It isn't going to happen though, is it?'

'Probably not.'

'I want Castlemora to be regained and I want my brother avenged, but I wish it could be done without loss to Glengarron.'

'It will be done with the minimum of loss to Glengarron,' replied Ashlynn. 'Iain will see to that.'

Isabelle pondered the words later, hoping with all her heart that they were true. While Ban kept her abreast of their plans in general terms, he hadn't gone into detail and certainly hadn't mentioned strategy, but then it probably hadn't occurred to him. Most men would consider it an unfit topic for a woman's ears. She smiled to herself, imagining his response if she were to ask. Not that she would ask. In a man's world such a question would be regarded askance or with amusement.

As the afternoon wore on she tired of sewing and laid it aside. Some fresh air wouldn't come amiss and with luck she might meet up with Ban and exchange a few words. However, that proved harder to do than she had hoped for when she sought him out it was to discover he had ridden to the village with some of his men. No one knew when he might return. For a while she hesitated but then it occurred to her that she could walk towards the village herself. It was no more than a mile distant. The day was fine. She would find him there or perchance might meet him on his way back to Dark Mount. The more she thought about it the better it seemed. There could be no objection if she went attended so summoning Nell to accompany her she set out.

It was a pleasant walk and the sweet fresh air lifted her spirits. The path wound round the crag of Dark Mount and thence along the glen parallel to the burn. With the hillside purple with heather it was a bonny sight. Below it golden stubble stood in the fields where the reapers had been working. Soon it would be burned off and the strips ploughed again or left fallow, depending on requirement. To her right a stand of trees marched down the slope and across the track to the burn. It was a pleasant place providing dappled shade, a welcome contrast to the bright sunlight. As they walked Isabelle scanned the way ahead for any sign of her husband or his men, but the track was empty. Her mind leapt ahead to his coming. He would be surprised to see her there but then he would stop and dismount, sending his men on ahead. Then they would walk together and she would tell him about her day and ask him about his.

She was so preoccupied with these thoughts that at first she did not see the horsemen in the trees, or the one who detached himself from the shadows and rode out to block the path. With a sudden jolt she registered his presence, thinking for a moment it might be her husband. A closer glance undeceived her. With a horrid chill of realisation she took in the dark clothing, the shaven head, the scarred face with its close-trimmed beard and, finally, the bow in his hands with the arrow aimed towards her. She heard the sharp intake of breath from Nell as the woman stopped in her tracks. The dark gaze swept over them both and came to rest again on Isabelle. Summoning all her courage she faced him.

'What do you want, Murdo?'

'You, Isabelle.'

'You know I'll never agree to that.'

His expression sent a shiver through her. 'It makes no difference. What is to stop me carrying you off now and doing what I wish with you after?'

'You have the power,' she acknowledged, 'but it avails you naught since I would take my own life rather than submit to the dishonour you describe. After that how long do you think you could escape the wrath of Glengarron?'

'I care nothing for Glengarron.'

'And yet it has cost you dear.'

'A price I am willing to pay to get you back.'

'I was never yours and so cannot be won back by threats or promises. You slew my brother.'

'Hugh was a fool. He got what he deserved.'

'Who are you to say what men deserve?'

'He was in my way. I removed him.' His lips curved in a cynical smile. 'I take what I want, Isabelle.' He raised the bow. 'Now I shall ask you for the last time: will you return with me to Castlemora?'

'Never.'

'Then if I cannot have you no one else will.'

Her throat dried. However, she would not give him the satisfaction of seeing her fear. Instead she lifted her chin. 'You are indeed a brave man thus to waylay two unarmed women.'

He ignored the gibe. 'You will die first and then the upstart who married you.'

Her heart thumped. He was well informed but then her marriage was common knowledge and no doubt common talk hereabouts. For a second she wondered about telling him she was with child but just as quickly decided against it. If he knew of the child it would likely fuel his wrath.

'You gain nothing by this, Murdo.'

'I will gain my revenge.'

'Let us go.'

'No.'

The word was softly spoken but carried a chilling malevolence. She searched his face for any sign of compassion but found none. He meant it all right. Frantically her eyes sought some possibility of rescue but saw only the shimmer of heat on the still land.

Murdo nodded. 'There's no escape this time, Isabelle, for you or your traitorous companion.'

He drew back the bow string and the arrow flew. Nell cried out. For a brief moment she was quite still, then her body slumped and she fell, the feathered shaft buried deep in her breast. Isabelle screamed, falling to her knees.

'Nell!'

With sick horror she saw the staring glassy eyes and knew that her companion was beyond help. She looked up at Murdo.

'Murderer! Coward!'

Grief mingled with fear and she rose slowly to her feet. Murdo took another shaft from the quiver and nocked it to the string.

'Farewell, Isabelle.'

The bow creaked. Instinctively she flung herself sideways and the arrow whistled past, expending itself harmlessly in a tree. Isabelle waited for no more. Picking up her skirts she ran, heading into the cover of the wood, dodging among the trunks, her heart pounding in wild terror. Another arrow whistled past, hitting the tree ahead of her. She gasped and fled on. The slope grew steeper. Hampered by her skirts she stumbled and fell. From behind she could hear the sound of voices and hoofbeats that announced pursuit. Murdo was going to kill her as he had killed Nell. Panic crowded in. She fought it. Panic was his ally. She wasn't going to make it easy for him. Scrambling to her feet she fled on up the slope, tripping on roots and jutting rocks, ignoring the branches and twigs that slashed at her. A hundred yards further on she paused, breathing hard, the blood thumping in her head.

Another arrow thudded into the earth just ahead of her. She knew then that Murdo was playing with her. He was an excellent marksman and if he missed it was because he meant to. He intended to draw this out a little to punish her. No doubt it pleased him to see her fear. Did he hope to have her at his feet, weeping and pleading for her life before he sped her at last? The thought stirred anger and hatred anew. Never would she give him that satisfaction. Pausing for an instant to look wildly around her she saw the horsemen coming through the trees. Ahead of her on the edge of the wood was open ground. If she tried to escape that way they would have her very soon.

She must keep to the trees. It was her only hope now. In her mind she saw Ban's face. He was in the village. He did not know that his wife was in mortal danger and he would not come to her rescue this time. They would never meet again in this life and she would never have the chance now to tell him how much she loved him. He would never see their child born. She swallowed hard. Behind her she heard a man shout. They had seen her. In desperation she turned and ran.

The cantering hooves came nearer and nearer. Desperate now Isabelle raced on through the trees but her luck deserted her for she ran out into a small clearing that removed all cover. Three horsemen burst out of the wood some fifty yards away, cutting off her route. She spun round to see two more barring her retreat. Up beside them came a powerful bay horse. Its rider reined to a halt. Her stomach lurched. For a moment or two Murdo surveyed her with quiet satisfaction, a faint smile curling his lips. She could only watch in helpless horror as he unslung the bow from his shoulder and drew another arrow from the quiver.

'I told you, Isabelle, that you'd never escape me.'

'You won't get away with this, Murdo.'

'No? And who will prevent it? Your noble husband?'

'He will hunt you to the ends of the earth. There will be nowhere for you hide.'

'I shall not hide,' he replied, 'and he knows well enough where to find me. All I need to do is give him the reason.' He levelled the bow.

Isabelle shivered. Still she could discern no trace of pity in his face, only a remorseless intent to kill. In horrified fascination she saw him draw back the string, heard yew creak as the bow took the tension. In vain she tried to throw herself out of its path; then cried out as the arrow buried itself in her side. She fell to her knees, one hand clutching the protruding shaft. The wood was silent all around her. Somewhere she heard a horse snort. Then she became aware of a shadow blocking out the sun and a bay horse filled her line of vision. She slumped to the ground before its hooves. The rider looked down at her for a moment, a second arrow aimed at her heart. Closing her eyes she struggled against the pain. Whatever happened she wouldn't beg. It would be over soon enough.

Murdo surveyed her closely but after that first cry of pain she made no sound. His face registered grudging admiration, silently acknowledged her courage, realising then she would not plead for her life. Slowly he slackened the tension on the bowstring.

'Death will not come quickly, Isabelle, not

until the barb is drawn. Time enough for you to remember me.'

From the trees a man's voice called out. 'Riders approaching, my lord!'

He took a last look at the woman on the ground before him. 'Farewell, my lady. It is good to know that your last thoughts will be of me.' Then he turned the horse's head and spurred away. In less than a minute he and his men were lost to view.

Isabelle heard the echo of the departing hooves and then how the silence washed back after. The clearing was still. Even the birds were quiet now, as if they knew death was in their midst. Once she made to rise but the pain knifed through her body and she fell back with a gasp, her face pale as bleached linen while grass and shrub and sky lurched crazily through her line of vision. She closed her eyes again until the sensation of sickness faded a little. She was going to die here in this glade. Now that it was imminent she was not afraid of dying, only of never seeing Ban again, never feeling his arms around her or his kiss on her lips. He would never know how much she loved him. She ought to have told him when she could. Once she had thought he might die and leave her. Now, ironically, it was she who would leave him. She didn't want to but the pain was great, a burning ache in her side. Murdo had intended her to die a lingering death. It was why he had not fired the second arrow. She had not known till now how deadly hatred could be. Yet love was stronger. Somehow she must see Ban again. Pushing herself on to one elbow she tried to rise once more. Icy sweat beaded her brow as pain stabbed afresh and she cried out from the agony of it. The patch of blood on her gown grew wider. Gasping, throat parched, she sank back into the grass while sky spun and then receded, drawing away to a mere pinpoint of light before darkness closed around her.

Chapter Eighteen

Ban held his horse to a steady canter. His business in the village had been concluded to everybody's satisfaction. He just wished his own affairs might so end but there was still the matter of Castlemora to be resolved. In order to live free of threat he had to defeat Murdo. The man was like a thorn in the flesh. It festered there and would continue to do so until it was removed.

A movement on the track ahead caught his eye and then he glimpsed mounted figures making off into the trees. He did not recognise any of them and no one from Glengarron would have behaved thus on hearing their approach. It smacked of covert action, of furtiveness. He frowned, reining Firecrest to a halt. Beside him Ewan and Davy followed suit, along with the remainder of his escort.

'Who was that?' Ban demanded.

'I dinna ken, my lord,' replied Davy. 'I didna recognise them.'

'Nor I,' said Ewan. 'The trees were too dense just there.'

'Keep your eyes open and your wits about you.'

Keeping to a gentle pace they proceeded further along the path. The feeling that something was amiss grew stronger in Ban with every step. It was the stillness that was wrong, the eerie uneasy silence that preceded an ambush or followed a battle. Automatically he loosened his blade in the scabbard. His companions followed suit.

At first they did not see the body lying in the dappled shade further along the path for their eyes were looking higher, up the slope and into the trees. It was Ewan who spotted it first and alerted the rest.

'My lord, over there!'

Something in the tone sent a chill through Ban's heart. Urging the horse forwards he saw what Ewan had seen. In moments the latter had reached the spot and dismounted. He knelt beside the body a moment then looked back at the others, his face grim.

'It's Nell, my lord. She's dead.'

'Dead?' Ban swung down off his horse and hastened to join him, but one glance at the shaft and the woman's staring eyes told him the sorry truth.

'What was Nell doing out here alone?' Ewan frowned. 'She always attends on Lady Isabelle. This makes no sense.'

'Unless she *was* with Lady Isabelle,' replied Davy.

As soon as the words were spoken the two younger men exchanged troubled looks. A terrible suspicion began to form in Ban's mind and he paled.

Ewan swallowed hard. 'There may be some other explanation, my lord.'

Ban shook his head. 'Spread out. Search the whole area. If my wife is here we must find her.'

He did not voice the terrible fear of exactly what they might find. His men hastened to obey and immediately formed a line to begin combing the wood. It did not take them long to discover the tracks of horses' hooves. Ban's fist tightened round the reins. The prints indicated half-a-dozen mounts at least by his reckoning. The trail headed away up the slope. Then he saw another arrow buried in a tree trunk and his blood ran cold.

Davy drew up alongside. 'Do you think it was Murdo, my lord?'

'I'm quite sure of it. That arrow is as good as a signature.' He looked swiftly around. Suddenly the quiet wood seemed infinitely more sinister.

'Follow the trail, but keep your wits about you. It could be a trap.'

He urged the chestnut on up the slope, following the tracks in the soft loam. The discovery of two more identical arrows only served to intensify his unease.

Beside him Davy looked at Ewan. 'What were they shooting at?'

'Or whom?' replied the other.

Ban's jaw tightened, his mind refusing to acknowledge the answer. They reached the top of the slope and then paused on the edge of a clearing.

'The prints turn back into the trees again, my lord,' said Davy. 'All the same, they've left a trail a child of five could follow; almost as if they meant it to be found.'

'That's just what they meant,' replied Ban.

'But why, my lord? They must have known it would be madness to venture on to Glengarron lands.'

'Murdo knew exactly what he was doing.'

'An act of provocation then.'

'No, an act of revenge.' As he spoke he became more certain what form that revenge would take, and for the first time in five years he felt horribly afraid.

It was another five minutes before they found Isabelle. Ban flung himself from his horse and fell on his knees beside her, seeing in frantic disbelief the arrow lodged in her side. Her face was ashen. No movement testified that she lived. With a cry he raised her shoulders from the ground and cradled her close, icy dread locked round his heart. Around them his men stood grim-faced, silent witnesses to the horror. Forcing himself to ascertain the truth Ban's fingers moved to her neck, seeking a pulse. For several hideous seconds he couldn't find one; then, very faint beneath his touch, he located it. Fear and rage swelled in his heart as he lifted his wife in his arms.

'Davy, bring my horse. We need to get her home. Ewan, take Callum and go and collect Nell's body.'

The journey back to Dark Mount was not long but to Ban it seemed to take for ever. As they rode into the courtyard he heard curious voices raised in question and then exclamations of shock and horror as the extent of the outrage became clear. After that was a tense and angry silence. The crowd parted to let Ban through. Carefully he bore his wife indoors and took her to the chamber they shared together, laying her gently on the bed. Her pallor terrified him. When he touched her hand it was cold.

'Ban? What is it? What has happened?'

He recognised Ashlynn's voice. 'He has killed her,' he replied.

There followed a sharp intake of breath as Ashlynn took in the extent of the injury. Then she rapped out a series of instructions to the hovering servants before turning back to her brother.

'Who has done this thing?'

'Murdo, who else?'

She shivered to see the expression in his eyes. Then he rose to his feet.

'Tend her, Ashlynn. I'm going after him.'

'Be careful, Ban. It's what he wants.'

'He'll get his wish. The murdering bastard has spent his last day on this earth.'

He took a last parting look at his wife and then strode to the door. He had no sooner reached the courtyard than he heard his brother-in-law's voice ordering men to arm and ready themselves, and saw the subsequent flurry of activity as they hastened to obey. Iain remained standing by Nell's body, now shrouded in a cloak. When he saw Ban he reached out a hand to clasp his shoulder.

'I'm sorry, Brother. I delayed in my pursuit of Murdo, thinking there would be time enough. I was wrong and I ask your pardon.'

Ban's face was grim. 'Let us find the coward now for he or I or both die this day.'

'We will have his head on a spear, I swear it.'

'Let it be so.'

In short order they were mounted and, accompanied by a contingent thirty strong, set out to follow Murdo's trail. After retracing their way to the scene of the crime it took little time to tell the direction the fugitives must have taken. Ban would have sent his horse after in hot pursuit but Ewan stayed him.

'My lord, he will likely return to Castlemora, will he not?'

'Aye. What of it?'

'There is a quicker way than his; an old drovers' trail across the moors. If we take it, we can cut him off.'

Iain nodded. 'Ewan's right.'

'Very well.' Ban met and held the dark gaze a moment. 'Lead on.'

Ewan turned his horse and set off a tangent along a path skirting the hillside. Spurring the horses on they reached the top of the slope and, when the ground levelled out, they gave the animals their heads. The horses settled into their stride, a mile-eating gallop that stayed for nothing. Ban's one thought now was to have Murdo within reach of his sword point. He could still see Isabelle's pale face turned up to his, feel the icy touch of her flesh. The shaft had been buried deep in her side. When it was withdrawn she would bleed, draining her strength further. Even if that were stanched the chances were that the barb had pierced some vital organ and she would bleed inwardly, her life leaching away by moments and with it the life of their child. He had lost them and the knowledge cut him to the heart. In that moment he understood what Isabelle meant to him; that he loved her more than life itself, and if she was gone then he cared not if he died too this day, but not before he slew Murdo.

Cold rage filled his breast and he rode like one possessed, guiding the horse with a sure instinctive touch, his body moving to the rhythm of the easy loping gallop. Beside him Iain rode too, his face a chilling mask that carried in it a sentence of death. Behind them their men rode as one body with one avowed intent, the desire for vengeance burning in their eyes. Glengarron had suffered a deadly insult this day and it could only be expunged in blood.

Some miles later they paused briefly to let the horses breathe.

'Murdo will assume by this that he is away and clear,' said Iain. 'He will hardly suspect we've stolen a march on him.'

Ban's expression was grim. 'It'll be his last surprise.'

They spurred forwards again until, at the top

of the next hill, Iain raised a hand and they reined in once more.

'Down there,' he said, pointing to the valley below.

Ban narrowed his eyes against the light and then his heart leapt in savage satisfaction as he saw the line of dust and half-a-dozen horsemen riding fast along the narrow trail.

'There they are.'

'Aye, we'll head over the top and cut them off in the trees further along.'

They sped along the track, plunging down the far side of the slope and into the wood below, ranging themselves along the trail they knew their quarry must ride. There they pulled their blowing horses to a halt and waited. They had not long to do so, for soon the breeze carried the sound of drumming hooves towards them. Ban loosened his sword in its sheath, his face grim. He heard Iain speak to his men.

'There will be no quarter. We take no prisoners this day.'

Grim smiles answered him, along with the soft scrape of steel against leather.

A blur of movement through the trees announced the riders' presence. The waiting men lifted their swords.

'Hold,' murmured Iain. 'Let them get closer.'

The foremost horseman was but fifty yards off

when the ambushers emerged from their cover and threw a cordon across the way. Amid cursing and warning shouts the riders drew their horses to a plunging halt, their hands going immediately to their weapons. Those in the rear turned sharply, only to see the path cut off behind. Seeing the vastly superior numbers one or two threw down their weapons. The gesture did not save them and they were cut down without mercy. Their fate steeled the rest who turned to face the assault, fighting desperately for their lives.

Ban spurred Firecrest straight at Murdo's mount, his horse's shoulder striking the other at an oblique angle. Thrown off balance the bay stumbled. Murdo rolled and came up fast, sword drawn. As he recognised his enemy he bared his teeth in a feral smile.

'I hoped you'd come after me though in truth I didn't think it would be so soon.'

'You have your wish.'

'Indeed I do, and now I shall kill you.'

'I am not so easy to kill.' Ban dismounted and advanced, sword in hand, his blue eyes like chips of ice as they swept over the other man. 'Unlike defenceless women.'

'I thought that would get your attention.'

'You murdering scum.'

'Did you really think I'd let you keep Isabelle?'

'I had no need to keep her. She chose me.'

'Much good it has done her. She will not live long enough to regret her choice.'

Ban's jaw tightened. 'No more will you. Prepare to die, you cowardly bastard.'

'It will afford me the greatest pleasure to carve you into little slivers.'

'This time you face those better able to defend themselves.'

'Say you so?'

Murdo circled slowly, looking for his opening. Then without warning he darted into the attack. Ban parried the thrust aimed at his shoulder and replied with a swinging cut. Murdo blocked it and then launched into a fierce assault. Nothing loath Ban went to meet it. He lost awareness of everything else around him, the world reduced to two blades and the man he hated most in the world.

He did not see Murdo's accomplices slain, or how the men of Glengarron gathered a little way off, standing in approving silence to watch this last battle. His whole focus was driven by the desire to avenge; his long apprenticeship with Black Iain evident in every move that he made. His sword arm rose and fell tirelessly, his enemy hard pressed to block the deadly blows that rained down upon him. However, a man with nothing to lose is the most dangerous foe, as Ban well knew. Murdo was alone and surrounded with no possibility of escape now. He would sell his life dear. Ban could feel the weight of that dark and mocking gaze. Its owner was enjoying the rage he saw reflected in his opponent's eyes, knowing only exultation in the understanding of why it was there, that his plan had worked and Isabelle was dead. All that remained was to take his final revenge on the man whose coming to Castlemora had been nothing but a source of trouble.

Murdo met his eye and grinned, and for several moments it was Ban who was forced back step by step as the master-at-arms launched a savage assault of his own. However, it was born out of increasing desperation: unbeknown to the observers, he had begun to feel the blooming ache in his side where Ban's blade had struck before. The wound had been infected for a while and was yet imperfectly healed.

Ban showed no sign that his own shoulder wound pained him at all. His rage sustained him. He lay on with a will and, seeing a chance, thrust past Murdo's guard to leave a bloody gash across his arm. Another slashing blow straight after it cut across his ribs. Warm blood flowed, the telltale darkening patch growing on his tunic. Both men were breathing harder now, their ragged breaths sounding loud in the silence beneath the trees. Still Ban came on, his sword like an extension of his arm, a deadly whirling arc of light showering sparks as it met the edge of the defending blade. And it was defending now, he could tell. Murdo was beginning to tire, his assault less controlled though no less savage for that. It was time to end it.

Ban feinted, giving a little ground, inviting his opponent in. Murdo saw it and smiled. Then he lunged. Ban sidestepped, narrowly avoiding the point, and appeared to stumble, falling to one knee. Murdo lunged again, closing for the kill. His opponent rolled, bringing up his own blade between them. Unable to check the impetus of the blow, Murdo rushed on to the point and the blade was buried for half of its length in his breast. For several seconds he hung there, his face a mask of shock, before he buckled and sank to his knees, his sword dropping from his hand. Ban pulled the blade free and swung it again hard. It severed Murdo's head cleanly. The body fell at his opponent's feet. For a moment or two Ban surveyed it with grim satisfaction, leaning awhile on his sword, knowing the savage exultation of victory.

Iain surveyed him for a moment before glancing at the head of the enemy; then turned towards the watching men. 'Bring me a spear.'

It was late when they returned at last to Glengarron, their tired horses lathered and blown. Ban, bone weary and sick with the knowledge that Isabelle was lost, dismounted and gave the reins to a groom. Then, with Iain beside him, he entered the hall. It was empty, save for the servants who hastened to bring ale and wine and food for the returning men. The mood was dark and subdued even though the enemy had been so soundly defeated. It seemed at best a Pyrrhic victory.

Hearing a light footstep and the rustle of a gown Ban looked up to see his sister standing in the doorway. With a glad cry she hastened forwards to greet her husband and brother. Ban's face was pale beneath its tan, his eyes wells of misery as he beheld her face waiting for confirmation of all he dreaded most.

'Isabelle?'

'Lives,' she replied.

For a second or two it was hard to take in and all he felt was the painful thudding of his heartbeat. Then, no less painful, a tiny flicker of hope took root there too.

'She lives?'

'She's very weak but she's holding on.'

Ban swallowed hard. 'Take me to her.'

He strode along the passageway in Ashlynn's wake until they reached the chamber where his wife lay. As the door opened Meg turned to regard them soberly.

'How does she, Meg?' he asked, hastening to the bedside.

'She is weak. The arrow missed the vital organs but there has been much blood loss, my lord.'

His heart sank. 'Will she live?'

'I do not know.' Meg paused. 'Only time will tell us that.'

He knelt by the bed, his gaze taking in the deathly pallor of the face, the dark circles beneath the eyes, and he felt the chill of the hand he held. It seemed every bit as icy as the chill around his heart. If he could have given her his blood and his strength, he would have done it. As it was he could only look on helplessly and wait.

'Don't die, my love,' he begged. 'Please don't die.'

For several days it seemed that Isabelle's life hung by a thread. Meg tended her closely, aided by Ashlynn and the servant, Morag. Ban hardly stirred from her side. Sometimes he slept, only to wake with a start, fearing that she might have died meanwhile and he knowing nothing of it. Then he would catch sight of her shallow breathing and know she lived yet. He cursed himself that he had not returned sooner to Dark Mount that day. If he had he might have been in time to prevent the encounter with Murdo. Why had she and Nell been there? He had no idea. Nell could never tell him and perhaps not Isabelle ei-

ther now. All he could think about was the imminent, mind-numbing possibility of losing her.
His conscience though was far from numb. She
had once thought him self-seeking and that his
love of land and wealth came before any thought
of her. And she had been right—then. He had no
idea when that had changed because the change
had happened so gradually. All he knew for sure
was that it *had* happened. She had found a place
in his heart that only she could fill. If he lost her
it would be as though a part of his heart had been
ripped out. If only she might live so that he could
tell her the truth.

The thought of her dying and leaving him
alone sent a roiling fear through his entire being.
Life would not be worth living without her. Once
before, he had lost everything. Now it seemed
that by a malign trick of fate it was about to happen again. Even the wounds he had sustained in
the sack of Heslingfield hadn't caused the kind
of agony he felt now. 'Don't leave me, Isabelle.
My darling, I beg you, don't leave me.'

Isabelle struggled through a stormy sea, fighting to keep her head above the waves that threatened to draw her under. Every movement was
slow and painful, every breath an effort. Part of
her urged the futility of the struggle, a siren voice
that spoke of surrender. If she stopped fighting

and let the waters take her, the pain would be gone and in their depths she would find peace. Yet somehow, over that siren voice, she could hear someone calling her, someone she must reach. It was a man's voice, gentle and loving, summoning her back. She must keep swimming, but her strength was ebbing and only her will kept her going now. If only she could find the owner of the voice she would be safe.

Chapter Nineteen

One afternoon, a week after the drawing of the arrow, Isabelle awoke. For a while she had no idea where she was but then, gradually, familiar details began to impress themselves on her consciousness. She had been in this room before. The walls, the tapestries, the bed were familiar. How had she got here? Surely she had been somewhere else before. A memory surfaced of trees and men and a woman screaming. Her brows twitched together. She couldn't quite recall who they were. Then she was aware of another presence in the room with her, a man. He too was familiar somehow. He was sitting beside the bed but his gaze was elsewhere as though he were deeply abstracted. Eventually, sensing himself watched he turned towards her. Blue eyes met hers. The sombre expression changed in an instant to incredulity and joy.

'Isabelle?' He pressed her hand to his lips. 'Oh, my love. Thank God.'

'Ban?' she murmured.

For a moment it seemed he could not speak; then he seemed to rally. 'I thought I'd lost you.'

She stirred a little and winced as fiery pain shot through her body. Hearing the sharp intake of breath, he bent over her in concern.

'You must stay still, my love. You've been injured.'

'Injured how?' she asked as the pain began to subside a little.

'Someone shot you. Do you not remember?'

'No.'

Her mind was suddenly confused with lots of different images: sunshine and trees and an empty road. Then the road was no longer empty. Men blocked the way. She was afraid.

'It doesn't matter,' Ban said gently. 'Just rest now.'

Nothing loath she shut her eyes again. However, the images came thick and fast then. The quiet sunlit track had become a place of menace. Its focus was the dark-clad warrior with the bow in his hands. He was pointing it at her and Nell. As in a nightmare she saw the arrow leave the string, heard Nell scream and then the shaft was buried in her breast. She cried out but already knew it was too late. Her companion was dead. Then she had run but her legs would not move fast enough and the horses had drawn closer, cutting off the way both forwards and back. The dark warrior nocked another shaft to the bow and let fly. She moved but not fast enough. There was terrible pain and then nothing, until just now. Tears trickled from the corners of her eyes.

'Nell's dead, isn't she?'

'She is. I'm so sorry, Isabelle.'

'He killed her, didn't he? Murdo I mean.'

'Aye, that's right.'

'He tried to kill me.'

'But he has failed,' he said, 'for I will not let you die. He will not take you from me.'

'I don't want to leave you, Ban.'

'I should not permit it in any case.' He smiled. 'I love you, Isabelle. More than my life. I should have told you that before. I should have told you every day.'

'Do you mean it?'

'I mean it. If I hadn't been so blinkered I'd have realised it long since. Can you ever forgive me?'

Her heart constricted. 'Oh, Ban. There's nothing to forgive. If I have your love, that's all that matters.'

'You do have it, unconditionally and always.'

Then other bits of memory returned and she paled. 'Dear God, the baby…'

'It's all right. I've spoken to Meg.'

'Are you sure?'

'Quite sure. She says there's no sign of anything amiss. I think you must be carrying a future warrior.'

Relief flooded through her. 'I shall go to the church and light a candle to give thanks.'

'We'll both go, when you are well again.'

'What of Murdo?'

'He's dead, and by my hand.'

She seemed to relax a little. 'I am glad. He was an evil man.'

'That he was, but his days of persecuting innocents are over.'

Her eyelids closed again and presently Ban heard her breathing grow soft and regular and knew she dozed. Even so it was a while before he could get his own emotion under control as for the first time he found himself truly daring to hope.

Later, when Morag came to sit awhile, he rose and betook himself to the tower roof, needing the fresh air to clear his head. It was there that Ashlynn found him later on.

'She will live, Ban. I'm sure of it now. The worst is over.'

He nodded, not trusting himself to speak for a moment or two.

'It is her love for you that gives her the will to fight,' she went on.

'I cannot live without her, Ash. She means the world to me.'

'I know.' She laid a gentle hand on his shoulder. 'And you two will have a wonderful future together, never fear.'

Ban let out a ragged breath. 'I hardly dared to hope these past days.'

'Isabelle's will is strong.'

'Do I not know it?' He managed a wan smile. 'She has been through so much but it has not broken her spirit. Yet I fear that Nell's death will hurt her more than an arrow ever could.'

'It was a cruel and dastardly act, but Murdo has paid the price.'

'I never knew it was possible to hate so deeply till that day.'

'Hatred can be a useful tool,' she replied, 'but I think it is a bad master.'

'Meaning that I should let it go.'

'Murdo is dead, his men slain or fled. They belong to the past. Leave them there, Ban.'

'You're right. I know you are. Yet part of me still wishes him alive again so that I could have the pleasure of slaying him anew.'

'Forget him. Think about Isabelle instead. Help her to get well.'

'She will get well, Ash, won't she?'

'I truly believe it. After all, she has everything to live for.'

It seemed that Ashlynn's prediction was correct for by slow degrees Isabelle grew stronger and the wound began to mend. Ban spent the greater part of each day at her side, fearful of letting her out of his sight lest she suffer some unforeseen relapse. Eventually as she began to take nourishment and a little of the colour returned to her cheeks he felt better reassured. His guilt was not so soon alleviated. When he thought back on his original treatment of her he felt only disgust. What the hell had he been thinking? Her forbearance had been astounding.

Isabelle, comforted by his presence and his evident concern for her, knew there was something amiss. It troubled her. Once she would have talked it over with Nell, but that was no longer possible. She missed her former companion terribly; missed her shrewd intelligence and sound common sense. It was as though everything she had ever had from her past life had been stripped away. She tried to imagine what Nell would have said had she been there. In her mind she heard the much-loved voice: *Talk to him, child. Tell him what is in your heart.*

Thus it was that when next they were alone she summoned the courage to broach the subject.

'Something is wrong, Ban. Will you not tell me what it is?'

He turned to face her, his eyes troubled. For a moment he remained silent.

'Is it something I have done?' she went on.

'That you have done? Good Lord, no! How can you think it?'

'Then tell me, I beg. I hate to see you look so.'

'It is of our earlier relationship that I would speak.' He drew in a deep breath. 'I have thought of it often while you have lain there nigh to death, thinking that there might never be a chance to make it up to you.'

She had been listening to him in mounting surprise and concern. 'I understand why you behaved as you did. The pressure on you was great.'

'And so I put unfair pressure on you.'

'You are the last surviving male of your house. Of course it was crucial to you to produce an heir. It's important to all men but for you it was, quite literally, a matter of life and death.' She smiled sadly. 'I too am the last of my house. I know how it feels.'

He clasped her hand. 'You have been through so much on my account. Too much.'

'What matters is to have your love.'

'You do have it. Never doubt that again. I'll spend the rest of my life showing you the truth of that.'

'Then we may yet found that dynasty.'

'If we do I hope our offspring will take after you, that they will possess your goodness and your generous spirit.'

'I hope they will have the courage and the integrity of their father.'

'Not so much integrity I fear.'

'You're wrong. You never lied to me or gave me false expectations.'

'Maybe not, but it still pains me when I think of some of the things I did say.'

She grinned. '"We may grow closer in affection."'

'Ouch! And that was probably one of my least offensive remarks. I only wish I could forget them.'

'I think you should. Focus on being Laird of Castlemora instead.'

'That title still sounds strange to me.'

'I can think of no one better fitted to fill the role.'

He kissed her hand. 'I shall strive to deserve it.'

'There will be much to set right I fear, but if anyone can do that it is you.'

'Your faith makes me feel proud. Your late honoured father will be a hard act to follow.'

'Your whole life has been leading to this,' she replied. 'It is what you were born to do.'

'Perhaps. All the same, it would have been a hollow crown if you had not been there to share it with me.'

'But I am here and I mean to stay.'

'That's just as well, my love, for I will never let you go.'

Since it was clear that their plans could not be implemented for some weeks, Lord Iain sent a group of men ahead to hold Castlemora in the interim. The news of Lady Isabelle's intended return was well received, for Murdo's reign had been hated by the family retainers, and the thought of the rightful heir being restored was pleasing to all concerned. Thus Lord Iain's men were made welcome by the Castlemora servants until their lady should return.

For Isabelle it couldn't come soon enough. While she was grateful for the hospitality of Glengarron, the thought of living with Ban in their own home was irresistible. As soon as she was up again she told him as much. However, he refused to countenance a move just then.

'You are not fit enough yet, sweetheart.'

'It won't be long now. I am so much better already,' she replied. 'I left my sick bed days ago.'

'You need to recover your strength and give the wound time to heal completely.'

'It almost is.'

'Almost is not good enough.'

She laid a hand on his sleeve. 'But, Ban...'

He was not to be coaxed. 'No, my darling, you're not going anywhere as yet.'

The tone was gentle but it carried a note she had learned to recognise. 'You sounded just like Lord Iain when you said that.'

'Did I so?' He smiled faintly. 'And just how does he sound?'

'Like a man who intends to get his own way.'

'I do mean to get my way.' He took her shoulders in a gentle clasp. 'I am your husband and I will be obeyed.'

Isabelle lifted a quizzical brow. 'Can I say nothing to persuade you?'

'Not a thing.'

'Perhaps there is something I might do then?' She twined her arms around his neck and bestowed a lingering kiss on his mouth. 'Was not that persuasive, my lord?'

'Aye, it was.'

'Good.' She kissed him again, a deeper and more intimate embrace. His arms closed gently around her, drawing her closer, and he returned the kiss with slow, contained passion. Then he drew back a little and looked down into her face.

'Even better, but it has not changed my mind. You're staying here.'

'You can be so stubborn.'

'When it comes to your welfare, my sweet, I can be downright intransigent.'

It drew a reluctant smile. 'All right. You win, for now.'

His eyes gleamed. 'I'd to think I'll win all the time but I doubt it somehow.'

'So do I.'

They both laughed. Then her face grew earnest once more. 'But Ban, I hope we will not wait too long. I would so like our child to be born at Castlemora.'

'There is no reason why he should not be.'

She hugged him. 'Then I am content.'

It was some weeks later before they set out for Castlemora. Although she was looking forward to their return Isabelle was sorry to say goodbye to Ashlynn, if only for a while.

'Fortunately the distance is not great so I feel sure that we shall meet again before too long.'

Ashlynn smiled. 'I am determined that we shall.' She looked meaningfully at her husband. 'When next my lord has occasion to visit Castlemora I shall accompany him.'

Iain glanced at Ban. 'You have been warned, Brother.'

'So I have.' Ban leaned closer. 'I suppose there's no chance of a reprieve?'

'I seriously doubt that.'

'So do I.'

Both men grinned. Ashlynn surveyed them in mock indignation.

'You are right to doubt it. I am going to become an aunt and I shall not be kept away.'

'That's it then,' said Iain. 'We've been told.'

Ban gave his sister a hug. 'I sincerely hope you will come and see us soon, Ash. There is much to show you.'

'I look forward to seeing it.' Ashlynn smiled at Isabelle. 'In the meantime, I shall miss you. Nor would I lose your friendship so soon.'

'Or I yours,' replied Isabelle. 'I shall never forget your kindness to me.'

The two women embraced warmly. Then Ban took his wife's hand.

'Come, my love. Let's be on our way.'

Since Isabelle could not ride she travelled in a wagon specially prepared for the purpose. Two women servants accompanied her. When his wife was comfortably ensconced, Ban mounted Firecrest. He raised a hand in farewell and then they set off, an armed escort riding behind.

The pace was necessarily slow but Isabelle

didn't mind it. She would do nothing that might put her unborn child at risk. Her pregnancy was beginning to show now, a circumstance that delighted her. Moreover, Ban was solicitous over her comfort, insisting they travel by easy stages, stopping frequently to let her rest.

'I have never travelled in such cushioned splendour,' she told him. 'I shall grow spoilt.'

He grinned and glanced at her belly. 'You will doubtless grow, my love, but spoilt never.'

Isabelle returned the smile. 'I wouldn't be too sure about that. I must be one of the most pampered ladies in Scotland.'

'You deserve to be pampered. Anyway, I enjoy it.'

'Then far be it from me to rob you of enjoyment.'

They lapsed into companionable silence for a while and she settled back to look at the slowly passing landscape. It was impossible not to recall that the last time they had travelled this country they had been hunted fugitives and every rock and tree potentially sheltering an enemy. Now their enemy was defeated, albeit at a cost. This time the mood was light and the escort strong. This time there was no danger. Ban also looked thoughtful and she guessed that he too was remembering.

'Between Castlemora and Glengarron we shall make this area safe again,' he said.

'The border lands have always been wild and lawless.'

'So they have, but this bit won't be if I have anything to say about it.'

'It'll take a strong force to accomplish that.'

'We'll have one, but it'll not be composed of mercenary thugs this time.'

'I'm relieved to hear it.'

A few miles further on Ban called a halt for a while. 'I would not have you grow too tired, my sweet.'

Isabelle was both touched and amused by his consideration. 'I am quite well, my lord.'

'I intend to see you stay that way.'

'You must not be so protective.'

'I am your husband. Who else should protect you if not I?'

'Your men will think you hen-pecked.'

'Let them think what they will.' He grinned. 'It could not change my determination to keep you safe, for you are most precious to me.'

'As you are to me, my lord.'

He raised her hand to his lips. 'The most precious thing in the world.'

Isabelle's heart was full when she remembered how once she had never thought to hear him say those words to her. Now the wheel was turning full circle. Out of sorrow and pain had come triumph and love. She laid a hand on her belly, swelling gently now beneath her gown. One day, not so far distant, their child would be born. It would be followed by many more; fine children to continue their line and hold Castlemora for posterity.

It took several days to complete the journey but as the mood was cheerful and the company in good spirits it did not seem overlong. Nevertheless, it was good to reach their destination. To Isabelle it was a longed-for homecoming. At the sight of the old manor house and its rambling outbuildings, its fields and its orchard set in the bowl of the surrounding hills, her eyes filled with tears. The welcome from her people was warm and sincere and they lined the courtyard to welcome her and her new husband. The news of their forthcoming arrival had been well received, for it underlined the fact that Murdo's hated reign was really over.

Naturally there was intense interest in Isabelle's marriage and in her present condition. Though he was a Sassenach, her lord's connection with Glengarron was a point decidedly in his favour. That he had also slain Murdo was another. His coming was seen as a fresh start, one that raised hopes and created a feeling of cautious optimism among the local people.

Since Ban looked every inch the part of a noble lord, and was besides young and handsome, he raised many a sigh in female breasts. However, he had eyes only for the woman at his side. Isabelle returned his smile and, on being lifted gently down from the wagon, accompanied her husband into the hall. All trace of Murdo and his mercenary force had been removed and the only thing that marred the occasion for her was the absence of Nell among the servants.

'I wish she could have been here to see this.'

'How do you know she isn't?' replied Ban.

She smiled, albeit wistfully, for the thought was pleasing. Even now she half-expected to hear a footstep and see Nell's familiar figure descend the stairs or stand in the doorway.

'This would have pleased her so much.'

'Would it?'

'No question. She liked you.'

'I am honoured.'

'My father too would have been pleased. You were his choice of husband for me after all.'

'Then I am twice honoured.' He paused. 'If you wish we will go and visit his grave later on. His and Hugh's.'

'I would like that, though I think it will take a while to lay the ghosts.'

'I know.'

'I truly believe Murdo to have been capable of any outrage.'

Ban took her hand and turned her to face him. 'Murdo is dead, love. He cannot hurt us now.'

'I know yet he is hard to forget.'

He drew her into his arms and kissed her. 'We may never forget, but we can leave him in the past where he belongs for we have a future to build together.'

The new laird and his lady dined in their own hall that evening in company with the captains from Glengarron who had accompanied them thither. It was a lively and pleasant occasion, the company universally cheerful, jests and banter flying as the ale cups were drained. Ban looked about him with quiet pride but most often of all his gaze fell on the woman at his side, the lady he had so nearly lost. When he had last left Castlemora he had little thought to return in triumph as its laird. What had gone before was just the easy part, he now realised. The real work lay ahead but he relished the challenges involved. Ultimately the common people would judge him by what he did, but he determined that their lot would improve. Isabelle was right. It *was* what he had been born to do and he would justify the faith reposed in him. Castlemora would be strong and respected for all the right reasons. Strong too would be its ties with Glengarron. What Archibald Graham had begun Ban vowed to continue.

Somewhere amid these private thoughts he became aware that he was being observed and smiled to see Isabelle's gaze on him. Taking her hand in his he raised it to his lips. In her shining eyes he read love and trust and a silent promise for himself alone. Then she refilled her cup.

'I would like to propose a toast.'

'What shall we drink to?' he asked.

'To you, my lord.' She lifted her cup. 'The new Laird of Castlemora.'

* * * * *

The World of Mills & Boon®

There's a Mills & Boon® series that's perfect for you. We publish ten series and, with new titles every month, you never have to wait long for your favourite to come along.

Scorching hot, sexy reads
4 new stories every month

By Request

Relive the romance with the best of the best
9 new stories every month

Cherish™

Romance to melt the heart every time
12 new stories every month

Desire™

Passionate and dramatic love stories
8 new stories every month

Join the Mills & Boon Book Club

Want to read more **Historical** books?
We're offering you **2 more** absolutely **FREE!**

We'll also treat you to these fabulous extras:

- 🌹 Exclusive offers and much more!

- 🌹 FREE home delivery

- 🌹 FREE books and gifts with our special rewards scheme

Get your free books now!

visit www.millsandboon.co.uk/bookclub
or call Customer Relations on 020 8288 2888